A SMALL PART OF HISTORY

A SMALL PART OF HISTORY

by

Peggy Elliott

Magna Large Print Books
Long Preston, North Yorkshire,
BD23 4ND, England.

British Library Cataloguing in Publication Data.

Elliott, Peggy
    A small part of history.

    A catalogue record of this book is
    available from the British Library

    ISBN   978-0-7505-2982-2

01/16

First published in Great Britain 2008 by Headline Review
an imprint of Headline Publishing Group

Copyright © 2008 Peggy Elliott

Cover illustration © Gordon Crabb by arrangement with
Alison Eldred

The right of Peggy Elliott to be identified as the author of this
work has been asserted by her in accordance with the
Copyright, Designs and Patents Act, 1988

Published in Large Print 2008 by arrangement with
Headline Publishing Group Ltd.

Magna Large Print is an imprint of Library Magna Books Ltd.

Printed and bound in Great Britain by
T.J. (International) Ltd., Cornwall, PL28 8RW

To Martin Manulis, who helped me start
my journey along the Oregon Trail.

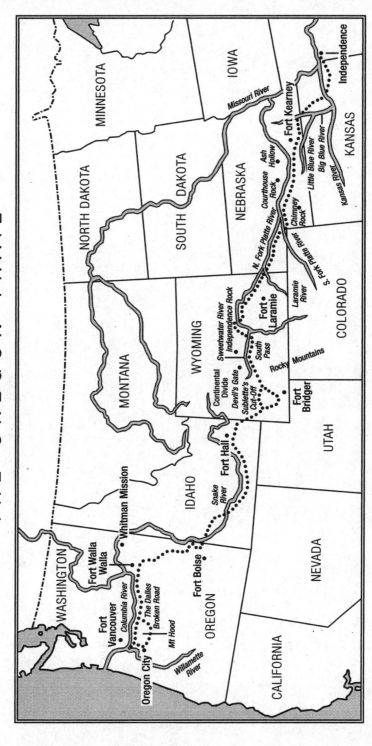

THE OREGON TRAIL

Part 1

Picking up Traces

Sarah

My Papa always told me it was best to start a story at the beginning when I confused him by jumping into things somewhere in the middle, so I am not going to talk about where I am today or even last month, because it all really begun back in June of 1845. A whole lot has happened since then, but when I close my eyes, I can still conjure up that June day in the summer kitchen.

It was more a porch than a real room, open on three sides. The sunlight poured through the poplars in the afternoon and reflected off the bottoms of the pots hanging on the side wall so bright I had to squint. I recall the smell of the fresh-picked peaches laying on the table, mixed in with the scent of alfalfa in the field out back, and just a trace of that moist, musty odor that wasn't there later in the year when it got hotter.

And I remember how the old oak table smelt, too, after all the years of spilled gravy and bacon grease and pastry flour settling down into the wood. Papa was one of the more prosperous farmers in Vermillion County, Indiana, and that table was long enough to seat well over a dozen at harvest time, and bore the nicks and scratches of thousands of meals and their preparation.

I can see me and Rebecca there in the summer kitchen arguing, which doesn't take much talent to remember since we were always arguing. By and large, I came out on top when we had a set-to. I had figured out that Rebecca didn't feel right lecturing me, since she was not my real mother, only my stepmother for just four months, and me already fifteen.

I never knew my mama. Never knew if I had had a mama whether I would have turned out different. My papa raised me the same as my brothers, though it was said by some he spoilt me. I don't see how just leaving a person be to do what they have a mind to is spoiling. I call that using good sense.

The fact is, I didn't think about not having a mother much. I had my brothers to look after me.

With Daniel, who got married when I was twelve, his eye was more or less only on me out of the corner, since he had other responsibilities, these being his wife Elizabeth and baby Betsy, who was named after her mama, Betsy being short for Elizabeth.

My brother Matthew was near Daniel's age, though he still liked to have fun now and then. Him and Daniel had a different mama than us – us being Willie, Joe and me.

Willie was only one year older than me,

and I had been following him around ever since I could walk. Papa said I would jump off the top of the barn if Willie told me so. and I got mad and said Willie would never be so mean or foolish. Later I understood he was just joshing, but I guess I *would* have done just about anything for Willie short of jumping off the barn.

Joe was three years younger than me and the apple of everyone's eye, with golden curls which he wished had been burdened on someone else. The rest of us all had Papa's black hair and dark complexion, but Joe had managed to have something of our mama. He may have been the youngest of the lot, but he never needed looking after, not minding being off on his own for hours at a time, even when he was a baby. He didn't cry and ask to go along with Willie and me, and since he was no bother, most always we did count him in.

If I had had an ounce of charity in me, I'd have owned there was no justifying getting mad at Rebecca for trying to take the place of somebody who had never been there in the first place. But I am ashamed to admit that by making her squirm, I could generally wiggle myself out of any task I found distasteful.

Rebecca wanted me to learn all the things a woman needs to know to run a household. Now, I not only didn't want to learn woman things, I didn't even like being a *girl* all that much. I liked to do the things a boy can do without much comment, but which are considered improper for a girl to do.

Nobody had made me stay at home and learn to cook and sew. My papa didn't stop to think that I'd be needing to, not having any woman around to point it out to him. Matthew and Daniel weren't but two and five when their own mama died, so Papa got married again soon so they'd have a woman to look after them. After Mama died having Joe, he didn't marry again so fast, even though the three of us were so young – I guess he felt he was a man plagued by bad luck.

We got along fine for many a year with Poor Lucy Marble coming to the farm two days a week. I reckon I was almost nine before I realized 'Poor' wasn't one of her Christian names. I was civilized enough to always call her Miss Marble, but one time the 'Poor' slipped out. I figured then that she didn't hear me so I got away with it, but I am wiser now, so I think maybe she did and pretended she didn't.

Poor Lucy had been kicked by a mule when she was a child and she drug one leg badly. It was also said she was slow. Whatever she was, no farmer would have a wife who couldn't share his work, so Poor Lucy was also Poor *Spinster* Lucy. Not a happy position in our community, where everyone agreed that the proper order of things was two by two.

We had three families of tenants to help on the property, but only Poor Lucy in the house, which by most standards I guess was sorely neglected. Poor Lucy gave things a lick and polish, but most energy went into her 'days'. Friday was washday, and one of our chores was to start the fires in the kitchen yard early in the morning. Then me and Willie and Joe would haul buckets of water from the pump, it taking quite a few trips to fill the big tubs simmering over the coals. Then it was more hauling for the rinsing. Our farm sat in a valley, which tended to trap the mist, so some washdays you could scarce see the hand in front of your face, with steam rising from the tubs mixing with the fog. When it rained, we went dirty another week, except when it caught us late, at which times we had to put up with dripping wash-lines strung all over the house.

Monday was baking day, and even though Poor Lucy Marble was a sorry baker, by the first of the week everyone was starved for fresh bread and sweet doughs, and it was all she could do to prevent us 'wild injuns' from making off with whole pies.

We had a hideaway under the roots of a big old oak where the creek had washed the soil away in a hundred-year flood. A thick grove ran all the way down to the banks of the creek, with wild grapes, plums and berries tucked in among the trees, growing so thick there was a sweet rotting smell all around from the droppings, and the bees and other bugs got drunk from their feasting, so didn't do us any harm. We would sneak cream from our dairy and weigh the pail down in the creek where it could stay nice and cool while we went berrying.

We'd end up covered in prickles and dust from crawling around in the bushes and there wasn't any cure for that but taking a swim, seeing who could swing the farthest out on the grape vines before we let go. Joe broke a bone once that way.

Afterwards, we'd make a feast with the fruit and cream or the pies we'd stole, while our clothes dried on our backs.

Oh, but those were fun times! And I am not going to cry. Rebecca said she wrote things down so they wouldn't be forgotten, and I don't want those times to be forgotten.

We had other chores beyond helping Poor Lucy. We drove the cows to pasture and then back home, which gave me real pleasure as I was always plum crazy for animals and didn't even mind feeding the chickens, which most people do not like at all. From an early age, I pailed the cows, which I loved, but I also had to churn the cream, which was most tedious and hateful.

But after chores, we'd be off again all over

God's creation, hunting for beehives or tracking each other in the woods or looking for arrowheads along the creekbeds. We found some in a cave one time. Shells, too. Once we saw some injuns, but they were tame ones. Tippecanoe beat the injuns in 1811 and the white people in Indiana haven't had any trouble since.

The best game was pretending we were spying against the British army. That meant crawling around under folks' porches and other places we shouldn't be, laying comfortably on our backs on the cool soft dirt and straining to hear what was being said over our heads that wouldn't be said if spying was suspected.

Bees made for good spying occasions. Though Papa claimed the county was becoming 'too d***ed crowded', it took nearly half a day to get to the nearest neighbor, so the women in the community looked forward to a bee, where they could have a good long gossip together, only they called it 'catching up'.

One time, when the women were husking corn in the kitchen while the men tended to hog-killing, the talk above the floorboards turned to our papa.

'I don't know why John Springer never married again.'

'Maybe two wives in a row was too much for him.'

'John Springer is a very self-sufficient man.' I recognized Miz Macklin's voice. She could always be relied upon to look to the positive.

'He can take care of just about everything on that farm by himself but his own loneliness,' put in Miz Parrish, whose husband ran the General Mercantile in town and who believed in grabbing a bull by its horns.

'There's something about being a man that makes him incomplete unless he has a woman with him,' said another lady, who had always been spoken of as being somewhat romantical in the head.

'Amen. It's in the Bible.'

'The Bible says the same is true for a woman, but I'm not too sure the Good Book's right about that,' piped up old Miz Jenkins, who had lived eighty years and said just about anything she felt like saying.

All the ladies cackled over this, since there weren't any men present to disapprove.

'Perhaps the Good Lord was speaking in practical terms. It is awfully hard for a woman to get along in the world on her own,' said Miz Parrish, in an effort to turn the conversation back toward gentility.

I lost interest in the thread of things for a while, but then Miz Parrish upped and said, 'Sarah is far too old to be traipsing all over the county without a chaperone.'

Joe and Willie both gave me a poke in the

ribs and I had to poke them back and make them shush or we'd be found out.

Miz Parrish's daughter, Letty, was my age and we were best friends at school, but she lived in town where her mama kept a close eye on her. There wasn't much of fun to do in town anyway, with people always around to tell you to stop whatever you were doing or even thinking about doing.

'Someone should talk some sense into John Springer. It's not natural for him to be living the way he has all these years.'

'Try talking to a turnip,' snapped Miz Parrish. 'You ever heard John Springer do anything other than listen to his own mind? And take his own sweet time about it, too.'

'Well, I'm sure a man like John Springer can be choosy and take his time,' Miz Macidin noted in her usual optimistic way. 'He is just about the most prosperous farmer in the county.'

So you can see I am not just bragging when I talk about our property.

'Maybe he hasn't found anyone yet he can fall in love with.' This was from Miz Macklin's niece Dora, who was visiting from Illinois, where it was known there were forward ideas.

Miz Macklin quickly set her right. 'You know very little about love, Dora, and less about practicality. Marriage is a matter of practicality.'

'Marriage is an absolute necessity,' all the women agreed.

Most of that talk just rolled off my back as I didn't give any thought to my papa marrying again. This was before Rebecca, of course. She wasn't even at that bee. Being the oldest in her family and the only girl meant that when her mama got sick, she was the one who took care of the little ones along with her mama too.

But it wasn't too long after the bee that Miz Stevens finally passed away and I have a hunch that somehow Papa became convinced of Rebecca's good qualities the very day of her mother's funeral, because it wasn't long after that he upped and married her – which wasn't his nature at all. He always said it was important to give all alternatives equal time, and it sometimes seemed to me he took his own sweet time doing his considerating over these alternatives. There had been no hint Rebecca was an alternative and my first reaction was to consider Papa marrying her was an act of charity on his part, as Rebecca was past twenty-five and would probably never have another chance.

I couldn't really see the sense in it. Even if Papa was being charitable, wasn't it just the same thing to Rebecca all over again, but this time taking care of children that weren't even her flesh-and-blood kin? At least none of us was sickly, though, so in balance she might've felt she was better off.

But I was uneasy: I just knew the coming of Rebecca would mean changes, and a charity or not, Rebecca's notions of how to run our household turned out to be no charity to me. At first she left me alone as she was busy getting a handle on all there was to do about the farm, which was much bigger than her father's and the house more grand, with both summer and winter kitchens, a formal parlor and a wing added on for Daniel and his family.

After rearranging the entire kitchen, Rebecca went through the bed linens. Then the kitchen garden wasn't to her liking, so she set Joe and Willie to replanting it. I would have been happy with that chore, but she set me to tasks largely of the domestic variety, an area in which I had no knowledge or interest, and in which she was determined to en-lighten me.

Sarah had been in the barn, playing with a new litter of kittens, when she heard Rebecca calling her name. She pondered ignoring the summons, but knew that trick was growing old. She prolonged the journey of less than fifty yards along the well-trod path from barn to house as long as possible, shuffling her feet to watch the dust clouds rise.

Rebecca had set three bushel baskets of early peaches on the table, which had taken a lighter hue after daily scrubbings and applications of beeswax. Sarah was used to everything in the kitchen being dark and homey and the new era of sanitation needled her. She was the only article in the room not yet spic and span, and Rebecca's attention now seemed to be focused entirely upon her.

'Mind your feet. I have just done a mopping.'

Sarah took Rebecca's words as a challenge. In response, she shook out her skirt, sending a cloud of dust to join her muddy footprints on the floor. She waited for Rebecca to say something sharp, which would give Sarah the advantage, since her papa always said that he who lost their temper lost the argument. But Rebecca only nodded toward the peaches, her lips set in a tight line.

'We talked about doing something with these today.'

'It was just you doing the talking.'

Sarah had no way of knowing that Rebecca had resolved not to react to either her sassing or her surly behavior. It was but the latest in a series of resolutions when it came to coping with her new life.

'I thought you might find it interesting to learn how to make preserves,' she said, feigning a cheerfulness that immediately made her feel self-conscious. She was acting as if she were offering a taffy pull – why did Sarah have this effect on her?

26

'I have more interest in eating 'em than making 'em.'

'They can't get eaten unless they get made,' Rebecca replied, sharpness edging its way past her resolve. 'Taking the hard as well as the easy is part of life, Sarah.' The resolution was crumbling. Now she had begun to lecture!

Sarah sat with bad grace, plopping down heavily and tucking her legs around the rungs of the chair. With a scowl, she attacked a peach, turning it quickly into pulp. She licked the rich juice from her fingers, then wiped her hands on her smock, inviting criticism.

Rebecca pretended to examine the edge on a knife while she wrestled with her own sharpness. She had no heart for confrontation. Instead, she was quick to find fault with herself and make excuses for those who punctured her thin skin.

It was no wonder Sarah was unruly, being allowed to run wild with her brothers instead of taking the hour's ride to the schoolhouse. Not that regular attendance would have advanced her education that much: Mr Duggin, the schoolmaster, was largely incompetent, but the best Vermillion County could afford, being so far from any metropolis. Rebecca steered her wandering mind away from making excuses for Mr Duggin; it was Sarah's future that concerned her.

In most households, mothers made up for

irregular schooling, but Sarah would not stand for Rebecca drilling her in math and spelling if she would barely tolerate peeling a peach at her behest! The solution suddenly dawned on Rebecca: it lay beyond herself.

She sat down opposite Sarah. 'Somehow we have gotten off on the wrong foot with each other, Sarah. I would like to do better – to know where your interests may lie, whether you believe me or not. I am not just talking about cookery or housekeeping. I am not a fool; I know you have no interest there. But there's a lot to be learned of good benefit if you take a chance. If you had the opportunity, Sarah, would you be willing to take a chance?'

'Depends on what I'm taking a chance *on*, I guess,' Sarah replied warily.

'Your future.'

Sarah felt her suspicions confirmed. 'You mean my chances to turn into a proper lady so I can make a good marriage for myself?'

'Right now, you don't have to think about that. You are blessed that your father has been so successful. He can afford you the opportunity to attend a proper school.'

The expression on Sarah's face told Rebecca how much she had miscalculated. Too late, she realized she had unthinkingly put Sarah in her own shoes, assuming this wild girl possessed some of her own aspirations at the same age. A 'proper school' meant an academy in Oberlin or Columbus; to Sarah it wouldn't mean the escape such a dream had meant to Rebecca. It would be an indication that Rebecca wanted her out of the house. How foolish she had been!

'Is that what Papa wants?' Sarah stammered.

Rebecca tried to find a way forward instead of slipping further. 'I wouldn't talk to him about it without discussing it with you first.'

'There's nothing to discuss! I'm not going!'

'Don't be so quick to make a decision, without weighing the advantages along with the disadvantages.'

'There's no advantages to me! I already know everything I need to know!'

'Then I am certainly admiring of you. Not many can say that.'

There was a pause between them; they had both gone too far: Sarah knew she had said something stupid and Rebecca knew she had compounded her own error by pointing it out to her. But while Rebecca made yet another resolution to measure her words more carefully in the future and find a way to repair the damage, Sarah chose to throw all caution to the wind.

'Just because folks aren't prepared to go along with your ideas doesn't mean they are in the wrong! There wasn't nobody found fault with the way things were around here until you came along. Why are you trying to ruin everything?'

Sarah had inadvertently opened the door to real discussion for the first time, and Rebecca considered her response carefully. Should she admit to dressing Sarah in her own lost dreams? She had kept her frustrations to herself her entire life. How could she voice them for the first time to someone who seemed determined to hold power over her?

Sarah waited, trembling with rage. Rebecca hesitated, feeling her face flush.

She started when she heard the distinctive creak of her husband's wagon. Was it already that late or was John early? Automatically, her hand went to her hair. She always attempted to greet his homecoming with a freshly washed face and neatened appearance.

'Your father's home. I'll get supper going.'

She started to clear the peaches from the table, tossing them back into the basket so briskly, she bruised more than one.

When John Springer appeared at the door, he didn't seem to notice either his wife's agitation or Sarah shrinking into her chair, unsure whether Rebecca would get her in Dutch with her father. His two oldest sons, Daniel and Matthew, entered close behind John. All three men seemed to share the same high spirit, something almost mischievous in their expressions – astonishing

30

in such solid farmers.

'We need to sit down and do some figuring,' John announced. 'Daniel, fetch me writing material.'

Rebecca had to rescue her preserving jars before John swept them off the table as he cleared a work space. What had possessed him? She was still too shy of him to inquire, but she had no need as he was bursting to inform her.

'Rebecca, we are going to Oregon!'

For once, Rebecca and Sarah were in harmony, their gasps almost in unison.

Rebecca sank into a chair, astounded. 'I had no idea you were even thinking of Oregon...'

'I have been considering it for some time.'

Sarah instantly embraced the idea. 'And you were just waiting until you got all the facts, right, Papa?'

'That's about the size of it.' John smiled, pleased that Sarah had heeded his lectures on prudence.

'It was really me had it in mind first,' Daniel added with pride. 'Then Matthew said he wanted to be in on it, so we decided to ask Papa what he thought.'

Daniel drew a thick pack of papers from his jacket pocket and spread them on the table. Sarah eagerly snatched one up: a handout illustrated with snowy mountain crests and giant fish leaping skywards from a waterfall.

Matthew added a stack of guidebooks: *The Emigrants' Guide to Oregon and California; A Route Across the Rocky Mountains, with a Description of Oregon and California; Mr Lansford Warren Hastings' Traveler's Guide; Overton Johnson and William H. Winter: A Journey West.*

As John made his own contributions, the table became covered with glowing statements from trappers of the Hudson's Bay Company, Oregon societies and missionaries; government reports containing columns of statistics; and copies of letters of endorsement. With the exception of the government documents, each tract was punctuated with stars and exclamation points.

Sarah was absorbed with wonderment over the assortment, but Rebecca remained sunk in her chair, struggling to find the right words.

'But the *farm,* John...' she finally ventured cautiously. 'You are contemplating leaving the farm?'

'There's not enough acreage here to provide for Daniel and his family, let alone the other boys.'

'You have spent half your life building this place up ... it is a fine property and you talked about adding on...'

John pulled a chair next to hers, sat down, and took her hand. 'Haven't I been telling you it's not the same any more? People are settling all around here now, right under our noses. Winters it's frost and snow to freeze a body solid and summers the overflow from the river drowns half my acres.'

'The weather's a wonder in Oregon, Rebecca!' Matthew exclaimed. 'The Captain's seen it for himself!'

Rebecca was confused. 'What captain?'

'Captain William Stokes,' Matthew explained. 'He was with General Harrison in 1812. He went out west to fight the injuns and wound up going all the way to the end and settling there. Now he's come back to get more people to go to Oregon.'

'Specifically *anti-slavery* people, Matthew,' John pointed out. 'The Oregon country could tip the scales on the side of right one of these days.'

'And if there's more people out there, there won't be any problems with the injuns,' Daniel added.

'Don't go frightening Rebecca and Sarah with talk of Indians,' John chided. 'The native population in Oregon is small and devoted to fishing, according to Captain Stokes.'

He turned back to his wife. 'In Oregon, I can get a square mile for myself and a quarter section for each of my sons. They even say there's talk of allotting partial sections to women, but I don't know if anything will come of that. But the time has come to move on.'

'There ain't nothing like it!' Daniel enthused. 'They say in Oregon country, they got wheat so high you have to stand on the back of a horse to see over the top.'

John frowned. 'And the pigs come already cooked, with knives and forks sticking in them. I choose to concern myself only with facts, Daniel.'

Daniel reddened. 'I am not a fool, Papa. I am just repeating what they are saying...'

'They have been saying a great deal, that is for certain,' Rebecca cut in. It had not taken her long to note that her husband and his oldest child were like oil and water, with conversations turning into arguments if someone didn't step in to turn things in another direction. Rebecca seemed to have a natural ability to temper their disputes, perhaps because she had so often arbitrated her brothers' squabbling.

With her husband's careful nature, she felt certain the idea of Oregon must have been going around in his head for some time. She felt no resentment that he had not chosen to share his ponderings with her; it was a man's business and a man's decision. And she didn't know him well enough to expect confidences.

No doubt the fact that Daniel had caught the Oregon fever first had caused John to think about it even longer. The two were opposite sides of the same coin; they even looked alike, with thick brows, turned-up noses and large hands. And Daniel was beginning to develop the same furrows in his cheeks.

'There has been a great deal in the newspapers for and against Oregon,' Rebecca went on in her attempt to deflect argument. 'Some say Americans have to get there so it won't go to the British.'

It was easy to sidetrack John, who was in the habit of bringing home the news and debating it, taking both sides himself if necessary. 'And others claim the USA is big enough and it's a fool's mission to try to get over the mountains,' he quickly responded. 'Well, the Captain has seen those mountains and he says they are nothing much to speak of.'

Daniel also took Rebecca's bait, resentment of his father's reprimand forgotten. 'Captain Stokes came back from Oregon to collect the rest of his family and he'll be leading a new wagon train back out of Independence, Missouri, next spring.'

'But still... I can't imagine it can be that safe ... and it is so empty...' Rebecca shrugged helplessly, feeling she had become argumentative herself, which was not proper for a wife, particularly a new one, even though her world was being torn apart.

Haltingly, Sarah read aloud from one of the brochures: '"In 1841, Jesse Applegate led nine hundred people overland to the Pacific slopes and the very next season, twelve hundred more followed."' Reading wasn't easy for her, but she had to refute Rebecca's naysaying.

'There's a whole heap of folks going this year, Rebecca,' Daniel encouraged, 'and if we don't pick up our traces soon, the best land will be gone!'

'Don't be exaggerating, Daniel,' John advised, but not crossly. 'It will take us close to a year to get ourselves ready for this trip. Oregon will wait.'

Rebecca removed herself from the conversation and began to string beans into a bowl braced between her knees. There was nothing more she could say.

When Willie and Joe arrived from their chores, Sarah took delight in announcing the news to them; being first to know was a real feather in her cap.

A dark shadow had lately appeared on Willie's upper lip, and he now took pains to behave in a way he felt befitting a man. He tried to restrain his enthusiasm, but Joe held no rein to his and peppered his father and older brothers with questions. Sarah still had plenty of her own and it didn't take long for Willie to break down and add to them.

It was Matthew who noticed Rebecca trying to clear a place on the table for her dishes and suggested they set it in order for supper. No one could deny Matthew. It was never openly acknowledged, but he made a strong link between John's first set of children and his second.

From his seat at the head of the table, John delivered a special grace for the projected undertaking, then continued to answer questions. He had agreed to meet Captain Stokes in Independence the following March, and the preparations necessary to move nine people from one end of the country to another would take up every minute in between. While Mr Lansford Hastings said it was best to travel light, Mr Overton Johnson took exactly the opposite view.

'Once we are on the trail,' John mused, 'we will find that much of what has been written is bogus. We will have to separate the wheat from the chaff and use our own heads.'

'To ride comfortably, we'll need four wagons,' Daniel considered, 'so right off, there is no traveling light.'

'How many oxen for each wagon? Eight?' Matthew asked.

'That's right, and a team to spare. How many does that make in all?'

John directed his question toward his younger children. Sarah and Joe looked sheepish, not having spent much effort in arithmetic, but Willie rose to the challenge, forgetting for a moment not to appear eager.

'That's five times eight which is forty!'

'That's a lot of animals!' Joe whistled.

'And don't forget the riding horses,' Matthew added.

'And a milch cow so's Betsy can have her milk,' Sarah volunteered.

John jotted yet another column of figures, a pencil stub in one hand, a fork in the other. 'The wagons, oxen and tack should cost a bit more than four hundred dollars ... and supplies another two hundred ... powder and shot maybe fifty ... and we'll need cash for repairs and supplies during the first winter...'

Willie shook his head. 'That's a powerful amount of money.'

'We'll be selling this property and everything on it, and I'll be calling in my debts as well.'

Sarah was impressed. 'I didn't know we were so rich.'

'The truly rich have no need to go to Oregon, Sarah. And the poor couldn't raise the money. It is people like us who are going.'

Rebecca took her husband's words without question, but if she had not been so caught in the turmoil of her emotions, she might have mentally amended them to 'men like us', and wondered what restlessness there was that caused that sex to seek the outward boundaries of the world while women clung to the comfort of familiar borders.

Women did not choose to go west. They went because their husbands or fathers chose for them. And as much as possible, they attempted to bring their homes with them.

It was a daunting task, but Rebecca would not have to tackle it alone. She had Daniel's wife as an ally. Even though she was the mother-in-law, the two were of the same decade. Elizabeth was of a timid nature and it took effort to bring her out, but she offered female companionship in a household filled with men – and one recalcitrant girl. Having a husband at her side would give Rebecca courage during the journey that lay ahead; the company of another woman would provide comfort.

Rebecca had her own timidity when it came to 'wifely matters'. She hoped one day she and Elizabeth might grow close enough for confidence, though some matters could only be couched in hints. Rebecca held anxieties she could scarcely form into words in her own mind. John overwhelmed her with his masculinity, and thoughts of those strong hands touching her privately in the dark sometimes crept into her mind during the routine of her daily chores.

Her mother had not prepared her; Rebecca had never known her other than sickly and involved with her own discomfort. A few cryptic comments were made by the more forward women when she was finally free and John had asked for her hand, but they only concerned forbearance and duty. No indication was given of what lay in store after the first painful nights had passed and she began to experience pleasure when his hardness entered her and she grew wet as his thrusts became deeper and faster. Was this shameful? She had no frame of reference.

It was easier to focus on familiar domestic chores than worry that her marriage was not normal.

For all her insecurity as a wife, Rebecca was confident when it came to domestic chores. Even with her heart not in it, there was comfort in efficiently executing the myriad tasks necessary to prepare for the journey. The kitchen was filled with the smells of canning and preserving and cluttered with jars and sacks, as well as looms and spindles. Neighbors filled every chair around the table most days, and some days there were enough women working to fill the good ones from the parlor as well. There was a constant murmur: spinning wheels whirring, boiling water bubbling, glass jars gently clinking together, the tea kettle whistling, and always the sound of women talking.

'Surely not dark blue for the sheeting!' Leticia Parrish always had something to complain about.

'The guidebooks recommend dark calico for pillows and sheets,' Rebecca explained.

'White goods won't be suitable with the dust and dirt on the trail.'

'It goes against the grain not to sleep on white,' Leticia sniffed.

'I agree,' Rebecca nodded, 'but the advice is sensible and we might have to bend a few of our housekeeping rules. But there are limits.' She paused to pass the scissors.

'The guidebooks have no use for finer things,' she continued, 'but there is no reason not to have a few linen coverlets and tablecloths decorated with close work to remind us we are still civilized people.'

'The guidebooks were all written by men, who don't know anything about the proper way to maintain a household,' Aggie Macklin said, and the other women tittered as there were no men around to hear her impertinence.

'Elizabeth and I are determined to hold on to as much of our life as possible,' Rebecca said, taking care to include her daughter-in-law. 'When we are thousands of miles away from all we knew before, we will still use the same tablecloths we have used here at home and lay out our good dishes and candlesticks on the Sabbath, even if it will be celebrated in a desolation. We can still stick to our regular routine and urge our family to not be lax in that regard as well. That way, it will seem we have brought a sense of home with us.'

Sarah

I had always turned up my nose at sewing, but covers for the wagons had to be made by hand out of doubled sailcloth – the devil to work with – and I took pride in conquering the task, punching a thick needle through yard after yard. I refused a thimble, and there were spatters of blood on the canvas until calluses grew on my fingers.

There was so much sewing, preserving, soap-boiling and general sorting-out of our household goods that for months practically every woman in the county pitched in for a series of bees, even Poor Lucy Marble lending a hand – she had quite a knack for embroidery. And now I wasn't shooed off when the gossip got interesting. As the sole person willing to tackle sailcloth, no one had a right to begrudge me a place.

And in the middle of all this, Matthew upped and got himself engaged! Now it was no surprise a girl would be sweet on him, because Matthew was generally considered the nicest and gentlest of all the young men around. The surprise was that it was Letty Parrish who had set her eye on him, and that Matthew was sweet on her in return!

I am not about to be saying anything unkind about Letty, who, after all, was my closest female friend. But I had thought we held similar convictions when it come to making moonies over boys; it had only been a few months ago that she had said she'd sooner kiss a toad than a boy!

Then, without any hint that things had changed, I caught Letty kissing my *brother* of all people! And what had possessed Matthew to so suddenly get sweet on someone he'd paid no attention to before? Letty hadn't changed into a new person overnight, as far as I could see.

Me and Letty weren't so close after that. We didn't have a falling-out or anything, but Letty now preferred Matthew's company to mine, and even when we were together, she didn't have much of interest to say. It was all Matthew, Matthew, Matthew, and I knew all about him already, having lived with him all my fifteen years. Willie said maybe the fact Letty was almost seventeen made the difference, but I didn't see it.

To my mind, Letty had been fussed over by her parents to the point where she had not developed any real toughness to her spirit. Miz Parrish was hard on just about everybody in our community *but* Letty, and Mr Parrish gave his daughter anything she wanted out of the stock in his store. Some people claimed the Parrishes were more genteel than their neighbors, and I suppose if that meant they didn't know much about farming and were used to store-bought goods, it was true.

Anyway, when Matthew told Letty she should marry him and come to Oregon, there were all kinds of fits in the Parrish household. The Parrishes didn't like the thought of their only child going so far away with nobody for her to associate with but savages. Mr Parrish even went so far as to say that some very prominent people, including US senators, were calling the whole Oregon movement a 'mass act of insane people'. It was still a question whether it was going to the British or the US of A.

Well, you can imagine my papa had very little patience with that kind of talk, but he didn't say anything for Matthew's sake.

All the arguing made Letty skittish. She went around for weeks with red, rabbity eyes, first thinking one way and then another. Finally Matthew, who couldn't bear arguing, screwed up his courage and laid down the law: he was going to Oregon, with or without her. That tipped the balance and they set a wedding date for just before it was time to leave.

Now all the ladies coming to our house had even more to gossip about: this upcoming wedding along with our trek to Oregon constituted the most excitement there had ever been in our community. Of course Letty was part of the bees and everyone jibed her because she had taken it upon herself to sew up what Matthew would be needing for the trip, even though her papa could have provided everything store-bought. But there was a tradition that a girl should gift a boy a shirt she'd made with her own hands the day of their wedding.

It took months to put the wagons together – solidly built of seasoned hardwood so they wouldn't fall apart on the trail. There weren't any real roads and the way was poorly mapped, with very few forts to help with bearings. Once constructed, the wagons were waterproofed with tar; they would have to be lifted off their wheelbases and floated across untamed rivers.

It was necessary to have extra wagon tongues and spokes and axles and wheels, as well as grease buckets to keep the wheels from binding, and ropes and chains and other gear to haul these magnificent wagons up and down the mountains.

And then there were provisions: two hundred pounds of flour, a hundred and fifty of bacon, twenty of coffee and sugar, ten of salt, along with chipped beef, rice, tea, dried beans, fruit, baking soda, vinegar, pickles, tallow, gunpowder, and whiskey for medicinal and celebratory purposes. There were hams and cheeses and dried fruit and a barrel of crackers. In addition to oxen and horses, there would be milch cows and chickens. They needed barrels for water, a washtub, a churn and kitchenware: a kettle, fry pan, coffeepot, tin plates, cups, knives and forks. It made for more than a ton of goods to be prepared for a journey of five months.

During the summer, bushels of peaches were dried for the trip as a precaution against scurvy, and Rebecca put by a whole bushel of pits for a grove in Oregon. She cautioned the family not to spit their watermelon pips on to the grass, as she was collecting them for Oregon as well. In fact, there wasn't much eaten that didn't get chewed over more ways than one, considering whether any part of the leftovers might be of some use in Oregon.

After peaches, it was apples. The younger set of children cut up fruit to dry in kilns in the orchard and kept fires burning with dry fruit twigs which sent a lovely perfume into the air. The early fall evenings were sweet, eyes chasing the last of the fireflies and ears listening to the doves settling down for the night and the owls commencing to hunt. After the sun went down, there was a bit of a chill – but only enough to prevent feeling too sleepy after a big supper.

Before the winter rains churned up the roads too much to bear wagons easily, more congenial days were passed in the company of neighbors around the old oak table. If the stove was kept hot, it was still possible to enjoy some last moments in the summer kitchen, with a panorama of trees turning red and gold as backdrop.

There were few visitors in winter and the inside kitchen was cramped, with no open sides allowing activity to slop over into the yard. There was still much to do: the coarser flax and wool had to be separated out for towels and rags and a combination of linsey-woolsey to fasten on to looms to make more cloth for everyday trousers. These were wintertime jobs, when nothing was growing outside to be gathered and preserved or dried.

Though she could scarce afford to take the time, Rebecca was determined her first Christmas as John's wife would be celebrated properly, with popcorn and berry garlands, fresh greenery and family passing around the Bible to read of the miracle in the manger. It was their last holiday in their home, but it was only Elizabeth who wept.

Later, she told Rebecca she had just learned she was pregnant again.

January was an inside, closed-in time. Elizabeth often felt sick, but she managed to help Rebecca go through every cupboard and press, noting what still was needed. To aid this project, they had asked the rest of the family to prepare clothing lists. Sarah's was a scrawl, filled with misspellings.

'Do you have enough rags for your monthlies?' Rebecca asked her.

'I'm not a child.'

'If I thought you were, I wouldn't be asking the question. We have to take everything we need with us, Sarah, and it would be an embarrassment to run short – far more of an embarrassment than discussing it now.'

'I can take care of myself.'

'Elizabeth and I will be making rags this afternoon – and napkins for Betsy. You can join us just to make certain you are well supplied.'

Sarah complied without further argument; Rebecca knew it came from enthusiasm for the emigration rather than her own authority, but she had no time to remain troubled by their lack of amity in the midst of so many tasks.

February flew by as hard choices were made. There was only so much the wagons could hold; everything must be of some use either on the trail or in Oregon. 'Don't pack anything worth less than a dollar,' John advised, but the criterion was of little help when it came to emotional attachment.

Soon there were only patches of snow in the yard, and the dry areas began to fill with stacks of goods – some set aside as possibilities for the trip, others still needing sorting. Cast aside in a jumble were old toys, broken china, bric-a-brac too fragile for the trip, and a drawing someone (no one remembered who) had made of the barn years before.

The necessities of everyday life, such as water barrels, washtubs and tin cups, had their own place, and each member of the family dealt with their personal hoard of 'undecided' possessions.

John Springer had enlarged his house and his possessions as his family grew, and it seemed nothing had ever been discarded along the way. As objects were mined from attic and cellar and forgotten corners, Sarah wondered if some of them had belonged to her mother. She shook off the pinch in her chest as not being sensible; her mama had passed such a long time ago, and there wasn't any point in asking her papa if he recognized anything because it was not the way of men to dwell on sentimentalities.

Unwanted items were stored in the barn to sell. John interpreted 'unwanted' as 'not an absolute necessity', though if left to their own devices, Rebecca and Elizabeth would have transported the entire contents of the front parlor to Oregon. Since neither had any desire to leave home, recreating it in their husbands' promised land would make a second best.

With pregnancy, Elizabeth had become

even more timid and acquiesced to all demands, but Rebecca was troubled as John relegated more and more to auction. Would it be insubordinate to quietly tuck a few small reminders of home among the linens?

She carried a basket into the barn, feeling like a thief as she scanned the shelves: a smaller flatiron would be useful for collars and sleeves. A pair of brass candlesticks would lend grace to whatever crude table with which they would have to make do.

Rebecca was contemplating a cut-glass vase and a lace tablecloth when one of the large barn doors creaked open, and a bright shaft of daylight spread across the floor.

She recognized John's silhouette against the light, pushing a small wagon loaded with sacks of rice.

Rebecca could not lie to her husband.

'John, I have not been a good wife. I have gone behind your back and I shall not do it again. I hope you will forgive me.'

John was puzzled; he could not imagine what transgression gentle Rebecca had committed, and the flicker of fear in her expression wounded him.

'Rebecca, you must not be afraid of me. Knowing your nature, whatever misstep can easily be remedied.'

In answer, Rebecca revealed the contents of her basket. 'You have marked these for sale, John, and I had intended to hide them among the goods bound for Oregon.'

John regarded the candlesticks. 'But we have a good stock of lanterns.'

Rebecca sighed. How could she explain? 'It is my task to keep house, John, and I hope to continue doing the best job I am able, even in a wagon. These may seem small things to you, but to set a nice table and have a crisp apron in the morning means all the world to me.'

John shook his head, still mystified, but relieved that Rebecca's sin was so trivial. 'Well, I see no real harm in letting you have your way in this, Rebecca. Housekeeping is your charge and you know best how to go about it. But I don't want to see you slipping the breakfront on to the wagon.'

'I promise you that I will not fill even one trunk, John, and I thank you humoring me.'

It touched Rebecca that John insisted upon carrying her laden basket back to the house. Though her shyness with her husband had not entirely disappeared, her warmth toward him grew daily; he was a good man.

She was not aware that Sarah was in the hayloft, playing with the barn kittens.

Sarah

It had been a deep disappointment to me not to be able to take at least one kitten to Oregon, or a perfect set of antlers I had found in the woods. But everyone had to part with something they treasured, so it was fair that I had to as well. But there was Rebecca breaking the rules and Papa allowing her to have her way!

It was unsettling to be a spectator on auction day watching strangers walk away with the things I had known all my life, even our beds and the pine table everyone had worked around for months. People came from all over; it was a big event in a place where everything had to either be bought miles away or made by hand. Many brought picnic lunches, though it was too cold yet to sit on the ground. The goods to be auctioned were in the yard, so folks had to leave their wagons along the road or even in the pasture, where a couple of them got bogged down in soft places.

'It don't hurt so much when it's neighbors buying our things,' Willie said, but I think he was just trying to put on a brave front as he was giving up his arrowhead collection – but not to auction. Him and Joe and me had decided to give what was really special to us to our friends. Papa said that was all right, and even that it was a good idea, one that he might consider doing himself as he had made several mighty good friends through the years and felt a memento was appropriate.

I gave away my antlers, but nobody wanted my kitten, Little One. A dog could go to Oregon, but a cat would never stick to the wagons. A couple of boys had expressed interest, but I knew they had torture in mind. I sat on the porch cuddling Little One as the auction got underway, feeling her purring against my chest.

Poor Lucy made herself a seat next to me, angling her bad leg. 'That's a sweet little kitten you got there.'

'She's near grown. She was the runt of the litter. I fed her with an eye-dropper.'

'My, my, and a good job you did as she sure looks healthy now.'

'A lot of good that will do her.'

Poor Lucy looked startled, I had spoke so bitterly.

'Begging your pardon, Ma'am,' I quickly went on, 'but she's been spoilt for living like the other barn cats now. I don't know what's going to happen to her once we leave.'

'I guess a wagon is no place for a cat,' Poor Lucy said thoughtfully. 'May I?' She reached out her arms for Little One and I passed her over once I saw Poor Lucy was capable of holding a cat proper.

'I have always been partial to cats,' she said. 'A dog will run you ragged, but a cat is easy as long as you don't expect too much of it.'

Poor Lucy didn't have much to say around the other women, but she had never held back her opinions with us children; perhaps because she'd grown so used to being treated like a child herself.

'How much you asking for this cat?'

'How much?'

'You are selling everything you ain't taking with you, correct?'

'Yes, Ma'am.'

'Well, you said yourself you ain't taking this cat, so how much do you want for her?'

My gloom started to lift. 'Why, if you'd be willing to look after her, Poor ... *Ma'am*, she is yours for the taking!'

There was a burst of applause which seemed to be for our benefit, but it had come as a result of the remarkable price our farm had fetched.

Papa was somewhat embarrassed by such a high bid, and tried to be modest when he was offered congratulations.

'It all evens out in the end – some folks have got themselves real bargains and a few of them have done as much as tell me so. There is no reason to cheat our neighbors and leave them thinking poorly of us, even though we'll be needing the money.'

'I reckon most transactions are going to be by barter on the trail,' Daniel remarked.

'Maybe so,' Papa replied, 'but I feel better with a belt of dollars around my waist.'

'There ain't no stores in the wilderness,' Daniel just had to say, riling Papa.

'The man that gives up and wants to return home has no use for his goods and much use for dollars,' Papa came back at him. 'Mark my words, Daniel, there will be bargains to be had from the go-backs.'

Well, it looked like they were going to get into another of their set-tos, but Rebecca stepped in just then with a list of things that still needed to be purchased, which relieved Papa of some of *his* dollars and kept the peace betwixt him and Daniel for a while at least. I do have to hand it to her – she had caught on right away to Papa and Daniel's problems, and had a knack in dealing with them.

Our house was left nearly bare after the auction, save for a few things that the purchasers had agreed to let us keep on loan until we left. We'd be sleeping on the floor now, on new mattresses specially made for the trail. Just about all our other possessions were already packed in trunks.

There was only one item of business left, which was Matthew and Letty's wedding.

Rebecca and Letty's mother had a big set-to over it right in the middle of our bare parlor.

'I know it is not the custom, Leticia,' Rebecca said, 'but it would mean a lot to me to give the wedding dinner as it will be our farewell dinner as well.'

Miz Parrish didn't like that. 'But it is our place to stage the event, Rebecca.'

'I don't think you would wish to deny me one last meal in my own home.' That was another thing about Rebecca: she was a good debater, and I say that from having tangled with her myself.

'If you're going to put it that way, I reckon I can't,' Miz Parrish said somewhat huffily.

'Of course, I can't do it without your help – all our good china is gone; not that I had anything to compare with yours.'

Rebecca was offering Miz Parrish a crumb, and she bit right into it, seeing a way to keep herself at the center of things. 'Well, my own matching service is for sixteen and Edgar could extend it from his stores,' she said, trying to sound reluctant. 'And of course I will lend my silverware and crystal punch bowl, along with the cups and glasses. They won't all match, but I don't think anyone will notice if I pretty up the table with a few special pieces – there is the tiered server I inherited from my grand-mother: it would look nice with candied fruits and nuts, don't you think?'

Letty didn't like being left out of the decisions. 'But the weather's still so cold and drizzly to have folks come all the way from town,' she whined. She turned into such a fly girl once she got engaged.

'I am sure the Good Lord will allow the sun to shine and the roads to dry and both things to celebrate will get off to a good start,' Rebecca said firmly, and that was that.

Having won the day with Miz Parrish, Rebecca set right to work, getting the folks that bought our fine cherrywood dining set to lend it back. We'd already been loaned the set from the kitchen. The chairs for both sets would go against the walls for the older folks to sit on and the tables put together down the center of the parlor. Since there wasn't any other furniture in the house, there'd be plenty of room for everybody to fit inside if the weather didn't hold.

Willie and Joe were set to scrubbing and polishing the flooring – Rebecca said it looked disgraceful now that it wasn't covered with rag rugs. I got a good chore for once, which was scouring the orchard for early-blooming branches to use. for decoration. Most else I had to do was as onerous as usual.

The menu included three kinds of salads – three bean, apples with celery and walnuts, and carrot – to go with braised beef, fried chicken and a fresh ham. There were biscuits and cornbread, and wedding cake to be served with ice cream. Everything called for a great deal of cream and butter, and before you knew it, I was back at that hateful churn, but Joe spelled me.

The morning of the wedding, we all got up earlier than usual, hurrying through our chores so we could pay full attention to all the last-minute things that needed to be done. Joe and me helped Willie crank the ice cream and we licked the paddles clean. Rebecca was too busy supervising everything else to give us a lecture about hygiene.

The Parrishes came early, bringing Reverend Davidson with them. Letty wore her mother's wedding dress, which had been her mother's before her. It had been bleached back near to its original white and tucked and pinned in quite a few places, since Miz Parrish was a big woman and Letty had been so nervous over the wedding and going to Oregon she had gone off her appetite. She wore a wreath of early cherry blossoms in her hair, and though to my mind she possessed too sharp a face to be called a beauty, I had to agree with the old saying that on her wedding day a girl is never more lovely.

Reverend Davidson said to Matthew, 'Give honor unto your wife as she is the weaker vessel.' He had Matthew tell Letty, 'With all my worldly goods I thee endow.'

These weren't much, but she was still getting the better end of the deal, I thought. Of course, he also had Letty tell Matthew, 'Whither thou goest, I shall go,' so he made it clear Matthew was going to be the boss.

Daniel stood for Matthew, which was right as he was his full brother, and Letty had her cousin who came in from Terre Haute stand for her. I admit I was a little disappointed she hadn't asked me as we had been friends, but I didn't say anything and acted as friendly as could be, and kept telling myself blood was thicker than water.

Rebecca had been up before dawn to start the ham and beef slow-roasting, and she and Elizabeth ducked out from the ceremony on the porch steps the minute Letty and Matthew were pronounced man and wife so they could have everything laid out piping hot. Poor Lucy helped me carry the dishes from the kitchen to the tables.

More guests kept arriving, not really minding they had missed the ceremony; it was the wedding dinner that mattered. There were so many, they spilled down the steps and into the yard, trampling what was left of Rebecca's flowerbeds after she had sacked the best of the bulbs. The skies stayed clear, though no one removed their overcoat until they were able to crowd into the house, and folks kept tripping over the umbrellas that had been left on the porch just in case.

The older generation clustered in the parlor, but the younger set spread out through the house, taking possession of the empty rooms. It gave us the opportunity to play games like hide and seek, which with all the nooks and crannies in the house, was just the thing. We played singing games as well, which some of our more religious elders frowned at, saying they were just dancing in disguise. But no one was really going to be too severe on a wedding day and what noise we made got swallowed up by all the yammering going on around the buffet in the parlor.

Matthew and Letty were able to slip away from the well-wishers long enough to join in for 'Skip to My Lou', and sing the chorus of 'Wait for the Wagon'. Willie got a bit rambunctious with 'Pop Goes the Weasel', and everybody shushed him lest the hi-jinks be shut down.

'The parson's just two rooms over and you know how he is!'

Of course it really was dancing and there was flirting as well. I joined in, but I didn't allow any boy to be too cheeky with me. I danced mostly with my brothers or some of the younger girls who were too shy to find a boy to partner. Even on such a chilly day, everyone's hair got plastered to their foreheads with sweat and Letty's cherry-blossom crown left pink petals all over the floor.

When people commenced hollering for the newlyweds to come cut the cake, we all took a moment to make ourselves presentable, then streamed back into the parlor for the ceremony. The moment was interrupted when Mr Macklin burst in to report that several little boys had disappeared with the guns Papa had purchased for the journey and which everyone had been inspecting earlier. They had told one of the little girls they were going to play 'going to Oregon'.

Young and old alike joined in the chase. No one was over-concerned as these were farm boys respectful of firearms, even at their early age, and they were caught before they did any harm.

The bride and groom were seen off in the Parrishes' closed carriage, under a shower of rice and catcalls from Matthew's friends, who didn't care what the preacher might think.

'Don't get too cozy in that feather bed! You'll be sleeping on the ground soon!'

'You only got two days! Make the most of them!'

Letty and Matthew were only taking themselves as far as the Parrish house in town. They'd be better off there than sleeping on the floor with the rest of us; their real honeymoon would be on the road to Independence.

Daniel had dubbed the wagon set aside for

them 'the honeymoon wagon', and he and his chums pinned embarrassing signs on the canvas cover. He made sure it was sitting in plain view in the yard so all could see it, which added to the merriment.

It took a full day to put everything back in order after the wedding, and Rebecca made us dust and polish the tables and chairs, then sweep and scrub the floors all over again!

'I don't know why we have to do this,' I complained. 'It's not like we're ever going to see it again.'

'It wouldn't do for the new owners to think us sluts,' Rebecca said sharply.

Departure day finally arrived. Without any plan, everyone in the family rose early and found an excuse to take one more turn about the yard and one last look in the barn. So thorough had the months of preparation been, there was really nothing left to do but wait for Letty and Matthew to arrive.

But instead of a carriage carrying them both with Letty's trunk, Matthew rode up alone on a borrowed horse. He was down in the mouth, not at all as a newly married man should appear.

'Letty won't budge,' he announced as he dismounted. 'It is her parents made her do it – they have taken the position that if she says she won't go then I won't go either.'

'It was a mistake letting them get their hands on her again,' Daniel said angrily. 'You should have just stayed out here on the farm.'

'And let you and Willie hoot and holler and send Letty into tears?' It was unlike Matthew to show temper.

Daniel shrugged disgustedly. 'Well, I reckon she is in tears anyway.'

'There is no use arguing over what might have been, Daniel,' John cut in. 'Matthew, we need to make Independence no later than the beginning of April. The muddy condition of the roads has already slowed us down.'

Matthew looked stricken. 'Just a day or so, Papa. I know I can change her mind.'

'Perhaps you could talk to the Parrishes, John,' Rebecca suggested.

'We have delayed too long already. If Matthew has not been able to change Letty's mind by marriage, he will not change it in two days more. Her parents are calling your bluff, Matthew, and the only way to persuade her is by calling their bluff in return.'

'Can I at least give it one more try?' Matthew begged, reduced by love and confusion to a child's wheedling.

'Some of our neighbors wanted to see us off John,' Rebecca added. 'We don't want to disappoint them, and Matthew's horse is the fastest one around.'

'Well, just don't break your neck while

you're at it,' John grumbled, not entirely hiding his desire to give his son as much slack as possible.

Matthew quickly saddled his own horse and left before his father could change his mind.

Elizabeth took the courage to whisper to Daniel, 'Will you take your time in drawing up the wagons? I have so counted on having another woman in our circle.'

Elizabeth had been filled with dread since she had found out she was expecting, so he held his tongue and attempted to comply, even though dawdling was not in his nature.

Pink, one of the Springers' tenants, helped Daniel and John bring the wagons in line.

'I reckon handling all these animals and wagons is going to be quite a chore,' he remarked, as they went from team to team checking the buckles.

'We'll be taking it slow until we get the hang of it. The roads are good to Independence,' John said confidently.

'Still ... who's going to be handling that spare wagon for you?'

'Willie's up to it.'

'But don't he have to keep his eye on the stock?'

John stopped working for a minute. 'What are you trying to say, Pink?'

'Well, if you have need of it, I could drive as far as Independence and maybe make up my mind once we get there if I want to go all the way or not.'

'You caught the Oregon fever too, Pink?' Daniel laughed.

'Didn't think so, but seeing the bunch of you starting to head out gave me an itch something fierce.'

John shook Pink's hand. 'It sits well with me, Pink. You're a good man to have around. But we'll have to come to a quick agreement over wages, as I don't have time to waste.'

'The ride's enough for me.'

'But not for me. Three dollars and board?'

'That's more than fair.'

Joe and Sarah joined Willie to gather the rest of the stock: a spare team of oxen, four milch cows, a calf, and four good horses.

'These beasts would take today to choose not to be ornery,' Willie said, trying to make more time for Matthew.

'I could hit Bessie in the rump with a rock,' Joe offered.

'Papa will see and he will whup you good.'

Some closer-living friends and neighbors began to gather in the yard. Nannie Hawkins, Elizabeth's mother, had hitched a ride, and she and Elizabeth sat the porch with Betsy to have a good cry where Daniel couldn't see them.

Most of the women who had helped through the months of preparation also came to pay a last call. They huddled together whispering, then pushed Poor Lucy Marble forward.

'Now you didn't know it,' she said to Rebecca, 'but all the time we was working with you, when you wasn't looking, we also did something special.' She thrust a bulky paper-wrapped bundle into Rebecca's hands.

Rebecca had never been the object of such attention. Embarrassed, she stared at the parcel in her arms. Poor Lucy was so impatient to reveal the surprise, she undid the knots herself and the paper fell off to reveal a friendship quilt. The other women couldn't contain themselves any longer either, and rushed up to help Rebecca unfold the quilt, all talking at once.

'See there? That's my sprigged muslin.'

'And here's my gray gingham.'

'We all put in a bit of our favorite dresses.'

'Around the edges we each embroidered a sentiment, asking you not to forget us.'

'As if I ever could,' Rebecca managed to finally say, tears glistening in her eyes.

'Most of the work we do is the kind that "perishes with the using", as the Bible states,' Abbie Macklin said. 'When we're dead and gone, nobody's going to think of all the floors we've swept, the tables we've scrubbed, and the stockings we've darned. But when you put something of yourself in a quilt, why, you live on. Your grandchildren and great-grandchildren will see it, so

66

wherever we might be then, we won't be forgotten for certain.'

The women hugged each other tearfully and the men shook hands without tears. Finally John announced they could wait no longer and the Springer wagons moved out of the farmyard, many of the other wagons and carts choosing to follow.

First came Daniel's wagon in the lead, then John's, followed by Pink with the wagon that would serve the rest of the family. Matthew's 'honeymoon wagon' brought up the rear with Willie driving, though no one called it by that name now.

Other neighbors gathered here and there along the main road to wave goodbye, and the leavetaking began to turn into a parade, with dogs and little boys running after the wagons. Everyone waved, some with handkerchiefs, and others with American flags, as emigrating to Oregon was considered a patriotic act.

Sarah and Joe pushed their horses to the front, ahead of Daniel's wagon, and led the parade, waving and bowing to everyone they passed.

The only person not joining in with the waving and the hollering and the general high spirits was Matthew, who joined the parade further down the road – alone.

Journal of Rebecca Springer

March 12, 1846

The first day of our journey to Oregon country.

Our party (all lately of Vermillion County): John Springer, 41.

Daniel Springer, 23, son of John Springer by Hannah Billings Springer (deceased).

Elizabeth Hawkins Springer, 22, wife of Daniel Springer.

Elizabeth (Betsy) Springer, 14 months, daughter of Daniel and Elizabeth.

Matthew Springer, 20, son of John Springer by Hannah Billings Springer (deceased).

William Springer, 17, son of John Springer by Mary Simmons Springer (deceased).

Sarah Springer, 15, daughter of John Springer by Mary Simmons Springer (deceased).

Joseph Springer, 12, son of John Springer by Mary Simmons Springer (deceased).

Rebecca Stevens Springer, 27, daughter of Rachel Cummings Stevens and Paul Stevens and wife of John Springer.

Also with us, Pink Adams, 22, who will drive for us as far as Independence, Missouri, and maybe more.

The weather is brisk, but sunshiny. Dinner: the balance of the cold meats from the wedding, a salad of pickled vegetables, biscuits and soup. Dried apples for dessert. This was taken near a stream.

Rebecca was pleased how well the first day proceeded. She had planned carefully, stowing tin plates, mugs and cutlery in the wagon box, which also served as a table, with a hole bored in each corner and four stakes cut to fit them. Her everyday cloth and a clean apron were on top of the baskets and biscuits kept warm next to a jug of soup taken piping hot from the stove in the morning. The table was set by the time the men had a fire going. It was but a step after dinner to put the dishes into a wash kettle heating on the embers. After doing a rinse in the cold stream, Rebecca and Elizabeth hurried back to thaw out their fingers before the fire was smothered.

Rebecca felt proud. 'I reckon we set up, fed ourselves and the animals, and cleaned the dishes and stowed everything away in the space of an hour.'

Elizabeth shared her pride. 'And this our very first day!'

'The men ate well, except for poor Matthew,' Rebecca added.

'Well, and no wonder...' Elizabeth's eyes began to well with tears, thinking of leaving her mother.

'It is unnatural for a wife to prefer her parents to her husband,' Rebecca gently reminded her. 'I am dismayed to be moving forever to the far side of the continent, but women know when they enter into matrimony that God has given them a new obligation.'

But back on the wagon next to John, Rebecca still dwelt on Matthew's unhappiness.

'It is hard to hold my tongue while Matthew proclaims Letty's virtues. That girl is filled with shortcomings, the biggest being her leaving him in the lurch.'

'You clearly have no difficulty in holding your tongue with me, Rebecca.'

Rebecca flushed. She had become more at ease with her husband and had forgotten herself. 'I am sorry, John. Lack of charity is one of my many faults and I will try to be more considerate.'

'Just as long as you don't direct that tongue to me.'

Rebecca was relieved to note the twinkle in his eye. She had been in awe of John Springer practically since childhood and had only recently grown comfortable calling him by his Christian name. She sometimes still felt herself on approval; that she must convince him he had not done wrong in rescuing her from spinsterhood.

Everyone had proclaimed it was a blessing when her mother had finally been relieved of her suffering, but Rebecca knew that the well-wishers felt it would have been more of a blessing if she hadn't lingered for twelve years and ruined Rebecca's chances.

There had been certain benefits to her life as a caretaker. Her mother's father had been a circuit riding preacher, who had taught his only child the Bible cover to cover. From the boredom of her sickbed, she had passed on her education to her daughter, firing a thirst for knowledge in Rebecca which led her beyond religious tracts – but not as far as formal schooling would have allowed.

She still had Grandfather Cummings' Bible in her possession – three generations of the family carefully inscribed in the flyleaf. Now she would be able to put down her own children as well.

With John Springer in her life, she might contemplate children! She had not held high romantic expectations for herself, even as a child. It had been made clear to her that she was not pretty, though she had been told she had a 'strong' face.

In their brief courting, John had said he had been attracted to her 'settled disposition', which in the long years of marriage was perhaps more of an attraction than a face something more than 'strong'. Other words of affection were few, and seldom spoken after he had emptied himself in her and they lay side by side, she sometimes yearning for something more.

She had tried to respond to him physically the night he had announced they were going west, but for once her body remained cold and tight. 'Our home in Oregon will be truly yours,' he had told her afterwards. 'There won't be the ghosts of my former wives to contend with.'

She had attempted to be light. 'I hope you are not trekking to Oregon on that account, as I never was the superstitious kind. If I was, it might be doing me a favor to have a nice chat with your wives so as to get to know you better.'

She would never let him know it had been the near death of her to pick up traces and leave home.

Fourteen miles were travelled the first day, crossing the Little Vermilion River and heading south along the Wabash. John often called a halt to check the oxen's yokes for chafing and the wagonloads for balance. Daniel was impatient to gain as many miles as possible each day, and his father's methodical methods grated on him. Rebecca kept a watchful eye, alert for potential argument. She wondered why people said there could be only one woman in a household, when it was in men's nature for each to have his own way. Women, raised to be submissive, would always look for ways to get along with each other. With the exception of Sarah.

The first night was spent as the guests of

Mary and Abner Goodwin at their farm located practically at the very bottom of the 'shoestring county', as Vermillion was called, since it was so long and narrow. The Goodwins were cousins on Rebecca's mother's side and Rebecca enjoyed hearing tales of their mutual grandfather, the Reverend Cummings, and was pleased to find her love and respect for him was shared.

After all had been cleared, the men pushed the table to the wall so the visitors' mattresses could be rolled out before the hearth. Abner offered John the spare room as head of the family, but Rebecca whispered to him that Elizabeth might be more deserving in her new condition.

John knew it was the right thing to do, though he had looked forward to the pleasure he found in his wife's body. He had been so long celibate, he had to be careful not to think of her deep warmth during the daylight hours less an erection betrayed his lust.

Husband and wife lay chastely side by side on separate mattresses before the fire, neither easily going to sleep in spite of the long day. While John thought of Rebecca's firm breasts, still unmarked by suckling children, Rebecca worried about Elizabeth.

Poor Lizzie! There were dark shadows beneath her eyes and Rebecca could see pale blue veins throbbing in her forehead.

What words of comfort could she possibly bring her, not being a mother herself? To have a young child on the trail brought one set of worries, but to bring yet another into the world while still traveling must present even more of a burden.

Rebecca had been too young to assist at her brothers' birthings and had had no occasion to be at any other. What she knew was hearsay, and that was largely concentrated on the worst that might happen. But she understood Captain Stokes' wife had quite a few children, so could be of help to Elizabeth. The thought comforted her.

The Journal of Rebecca Springer

March 13, 1846

Second day on the road and close to leaving the state of Indiana. Tomorrow we leave the Terre Haute road and cross into Illinois. Today dawned colder but still dry. We were able to make 17 miles on a very good stretch of road. One horse caught a stone in its shoe, but John feels it will not go lame. All members of the party are well.

I thank You, Lord, for all the benefits You have granted me and ask for Your blessing and guidance. Take particular care of my good husband and bless the Goodwins,

74

along with the other friends and family we have left behind. Grant us good weather on the road ahead.

When John had traveled far afield to pick up supplies for their journey, he often brought home news of what others were saying about the great Oregon migration. It impressed Rebecca to know it was the topic of conversation in so many quarters. Like it or not, she was going to be a small part of the history of the nation. Feeling that merited marking in some way, she had sewn the pages of a journal together and bound it with oilskin, but wondered if her notations were of any value.

Men were making the journey with great enthusiasm. They did not seem content with the bounty they had, but were determined to seek something more at the other end of the continent. Sarah shared that restlessness, but she was still a girl, and, moreover, raised to think like a boy. Her life was so different from Rebecca's, who had had little freedom in her own youth. Her father doted upon her, while Rebecca's had never thanked her once for anything.

Rebecca was determined to find some understanding between them. It was not a new year, but it was a new beginning.

Discomfort soon supplanted Rebecca's contemplation: there was no room to turn around inside the wagon. It was ten feet wide and near twice that long, and the bows stood high enough that a person could stand in the middle, but bags of grain and flour and cornmeal were stacked two feet high along the sides and tubs and baskets were stashed between.

The canvas flaps were closed against the cold and the smell of the caulking pitch was nauseating. When Rebecca opened the flaps for air, the odor rising from the tar bucket hanging off the rear gate smelled even worse. And its constant clanking got on her nerves, along with the squawking of the chickens, pent up in coops on the wagon-sides. She questioned whether they would settle down to laying. As a precaution, she had put up two dozen eggs in the flour bags.

If she sat too long, her feet became chilled, so she decided to walk beside the wagon. The fresh air eased her nausea, and the thought that she would be spending the night with her best girlhood friend, Kitty Winters, lifted her spirits.

The Winters' farm was near Terre Haute. Matthew, Joe and Willie took accommo-dation in the barn. Sarah wanted a place there as well, which Rebecca told her was not seemly for a young woman. Sarah argued the issue, contending that since she would soon be sleeping on the ground, sleeping in a barn seemed downright seemly. Rebecca was too weary to engage in debate and gave way; it was so much easier dealing with stepsons, who had been reared to be respectful of women.

It was grand to see Kitty again; so many miles lay between their homes since Kitty had married. She had come to Rebecca's mother's funeral, but Rebecca's marriage followed too soon afterward to justify a second journey. But Kitty's presence at the sad occasion had meant so much, and the wedding had been but a simple affair, befitting a man who had married twice before.

Kitty and Rebecca huddled close to the hearth after supper, toasting salted nuts and giggling as if they were still young girls sharing secrets. Kitty had grown stout and content with three children, but to Rebecca's eyes and heart, she had changed little.

Kitty was the only one who understood and sympathized with how much Rebecca's life was constricted when her mother fell ill; it was she to whom Rebecca complained when she was low and her father showed her no kindness. And without a word exchanged, she understood how Rebecca's life had changed yet again – first with marriage, and now a journey into the unknown. And unlike Elizabeth, she felt free to discuss 'womanly matters'.

'Men are not shy at all about what they consider natural,' Kitty explained. 'If your

John is a good man, he will not subject you to anything that will demean you. And with time, it will all seem less awkward to you. I know it did to me – and look what I got out of it: three beautiful children!'

'They certainly are a blessing,' Rebecca said, not bothering with Kitty to hide her blush.

'That's right – each time he comes to you, just think he might be bringing you a blessing!'

'But Kitty ... is it natural to come to me each night?'

Kitty grinned. 'You must have a powerful hold on him. Now be honest, Rebecca, do you find it natural?'

Kitty did not continue to tease when she saw how flustered Rebecca had become. 'My darling,' she said, patting Rebecca's cheek, 'it is God's blessing to both give and receive pleasure in one another. I have no patience with women who moan about forbearance – others' unwillingness to be generous should not interfere with our own. Your husband seems a good man.'

'He is, Kitty. Oh, he is.'

'You are brave to be going so far away into the wilderness.'

'I am only two days into the journey. It is easy to be brave now.'

'Try not to think ahead; take each day on its own, and before you know it, you will be used to it and everything will seem more familiar, just as your husband's body will become familiar and bring you comfort.'

As her friend brushed her hair, Rebecca was certain Kitty privately thanked the Lord that her own husband had not caught Oregon fever, but only moved his wife a few miles from home where the land and people were still familiar.

When they left Kitty's farm the following morning, Rebecca knelt in the back of the wagon watching her friend until Kitty was just a speck – the last familiar thing her eyes would ever see. No one would know who she was or who her family was in Oregon. And she was going to this unfriendly place with a husband who was still largely a stranger, and a family that was not her own.

The Journal of Rebecca Springer

March 15, 1846

On our own in Illinois with no acquaintance. But we are on the National Road. Some rain today. Wind later. Found a good campsite with the stock boxed in by the wagons and the natural boundary of a stream so they can't wander.

Thank You, Lord, for making the start of our journey so smooth. I know the way will become more difficult, but an easy beginning helps ease the pain of leavetaking.

Keep us safe this first night sleeping in the open.

It started to rain and John covered the chicken coops with a tarp. Rebecca decided to put at least one bird out of its misery and combine it with biscuits and gravy for supper. Even if the rain let up, she didn't want to attempt too ambitious a dinner her first day cooking in the open. But the necessity of pulling it together while holding an umbrella amounted to as much as if a feast were being prepared. The wet firewood smoked badly and the smell lingered in her hair, which made her feel unclean.

Though the rain ended before supper, the weather did no kindness, as a stiff wind whipped up. The stew simmered in a Dutch oven nestled in the coals. When Rebecca stooped to lift the lid, a sudden gust sent sparks shooting everywhere, startling her so, she dropped the lid in the fire, sending billowing ashes into the stewpot.

Whenever a dish was passed at table, the cloth flew up and another dish had to be found to keep it from spinning away. As the table was being cleared, it did sail off with Willie chasing after.

Sarah came to table with a muddy dress, but Rebecca could not complain as her own dress and apron were filthy from wet ash.

With the wind and the prospect of more rain, John decided to shift the goods in the wagons and roll out mattresses, rather than pitch tents.

They had to do the dishes by lamplight and Rebecca was sure they would have to be gone over again in the morning. After starting the bread and washing out at least one of her aprons, she found her husband already asleep by the time she crawled into bed. She welcomed a moment alone to calm her mind from the small disasters of this day and to consider the next; tomorrow was the Sabbath and a day of rest. She had much planned for it.

She and Elizabeth rose before dawn to stoke the fire and put on the kettle, then rigged a windbreak while the flatiron heated; Rebecca felt better when she was able to tie on a fresh apron. Sarah had to be roused to do the milking, stumbling off half asleep with her bootlaces still untied. By the time the coffee was boiled, the men were up, anxious about the livestock, which were jittery in the wind.

Rebecca examined the dishes. Her fears were confirmed: they were speckled with bits of dried food from last night's meal. She stopped Sarah from pouring the milking pail into the pitcher.

'Give it a good wash first.'

'I washed it after supper.'

Rebecca pointed to the yellow drips of congealed cream streaking the sides of the pewter pitcher. 'Not very well.'

'It's not my fault it was too dark to see!'

'Well, it is broad daylight now, so go back and do it over, along with the rest of the dishes. I am planning a nice Sunday dinner and I will not have it spoiled by dirty dishes. It is all I will ask of you today, Sarah, so please accommodate me.'

Rebecca felt her customary guilt as Sarah stalked off. Her resolve to find common ground with her had not lasted long. Sarah, of course, was right – the state of the dishes was not entirely her fault. But she was not much help with any of her chores, preferring to tend the stock with Willie and Joe. And since Elizabeth often felt poorly, everything seemed to sit squarely on Rebecca's shoulders.

She gave those shoulders an irritated shrug: she had no time to stand around feeling sorry for herself! It started to rain again as she was rolling out pie dough. She could hear Matthew shouting in the distance and reckoned one of the oxen had escaped from the corral. But then she spotted a closed carriage coming up the road. Matthew was running after it, shouting and waving his hat like a madman.

Even through the sheets of rain, Rebecca

recognized the Parrishes' distinctive carriage, and as it grew closer, she could spy Letty and her father huddled inside. The driver – one of the clerks from the store – slowed the horses so Matthew could trot alongside. Letty reached her hand through the window and Matthew took it in his. She was crying and laughing at the same time and Matthew seemed to be crying himself, although it was hard to tell with the rain pouring down his face.

The entire family had been drawn by the commotion and gathered at the side of the road. The carriage pulled to a stop with a spray of mud that made everyone jump back.

Matthew helped Letty down from the carriage, leaving long muddy streaks on her dress, which she didn't seem to notice. Edgar Parrish remained inside, sunk deep into the leather cushions, his grim look drawing his long face down even further. John mounted the steps to lean in and put a hand on his shoulder.

'I promise to look after her as if she were my own child, Edgar. And she practically is, since I've known her since her birth.'

Edgar struggled to maintain his composure. 'Protect her,' he finally muttered.

Once Willie and the driver had unloaded Letty's trunk, Edgar didn't waste a moment in ordering his man to turn around.

'A quick execution is often kinder,' John noted to Rebecca.

Matthew put his arm around his bride and started to guide her back toward the wagons. Willie began to softly sing,

'I love my mama and my papa, too,
But I'd leave them both to go with you.'

Matthew and Letty paid him no attention.

Rebecca had mixed feelings, but it was necessary to act with consideration. 'We will have to make allowances for her with the chores,' she said to Elizabeth. 'She is entitled to a honeymoon, even though she was the one who has caused all the fuss.'

Elizabeth shrugged. 'She is made different from us.' She pondered for a moment. 'You reckon her mother has given her a proper talking-to?'

Rebecca shook her head. 'The only sure way a woman's got to keep from conceiving is not sleeping with her husband – do you want to be the one to go tell that to Letty in her honeymoon wagon?'

Part 2

The Jumping-off Place

Sarah

Willie and Joe and me had a fine time on the way to Independence. It was like things hadn't really started yet, as it was only our own family with everybody and their ways so familiar – more like an outing than a real journey. And of course we were on real roads with signposts and mile markers and no chance of making a wrong turn like could happen in the wilderness.

Except for keeping an eye out for the stock, we pretty much acted like the wild injuns we were always judged to be. Papa did set Willie his turn on picket and he took it real serious, but me and Joe only did what we were asked to do if those that asked had us in their sight. I know this burned Rebecca something fierce and I am big enough now to admit it and say I am sorry about it. But me and her were not on good terms.

Rebecca fussed a lot over how dirty all our things were getting to be. She had a constant war with dirt, and declared that with the mud and the ashes from the campfire, there wasn't a piece of linen among us that was not a disgrace, so we had to have a washday before we could properly present ourselves to the folks that were already gathering just outside Independence. There was grumbling, but Papa gave in to her whims. He seemed to be always giving in to her about something and it riled me. But to be fair, Papa said that we had been making good time and it was hard to see how Captain Stokes' train could leave without us as the weather had not held good two days in a row. The prairie had to be dry before it could carry so many wagons.

We started to see quite a few other travelers having the same destination as us. Rebecca said she did not like the looks of many of them, who were untidy at best. She said it was up to the few women around to uphold standards and she would not have the ones in our company appearing like sluts. This was mostly directed at me, I reckon. When we came to Independence, she said, it'd be important to join up with a train whose women were of like character, and we wouldn't want to be judged less than we were.

So that is how we wound up, only a mile or so to go before we made it to the big camp, having to stop and do a wash, with me hauling water again just like back at home. Clouds came closer and thickened up by mid-afternoon, but the wind came along with them and helped dry everything out before the storm hit. We all scurried about, plucking our laundry off the bushes and trees where we had spread it to dry. Willie said we had certainly found some unusual fruit to pick, though he wouldn't be wanting my petticoat in his cobbler.

There were more than five hundred wagons camped on the prairie outside Independence, their fires making a haze that spread far out across the open plain. Tent villages were dotted everywhere on the landscape, and men on horseback galloped back and forth among the various encampments. Hundreds of animals had to be provided with hay since the spring grass hadn't come in, and the stacks of bales also seemed like tiny villages. It was all temporary, but to the Springers, it was as impressive as a metropolis.

'This is just one of the jumping-off places,' John explained. 'There are more at other towns further up the Missouri River where there is good dockage for parties coming from further east.'

'What's a "jumping-off" place?' Joe asked.

'Well, Independence is the farthest that civilization has reached in this country,' Papa explained. 'Anything west of here, you're taking your chances. Folks say it's like jumping off the top of a cliff without knowing your landing place to take off across the prairies to Oregon.'

'At least we'll be in one place for a while now,' Letty said, 'and maybe find some interesting company.' She hadn't taken too well to life on the road, but Matthew was too lovestruck to mind her pouting.

More than half the wagons were bound for Oregon, with most of the rest going to California, although a few had plans for Texas. People had come from as far away as New York and New Hampshire, some already camping for months, waiting for kin to join them or for the prairie to dry out. The wagons and horses had churned up a sea of mud on the plain, but planks had been laid to walk on and the stock was kept well away from the campsites.

Many of the overlanders had painted slogans on their wagon canvases, such as '54/40 or Fight', the number of latitude the US was arguing over with England to create a new border. 'The Whole or None' meant America should not give one bit of Oregon to the British. But many were not so political, declaring 'Never Say Die' or, poetically, 'Westward the Tide of Emigration Rolls'. Some with no imagination simply put down their names and where they came from, while others demonstrated artistry, displaying drawings of buffalo and eagles and even lions and giraffes. There were several elephants, as 'going to see the elephant' was the saying for going to Oregon.

Even in all the confusion, the Springers were able to locate Captain Stokes, and John was pleased with the spot he'd staked out for his camp, above the mud and well drained. 'Gives me confidence in his leadership.'

Daniel agreed for once. 'Ain't much left for us to do here. We might as well go into Independence to collect the news.'

'There's going to be more rumor than news,' John replied.

'Well, we've got axes and shovels that need grinding, and I want to see if I can pick up a Colt revolver,' Daniel responded.

'They'll probably be wanting an arm and a leg for it. Don't go for anything fancy.'

It appeared that another argument was in the making, but this time Matthew stepped in to be the peacemaker.

'Well, I sure want to go with you, Daniel, even if Papa don't.'

'Now, who said I am not going?' John huffed.

'Matthew! You are not running off and leaving me here by myself, are you?' Letty protested.

Sarah cast Letty a dark look. She had Matthew tied to her apron strings already. She could have used them to strangle her!

'I figgered you had womanly things you wanted to do here in camp,' Matthew said sheepishly, the wind taken out of his sails.

Rebecca tried to help him. 'I for one can't wait to get these men out of our hair so we can meet our neighbors. There is going to be more company than we've been used to for a month.'

The prospect of gossip seemed to lift Letty's mood.

'Rebecca don't want nothing to do with the town because it is full of fancy women,' Willie whispered to Sarah.

Joe overheard. 'What are fancy women?' he asked loudly.

'I'll point 'em out to you.'

'You do and you'll be answering to me,' Daniel warned.

Sarah didn't say anything, but was hoping she might catch a look at one or two on the sly.

But first the stock had to be attended to, and hay purchased for fodder. Many travelers had taken on bachelors to help with their animals – men on their own who tied up with a family to obtain hot meals and a few dollars in exchange for a way west. Captain Stokes had hired several, and magnanimously offered to have them look after the Springer stock until the family settled in. This allowed Pink some time off, for which he was most eager.

Sarah teased him. 'I reckon as how you are our bachelor, you better not find yourself a pretty girl in town and get hitched.' They had an easy friendship and Pink took no offense.

If the Oregon Trail had an official starting point, it was Courthouse Square in Independence. The courthouse was built of solid brick, as were some of the more substantial residences around the square, and was set well back from the road, with a sturdy fence running around it. The square had an established feeling, unlike much of the rest of the town, with many mature shade trees. Wagons continually rolled through the muddy streets surrounding it and there were crowds of men: trappers, Indians, and emigrants; some looking prosperous with beaver hats and frock coats, and the emigrants sticking with their homespun hickory There were a few women who were fancily dressed, but Sarah couldn't determine if they qualified as fancy women.

The blacksmiths' shops were open from dawn until dusk, gearing teams for the trail and turning out freight wagons for the traders along the Santa Fe Trail, which also started in Independence, but headed south. The Santa Fe traders had Mexican mules to carry their loads of silver bullion and pesos. There was speculation how long this trade would continue if the US's differences with Mexico led to war. The overlanders heading for Texas and California, as well as the Santa Fe traders, were concerned.

'If the Mexicans agree to sell California to us, maybe bloodshed can be avoided,' John said.

'Us Oregon emigrants will be well away

93

from war,' Daniel maintained, 'unless we have to fight the English.'

John started to lecture him on patriotism, but both men were distracted by a fistfight that broke out practically in front of them. As many men wore pistols, the Springers wisely crossed to the other side of the street.

Much of the activity in Independence went on inside the taverns. There were dozens of them, erected hastily. No one seemed to mind that the floors were dirt, the lighting dim and the glasses none too clean, as there was a need for gathering places. Strangers needed to take the size of other strangers to learn with whom they might get along on the trail. They needed to decide which train to join if they hadn't come to town with a commitment already in place – and a great many men came to Independence with no real plan in mind.

Women and children were allowed in the family rooms, which was not where the serious discussions took place. Willie promised to fill Sarah and Joe in, and they sat outside on empty beer barrels sucking hard candy, which Matthew had been kind enough to provide. He had bought a whole bag to take to Letty but didn't think she'd miss a piece or two.

Whenever men got together, there were differences of opinion, and nothing seemed to cause more arguments than the subject of slavery. The Springers joined what appeared to be a congenial group, but it wasn't long before two of the men turned into instant enemies when their opposite opinions on the subject were expressed.

Daniel was inclined to put in his two cents' worth, but John insisted they move to the other side of the room.

Their new companions had only Oregon on their minds.

'Seems like everybody's off to Oregon, and I'll be damned if I'll be left out.'

'It's the best people that's going; the soft ones are opting for California.'

'California is not an orderly place and it is full of gamblers.'

Daniel joined in. 'A man's got to be tough for Oregon. It's going to be a job to take it away from the injuns and the English.'

'I feel equal to it,' another man responded proudly. 'My forefathers were pioneers and Indian fighters.'

'I am not as much alarmed about Indians as swollen rivers, lack of water and snow in the mountains,' John remarked. 'If we are kind to the Indians, they will not molest us.'

The Indians on the streets of Independence had been pacified, and wore ragtag clothes cast off from white men.

Joe was disappointed. 'Maybe the folks here made them put on those clothes as they can't go walking through the streets all naked.'

'Just you wait, Joe,' Willie told him. 'The injuns we'll be seeing in the wilderness'll be all dressed up in buckskin and paint.'

'Papa says if we don't bother them, they won't bother us,' Sarah said, hoping he was right.

The Journal of Rebecca Springer

April 16, 1846

We are camped just outside of Independence, Missouri. Captain Stokes has laid claim to a good-sized allotment, so we are not cramped by our neighbors. A brick fireplace has already been built and our sanitary arrangements are acceptable.

The Stokeses have three grown sons already in Oregon with their families. With them now is a daughter named Nancy near Sarah's age and Mrs Stokes' mother, who is quite elderly. I can see Grammy now across the way, rocking in the chair from which she has refused to be parted.

The Stokeses are also transporting a single woman from Massachusetts who intends to teach at a mission. It is a comfort to know the Christian faith is being brought to the savages, but I have never heard of a woman in the teaching profession before.

I hope the chickens will start laying now

we are settled in one spot for a spell. I am fresh out of eggs and they cost a fortune here. We will have beef stew for dinner and peach cobbler after. I am soaking beans.

For Matthew's sake, Rebecca attempted to take Letty in hand. She was a barrelful of emotions, so full of both tears and laughter she was always in danger of overflowing. Rebecca felt a person with so much feeling should not be so careless with it. She almost preferred Sarah's consistent sulkiness.

Added to the cross of coping with Letty was the fact that Rebecca was feeling under the weather. She had always prided herself on her robust health. At first she blamed the motion of the wagon and the smell of the tar bucket. But once they were settled in camp, she had to pay attention to what her body was trying to tell her.

A wave of nausea suddenly overtook her and it was all she could do to excuse herself from Letty's presence and duck behind a wagon before she started vomiting. Elizabeth found her sitting on the ground with her head between her knees, too shaky to continue her day.

'Don't be distressed, Lizzie,' Rebecca reassured her, as Elizabeth wiped her face with her handkerchief. 'I should have learned a lesson from you and not attempted breakfast.'

Elizabeth looked dismayed. 'You're in the family way?'

Rebecca nodded and managed a weak smile. 'It will be easier for us both to share our worries – and our joy in the miracle the Lord has chosen to send us.' She privately wished God's blessings had been bestowed at a more convenient time, but she would not question His will.

'How far gone are you?' Elizabeth asked.

'About seven weeks.'

'Then you will have your lying-in after we reach Oregon.'

Elizabeth's own baby would be born on the trail.

Rebecca tried to encourage her. 'It means a lot to have the companionship of someone to whom I am so attached, Lizzie. And you have had a birthing before so can educate me in the process.'

'I think no amount of education is of any use, Rebecca. It is just something you have to go through with.'

'Well, women have been going through it since Eve, and judging just from the number of people in this camp, they have mostly been doing it with great success.'

Impatient for entertainment, Letty hunted them down. 'Are we going visiting or not? I have been waiting for some time.'

Rebecca said nothing to her; Elizabeth could be trusted to hold a secret, but Letty was not reliable. She didn't want her husband to hear the news from any but her own lips.

Elizabeth chose to stay behind with Betsy, who was teething and fretful. For the rest of the morning, Rebecca and Letty went from wagon to wagon, making small talk to the other women.

Many invited them to inspect their wagons. They were proud of how they'd dreamed up ways to create extra storage space, or added beautifying touches, the inside of a wagon being a woman's province, as the outside was a man's.

One thing all seemed to have in common, freely admitted with no men about: each had hidden away a special treasure as a touchstone to their former lives – a figurine, a shell box, even face creams. Rebecca felt her own treasures looked downright practical against some of these vanities. And she had not hidden them from her husband; once he had caught her at it, to be fair.

Her nausea abated reliably, but her pregnancy remained on her mind, as she went over how she would tell John of her condition. She wanted the moment to be special, but there was so little chance to be truly alone. The only time was in bed – in a small tent, with the rest of the family's tents pitched only inches apart to share warmth. John still lifted her nightdress beneath the blankets, but they came together in silence.

He returned from town in fine humor, reporting what he had learned of the best date to depart, the state of the trail and the grass, and the best route to take. 'I have learned a great deal,' he considered, 'including whose advice is not to be trusted.'

Rebecca chose to change the evening's dessert to apple pie, John's favorite, and after two slices, he took kindly to her suggestion that they take a stroll to a small grove of cottonwoods further down the creek. There was no purpose in the walk other than pleasure, but since they would not be traveling for some days, he seemed capable of relaxing his zeal for productive activity.

It was lovely walking among the trees, which stood out clearly against the brightness of the moon. The silvery leaves shimmered in a slight breeze and nighthawks flitted between the branches. Spring was truly coming; tiny, pale yellow cinquefoil flowers were already dotting the grass, even though it was still brown.

John surprised Rebecca by asking, 'How do you feel Letty is getting along?'

'She and Matthew seem very much taken with each other's company,' she said carefully. In all honesty, she couldn't say more without being unkind, and she had swore to watch her tongue.

'I fear Matthew has put more on his plate than he can chew with taking on Letty.'

She wondered that John had taken note of Letty's character. She seemed more a person to irritate another woman than a man.

'I can see she is not much of a house-keeper,' he went on. 'That puts an extra burden on you and Elizabeth.'

'We try to help her.'

'I know you are doing your best, Rebecca.'

It was nice to be complimented. 'John, I don't want to worry you about anything.'

'Rebecca, you should know by now that you have married a natural-born worrier.'

'I am glad you take such care; it frees me of much concern.'

'If you tell me what your remaining concerns might be, perhaps I might relieve you of a few more,' John said with an affectionate smile.

'Well ... not really a concern...'

'Is something not to your liking?'

'There is something very much to my liking, John, and I'm trusting it will be to your liking as well. Only...'

'Only?'

'Maybe this is not such a good time for me to be carrying a child.'

John seemed dumbstruck for a moment, but then he gave a whoop, scooped Rebecca up, and whirled her around in his arms. Rebecca was startled, as he was ordinarily such a sober creature. He set her down quickly.

'I shouldn't be giving you a jarring.'

'I have already had a good jarring on the road to Independence, thank you.'

'I am more delighted than words can say, Rebecca. This baby will knit our family together as one. How soon is it coming?'

'I figure it will be born a citizen of Oregon, and I hope by that time Oregon will also be part of the US of A.'

'Now fancy that! We'll have to name her Oregonia if it's a girl.'

'Aren't you wanting a boy?'

'Harder to think of a suitable name for an Oregon-born boy, and I've got boys enough already. Boy or girl, there's plenty of space out there!'

They started to walk back, as it had begun to drizzle. John kept his arm around her waist.

'There's feather bedding for sale in town,' he said. 'You should have a softer place to rest.'

'Elizabeth has not asked for special treatment and she has Betsy to look after as well. I thank you for the kindness, John, but I am not a dolly.'

John laughed. 'I am happy to accommodate any whim you might have, Rebecca. And I will be having a talk with Sarah.'

John seemed to have observed far more of

the relations among the females in his family than Rebecca had imagined.

'I know I have not done much of a job in raising her,' he continued, 'but she will have to be of more help to you.'

'I think she would be more helpful if she was not commanded to be so, John.'

'If that is what you wish. I told you I would accommodate you in all ways. That is the privilege of an expectant mother.'

'And I would like to tell her about the baby myself – before we tell the rest of the family.'

Rebecca hoped sharing the news with Sarah first might help forge a bond between them.

The Captain's wife was waiting for her when they returned to the wagons. Though she had never been to Oregon, Harriet Stokes acted as if she were an old hand. This came partly by nature, partly from hearing her husband's experiences, and the remainder because army wives were used to taking command. She was a formidable woman in both conviction and bulk and appeared ready to take command of Rebecca if she allowed it.

'Do you think it's right letting your girl traipse all over creation?' Mrs Stokes inquired. 'There's nothing but men around here and most of them are up to no good.'

Rebecca agreed, but didn't like being told

her business – or that Mrs Stokes had observed her lack of control over Sarah. There were so many wagons consisting only of men, as well as hundreds of 'bachelors'. Sarah had already become far too friendly with one of them, Ben Cooper, just a year or two older than Willie and equally a charmer, with bright blue eyes that had the devil in them and a mop of sandy hair that seemed to beg for a girl to run her fingers through it.

Rebecca attempted to give Sarah a warning. 'That boy is far too fly.'

'He isn't a boy, Rebecca. He's a grown man.'

'All the more reason not to be so free with him. It is not in your best interest.'

'As it is my interest, I think I can be the judge of it!'

'You have not been around men and don't see how it will be taken.'

'You would rather I stick with Nellie Bingham, wearing a bonnet and gloves even when the sun isn't in sight?'

Nellie was the daughter of their close-by neighbors in the encampment, Reverend and Mrs Bingham, and near Sarah's age. Mrs Bingham seemed astonished that such a plain pair as herself and the Reverend could have produced a wonder like Nellie with her shining golden hair, and was determined to preserve this marvel like some curiosity in a museum. While Sarah didn't last a day without some rip or tear and her grooming was loose, to Rebecca's mind there was such a thing as going too far to the other direction.

'As a matter of fact, Sarah, I was hoping you might befriend Nellie so the poor girl might have a bit of fun!'

'I will choose who I like for friends. You want to boss me in everything!'

'I meant to pay you a compliment – to say I prefer the way you are to Nellie.'

Sarah scowled at Rebecca, her dark eyes icy.

It was the wrong time, but there never seemed to be no right time with Sarah.

'Sarah, we must find some way to live together as family. I am expecting a new brother or sister for you.'

Sarah grew rigid. 'Papa knows?'

'After him, I wanted you to be the first.'

'I don't guess what I feel about it makes any difference.'

'Sarah, surely you must have known your father and I would be adding to the family.'

'Our family was fine the way it was, until you came into it!'

Sarah ran off between the wagons, not wanting Rebecca to see the tears she could no longer hold back. Her mind was a confusion of feelings: shock, anger, betrayal – and, most deep, wounding jealousy that she was no longer her father's favorite.

Rebecca said nothing to John about the incident and went on to tell the rest of the family the news at supper. No one seemed much surprised. The older boys gave her a kiss, and Daniel and Willie teased Letty and Matthew about being next. Sarah claimed a bellyache and stayed away from the table.

The Journal of Rebecca Springer

April 18, 1846

I packed John a substantial pail for his dinner, as everything costs an arm and a leg in town. He is meeting Captain Stokes and some others to discuss our route. The Captain is already placing weight on my husband's opinion, which is not surprising to me.

Although the men fret over waiting in camp, I have welcomed this slower pace. I am quite enjoying making calls. This is a camp of women and children during the day, as the men spend most of their time in town.

Reverend and Mrs Bingham are already committed to Captain Stokes, so they will be with us all the way. I am glad we will be able to celebrate the Lord's Day with some proper preaching.

Joe has found himself a new friend named Bert Hansen, which pleases me, as Willie seems to want to spend more time with the men now. Bert's mother seems very cordial and tidy. There is a little sister, and a brother already married with a baby girl.

That baby was delivered by a Mrs Mc-Allister right here in camp three weeks ago. She is well known as a midwife, but is committed to another train. I talked to her a bit and she nicely gave me some of her physicking pills and a vial of peppermint essence. Also some good advice, which I passed on to Elizabeth.

I hope the Hansens will be joining us in our train.

Many folks here hail from Missouri, so they have not come that far. Others are from Illinois, Iowa and Indiana and quite a few have moved to free land before.

I have made the acquaintance of at least a dozen women. Not all of them are to my liking, but I do not wish to mention those by name – it might jinx me and cause them to choose to join our train.

Daniel often left for town even before John had completed his breakfast. He was too taken with 'flash', John confided to Rebecca. 'There are big talkers in town and his head is getting turned.'

Rebecca wondered in what direction, but John only shook his head and said no more.

Matthew lingered until the last moment,

then hurried to leave with his father, which put Letty in bad humor. In Rebecca's estimation, she had too much idle time and little inclination to fill it. When Betsy's teething kept Elizabeth up all night, it was Rebecca who took the baby, while Letty scarcely lifted her hand to darn a sock. She didn't know the first thing about wiving, let alone mothering. She didn't even think of Matthew's dinner, so Rebecca quietly put double in John's pail, not wanting to be so openly petty as to call attention to the oversight. At least Letty did a better job of dishwashing than Sarah.

She was sent off to the creek with this chore after breakfast, while Rebecca and Elizabeth attacked their men's shirts with the flatiron, using the wagon box as a board.

'I do wonder if this is all worth the effort,' Elizabeth said. 'Daniel doesn't even seem to notice if his collars are smooth.' She hurried to correct any misapprehension. 'Of course *I* know it is worth the effort, and that should be reward enough.'

'Now, don't be so harsh on yourself,' Rebecca chided. 'We will both take a break when Letty comes back from the creek and allow her a turn with the flatiron on those fine shirts she made Matthew.'

That made Lizzie laugh – a rare thing. Matthew's shirts had uneven arms and the buttonholes were so small, he had ripped them all. 'It will do Matthew a favor if she scorches them,' she said.

Rebecca untied her apron. 'You missed out on the visiting earlier. Let's pay a few calls together.'

They used each other for mirrors, tucking in stray hairs and wiping away small smudges.

'Am I presentable?' Elizabeth asked. 'This bodice has already grown too tight.'

'You have never looked better.'

'Liar.'

Even timid Lizzie had secretly packed a pair of satin sippers and some lace gloves among her bed linens.

'I wore them at my wedding,' she confided to Rebecca. 'I know I will never have occasion to use them again, but they are so pretty to look at.'

Elizabeth's hands were red and cracked from the lye in her wash soap and her feet were swollen from pregnancy. All that remained of the bride so filled with hope for the future was wrapped in yellowing tissue paper and hidden at the bottom of a trunk. As her mirror, Rebecca did lie to Elizabeth. The truth was too harsh.

The Journal of Rebecca Springer

April 19, 1846

The Sabbath. Some of the churches in town got together and put up a tent for camp services. It was all done very nicely with benches and two choirs. Three different preachers spoke, all saying our journey was pleasing to the Lord, which is of some comfort.

John says there will be a 'muster' to-morrow. The men wanting to be leaders each take a position and those wanting to go with them line up behind. The men with the longest lines win and the others have to join their lines up with them, or I guess go it alone. I told John it seemed like a child's game, but he said it would be one of the most important events ever to happen in our lives, so we will all go to witness it.

I thank You, Lord, for providing such a fine service. I will try to keep those ins-pirational words in mind when I am far away from any steeple.

John and Daniel were at loggerheads, and it was no small matter that Rebecca could easily paper over. Daniel had developed a dislike for Captain Stokes. He claimed there were at least a dozen leaders he had since met in Independence who were a cut above Stokes and that his father lent too much credence to the Captain's army record.

'It was you that first called my attention to Captain Stokes and you found his record impressive at the time,' John reminded him.

'Well, I have kept an open mind and I'm willing to admit a mistake, now that I have seen more of what is on offer.'

'And my mind is closed?'

'You seem to think it is unmanly to admit a mistake.'

'If you were not my son, I would consider that a grave insult, Daniel.'

'I don't mean to insult you, Papa,' Daniel protested, then proceeded to do exactly that: 'But I confess I am weary of your stubbornness. You can make whatever decision you like with your family, but I will make my own. I have decided to go with Mr Kelsey's train.'

'It is late, Daniel, and we should both sleep on this.'

Daniel shrugged. 'Sleep won't change anything, Papa. My mind is made up.'

'Then we will tell the rest of the family in the morning.'

John hoped a little reflection might change Daniel's mind without him having to publicly back down in front of the entire family.

Rebecca and Elizabeth sought each other out at the fire. Elizabeth was sick with fear. 'It mustn't be allowed to happen, Rebecca! We can't be parted!'

'Let's not talk about partings. This will all blow over like before.' Rebecca spoke with a conviction of which she was not at all sure. 'Daniel will see it makes no sense to be dividing up our goods. What sustains us together will not sustain us apart.'

'But Daniel will argue we should be together *his* way. He may well be right, Rebecca. He says Captain Stokes isn't the best leader. What if Mr Kelsey *is?*'

Rebecca would not disagree with her husband's decision, no matter her feelings for Elizabeth, but she would feel lost without her companionship – and what would they become if they lost all sense of family?

'Then Daniel will be proved right and John wrong, and it will not make much difference in the long run, as both Captain Stokes and Mr Kelsey will wind up in the same place,' she said firmly. 'We'll be together in Oregon, which is what counts.'

Elizabeth was close to hysterics. 'That is very nice for you to say, Rebecca Springer! You will be having your child with the entire family at your side in Oregon!'

'Just because I'm reckoning my baby will come into this world in Oregon doesn't mean the Good Lord won't decide to make His own timetable!' Rebecca snapped back, her own emotions swelling.

Elizabeth started to cry. 'I am just about at my wits' end with Betsy always crying and

Daniel and Papa John fighting! I don't want to go to Oregon! I want to be back home and have my mama with me when I have this baby. I want all my nice things around me and four walls with pictures on them. And don't go telling me I will have nice things once we get to Oregon, because there'll be dirt floors and sod houses and I wish I'd never heard of Oregon!'

These were thoughts Elizabeth had never allowed herself to say out loud before, so she cried even harder out of her shame in voicing them. Rebecca swore she didn't think the less of her for her words or consider her a bad wife.

'I know this journey is going to be filled with regrets, but we'll just have to do our best to make things homelike and natural, and bit by bit it will seem that way in truth.'

'There is nothing ordinary about having babies on wagons out in the open on the prairie.'

'Think about where Mary had her baby, with no woman about to help her.'

'That was not the same at all. God would not have let anything happen to Mary or Baby Jesus.'

'And God won't let anything happen to us and our babies.'

Rebecca insisted Elizabeth have a dram of whisky to calm her spirits. As an after-thought, she also moistened a cloth for Betsy to chew on. She couldn't stand the taste of spirits herself and tolerated her morning sickness better than the jigger of brandy she used to force down for her monthlies. But she wished she could find some relief for the pain of separation.

John was late coming to bed. He scarcely spoke, paying particular attention to the careful folding of his shirt and trousers. Rebecca knew neither of them would have a restful night.

'At least you and I can talk about it, John.'

'Rebecca, it is a matter of principle.'

'What principle would tear a family apart? Does it make that much difference if it is one man or another? Can you not swallow your pride if Daniel will not his own?'

For the first time in their marriage, John spoke to her harshly. 'Rebecca, this is not your province and I must ask you to leave this matter to me!'

He put out the lantern and turned on his side away from her. She tried to blink back her tears and calm her heartbeat. After lying rigidly for what seemed an hour, she gave up and went back to sit by the fire until the cold drove her inside yet again.

April 20, 1846

Lord I know You do not give us more than we can bear, but I am not that strong.

Without speaking to the rest of the family, John and Daniel rode off separately early the following morning. Rebecca felt it unfair that the men had left it on her and Elizabeth's shoulders and decided, since she had not been instructed otherwise, to say nothing.

Matthew hired a gig and took Letty in to Independence to see the sights before they went on to the muster. Sarah appeared at breakfast with Joe and Willie; hunger had finally got the better of her pride and she snatched spoonbread straight from the skillet when she thought Rebecca wasn't looking. Rebecca pretended not to have seen, concentrating on steadying her hands enough to break eggs cleanly and not burn the bacon.

'Pink ain't brought the oxen yet,' Joe said. 'Sarah and me can go and fetch 'em.'

It was almost like he was speaking another language. 'Why do we need the oxen?' Rebecca asked stupidly.

'So's we can take the wagon to the muster. It's getting late.'

'We're not going,' she told him, suddenly

deciding. 'We've got a lot to do around here.'

Joe was astonished. 'Don't you want to know who's going to be traveling with us?'

'We'll find out soon enough.'

Sarah couldn't contain herself. 'That's not even fair!' she shouted, but by then Rebecca had gone back to the wagon to cry, leaving the coffee to scorch on the fire.

When later she remembered her duties and returned to rescue the coffee pot, Sarah, Joe and Willie were nowhere to be seen. They had no doubt found a way to get to the muster and would see their father and brother taking stands in two different lines. What a cruel way to learn their family was splitting!

The day crept on slowly. Elizabeth remained in her tent with Betsy; Rebecca tried not to look across the plains at the huge crowd that had gathered for the muster, their murmur so strong it carried across to the encampment. By wagon or cart, on horseback or on foot, nearly a thousand people had gathered, some even sitting on top of the canvas wagon covers to get a better view. Later, the sound of cheering drifted across the mile or so separating the muster from the camp.

Matthew and Letty were the first to reappear, Matthew disappointed because Letty had lingered so long in town he had missed the muster. She was in high spirits.

'The clothes on the women in the streets are something to behold,' she exclaimed. 'I reckon they must come all the way from New York City! There was a black jet with a peplum I would give anything to have, only I don't know where I could wear it once we leave here. But I was saying to Matthew, I think there is opportunity enough right here without traipsing off...'

She would have gone on the rest of the day, but Rebecca could bear it no longer and cut her off with a reminder that she needed to prepare the potatoes for dinner. All around them, wagons were returning. Some families were already breaking camp to join their new trains.

Willie, Sarah and Joe appeared, riding two to a horse with Joe's friend Bert. Rebecca searched their faces, but could detect nothing but Sarah's usual look of disdain when they caught each other's eyes.

'You should have come, Rebecca,' Joe announced excitedly. 'We got there just when the muster lines was being drawed up, but there was so many folks, we couldn't see much, even though me and Bert was able to wiggle our way almost to the front.'

Finally John rode into camp, with Daniel not far behind him. Rebecca and Elizabeth stood by silently as they dismounted.

'How was the muster, Papa?' Matthew

asked in his ignorance. 'I sure wanted to be there, but, well...'

He shrugged, embarrassed to admit how much he was under Letty's thumb.

Daniel answered instead.

'You remember those two hotheads in the tavern a couple of days ago?'

'Redhead and a skinny fellow?'

'That's them,' Daniel confirmed. 'Named Hart and McAdam.'

'Arguing over slavery,' Matthew remembered.

'Yes,' Daniel nodded. 'They got in a fight and Hart near about took off McAdam's ear. Now McAdam's swearing he's going to fix him.'

'And damned if they both didn't muster for Kelsey,' John added.

Daniel nodded in agreement. 'There'll be no geniality in that group.'

John nodded back. 'That's the same thing I was thinking.'

John and Daniel exchanged a look and a further nod.

'I'm going to wash up,' Daniel announced, heading for the creek – and John followed on his heels.

Rebecca sensed John desired no more to be said on the subject. She felt forgiven when he turned toward her in the tent that night. The arousal that used to make her feel shy now gave her reassurance. She lifted her gown herself so he could suckle her blossoming breasts and rub his hand down her belly, which was still flat. When he opened her with his finger, she was moist and ready.

By the following morning, few of the great multitude of wagons were in the same place they had been the day before. The trains were quickly organized, the men meeting to elect a governing council for each. John became a part of their own. The councils then met to draw lots for departure dates; too many wagons at a time would turn the prairie into a sea of mud. Some impatient travelers had already ventured out, but they were mostly individualists unwilling to submit to any authority. The bulk of overlanders knew they had to rely on structure as well as discipline to see them through the following months.

The Journal of Rebecca Springer

April 22, 1846

Departed Independence today. Made eight miles. No more expected with so many wagons. Had to stand by several times to allow them to string out when they bunched up too much. Pink has decided to come with us, 'At least a speck more,' he says. Last night, McAdam ambushed Hart and split his head open with an ox yoke. The deed was done in plain view of several men, who tied up McAdam and delivered him to the General Council.

They sentenced him to death. Our route took us by the tree where his body still hung.

Andrew Hart, murdered April 21, 1846, lies in the Independence churchyard. His murderer will be buried in an unmarked grave, but no death should go without recording, so I am recording it here: Harold McAdam, died April 22, 1846. Ages of both unknown. I don't know where either of them came from.

It was Hart who was for slavery. McAdam was on the side of the angels, but he has killed for the devil. Lord, I pray our train will not receive divine retribution for our men taking Your law into their own hands.

Part 3

High Water

Sarah

I always liked to listen to what Papa and the other men had to say, particularly those subjects brought up when they didn't know I was around. The men in our parts tended to take the same view on slavery: it was an evil which was bound to lead to even more evil, as people were getting more and more riled up over the subject.

Papa wasn't about to let any of us see the hanging, which was a big event to folks not much used to entertainment. As it was, there wasn't much entertainment in it, because McAdam was strung up at the crack of dawn with nothing more than a short prayer, since all the men wanted to head back to their wagons and get going.

But the wagons passed right by the dead man swinging from the limb of a tree on the way out. I had only seen proper laying-outs before, the dead all peaceful like they were sleeping. There was no peace in McAdam, with his eyes and tongue bulging and his face purple. There was a bad smell and Willie said that was because they always dirtied their pants when the rope broke their necks. I never should have looked.

I was having trouble sleeping, but more because of personal concerns with Rebecca and the baby that was coming. During the day, there was so much excitement over finally 'hitting the trail', my black thoughts got pushed away, but at night they popped up again.

There was fifty wagons in our train and most of the folks were new to me. I knew Reverend Bingham and his wife and Nellie, and the Hansens. I hadn't made their acquaintance, but I knew a bit about a family named Prescott, as I had seen them when they arrived in Independence.

A steamboat was coming in on the Missouri River, and me and Joe and Willie went down to the landing to see the sight. By the time we got there, the boat had docked, laying heavy in the water, it held so many wagons, mules, horses and people. Everybody was pushing to get their gear off first: gamblers elbow to elbow with 'mountain men', and a party of Kansas Indians up against a big group of Oregon overlanders shouting at the black stevedores to roll their wagons first down the gangplank.

The Negroes there were both free and slave, and many of them were toting large trunks on their backs all the way up the steep bank from the landing. Slaves were allowed in Missouri.

It was a woman who had got off the boat

and was waiting for her husband to fetch their gear who pointed the Prescotts out to me.

'Those two are from Albany, New York,' this woman said, gossip spreading as easy in Independence as in Vermillion County. 'A woman's lucky to have a Yankee for a husband. They treat their women better.'

And indeed Mr Prescott did see Mrs Prescott and their son real gentlemanly down the gangplank. Then he went back up and started bringing a horse off. It was a thoroughbred, made real skittish by the noise and confusion. When it suddenly reared up, all the men who had gathered to view such a fine horse come to Missouri went running. So I was right curious when I saw them again as part of our train. Turned out Mr Prescott had a whole string of thoroughbred horses, along with all the gear necessary to equip them properly.

'Soon as the West starts to get settled, there's going to be a need for the finer things in life,' Daniel told me. 'Blooded horses, a good saddle and a proper hunting piece. That Yankee's going to make himself a killing.'

The Prescotts were bound for California, but would be going halfway with us, to Fort Laramie. Papa said that Fort Laramie was the first civilization we would see once we left Independence, and that about halfway through our journey. He said that every company stopped there and folks often did what Mr Prescott had in mind, which was to attach himself to a train bound for California.

Since Mr Prescott knew a great deal about horseflesh and riflery, he made a powerful impression on Captain Stokes. The two of them hit it off, both being military men, only Mr Prescott had resigned his commission and didn't want to be called 'Lieutenant'.

But a lot of the men didn't trust Yankees, or the kind of people that preferred California over Oregon, so there was some talk.

'That rig's too fancy to be of much use,' was the opinion on their wagon, which was pulled by horses instead of oxen.

'Them horses ain't going to be able to handle it,' was the opinion on that.

Papa said, 'I don't know how much of the man is hot air. He's a braggart – talking in the taverns about how good a shot he is and how important a politician his papa is back in Albany, New York.'

Daniel was one who held a higher opinion of the man, but he didn't get his back up at Papa; the two of them seemed to be going out of their way to cut each other some slack since the muster.

Practically everybody was farm people like us, but still the Prescotts weren't the only oddities to gossip over. There were also the LaForces from North Carolina, new-married like Matthew and Letty, but that was the only similarity they had with anybody, including the Prescotts, who weren't like the rest of us neither, but in a different way.

First off, the LaForces had *slaves,* two of them, Kitty and Semple. Miz Stokes said both had been wedding gifts and that the LaForces had been married less than a year and part of that year had been taken up with getting themselves all the way from the Carolinas to Independence.

Mr LaForce started out on the trail dressed real fancy, but he ruined his britches in less than a week – and was both good natured and rich enough to laugh it off, which made me take to him even if others were still wary. Miz LaForce, who wasn't but around eighteen, dressed in lace and ruffles, not doing enough to dirty them, but even if she had, I guess she would have paid it no mind as she had a slave to clean up after her.

Folks softened up toward the LaForces after a bit as he was so willing to go along with things and she was so pretty. She also had a baby coming and that always led to consideration. As the youngest of his clan, Mr LaForce had been picked to judge the prospects out west for investment, though I thought he was more out for the adventure than anything else.

Those slaves sure didn't look like they were feeling bad over their condition, so I figured there were different circumstances of slavery. But I decided to keep an eye on them anyway, so if they were whupped or otherwise treated badly, I could tell my papa and he would do something about it.

Willie was looking after our spare stock, with Joe lending a hand, and most of the time I joined up with them as I had my reasons not to stay with our wagons. The train moved so slow, it was easy to go back to our way of spying again, this time on the LaForces. It didn't take long to see that Semple was sweet on Kitty. He was supposed to be looking after the LaForces' spare mule team, but he mostly rode close to the tailgate of their wagon so he could chat with Kitty, who sat dangling her legs over the edge.

Mules are independent animals, and after a while they decided to go off on their own instead of keeping up. We didn't let them stray too far and bided our time until Semple remembered to look around for his stock. You should have seen the look on his face when there wasn't hide nor hair of them!

Then I hollered out, 'If you're looking for mules, I know where you can find a whole team!' That's how we became chums, though not in camp; just when the wagons were strung out and nobody could see what the next was up to. I didn't know how folks would take to the notion of me being friends with slaves.

Most wagons were pulled by oxen, except

the LaForces had mules, which I reckon was the southern way, and the Prescotts had their horses. Oxen were cheaper to buy and less likely to stampede or be stolen by injuns along the way. If they did get away, it was an easy job to catch up with them. And if they got killed somehow, they could be used for beef. They were better for the long haul.

I was especially good with our oxen, knowing all their names by heart, Buck and Bright, which yoked together, being my favorites. Most of the driving was done walking alongside. The best drivers never whupped their teams; it was just the sound of the whip made them go, along with saying 'gee' and 'haw' and of course 'whoa'.

I pestered Papa into giving me a turn at driving, and, in spite of all the laughter at seeing a girl at it, there was nothing said against my ability. And Ben Cooper taught me how to crack the whip like a man.

He was one of the bachelors. Another was Tom Miller, who Mr Prescott had hired. The men said Tom was a good man who would keep Mr Prescott from running their wagon into their neighbors. Tom was just about the shyest man I ever saw, too shy to be joining in on the other bachelors' hi-jinks.

And there was Mike, who played the mouth organ and was lots of fun around the fire. Another bachelor, Jake, had a fiddle and he added to the jolliness. Of course sometimes we didn't see the bachelors for days as they would be hanging back with the stock, but when they came into camp, we had lively times.

The day started even before dawn, so no one stayed up too late, but most folks enjoyed an hour or so around the campfire. The council set up a watch, and pickets guarded the livestock in shifts – Captain Stokes said there was nothing an injun liked better than to steal white men's animals. The men drifted in and out of the circle to smoke their pipes and speculate how many miles we covered each day and how many we might put behind us the next, or they speculated about whatever topic might be raised, just to pass the time.

'I hear tell the Mormons are gathering over at Council Bluffs.'

'I hope they don't come our way and give us trouble.'

'Them fellers ain't anything to worry about; any man wanting to take on an extra wife has to be tetched in the head.'

The Journal of Rebecca Springer

April 24, 1846

Our second day out of Independence. Made less than seven miles. When we made camp last night, we could still see where we had started from. I am used to the pace we kept to when we were on our own. The spring grass is just starting to come in, but we still need hay.

I reckon out of fifty wagons and almost two hundred people, we are fifteen women at most, not counting babies such as Betsy and the little Hansen girl, but I have heard of other trains faring much worse. We will need each other, so I do hope we can find one other's company congenial, though I have my doubts I can find much in common with either Mrs Prescott or Mrs LaForce. They have been raised to other ways of life.

The women made their own gossip around the fire. Harriet Stokes claimed Mrs Prescott did not know the first thing about house-keeping. 'I even saw her husband fetching the water bucket.'

Rebecca was determined to find only posi-tive statements to make. 'She dresses mod-estly and gives little in her appearance for remark.'

'She has the pale complexion that goes with red hair and will suffer greatly from the sun,' Ivy Bingham said with some satisfaction.

'At least they are abolitionists. All Yankees are,' Mrs Hansen said. Bert's mother was good-natured and not much given to gossip.

Cora LaForce's housekeeping could not

be criticized as she did none, having two slaves to do everything for her. Indeed, she scarcely set foot outside her wagon, spending much of her time on a feather-stuffed mattress. 'Her husband's name is Early, which is an old family name, well-known in the South,' Harriet Stokes informed them.

Rebecca thought it a most peculiar name for a man, but people from the South seemed to saddle their progeny with outlandish names.

Letty joined most of the men in admiring Mrs LaForce's beauty. 'Did you see those diamond drop earbobs of hers?'

'And there's a necklace to match!' Elizabeth added, also charmed.

'She puts it on in the evenings, just like they're going to a fancy dinner party, instead of eating beans at a campfire,' Letty went on, looking dreamy.

'That's just about the silliest thing I ever heard of,' Ivy Bingham sniffed.

'Well, I think she just wants to look pretty for her husband,' Elizabeth said defensively. 'He stays with her instead of joining the other men at the fire, and he shoots down ducks for the stew pot, which is more than most of the men can do.'

Rebecca believed shy Elizabeth had developed a crush! But she took her point, as she also did the best she could to make a nice appearance when John came for his supper. She was vain enough to think this might make his day a little sunnier and was all the more reason for regular wash days.

Rebecca noted that Ben Cooper was off duty and in camp, which made her uneasy. There were too many hideaways; too much opportunity for a man to push an impressionable girl against the side of a wagon, pinning her with his body and raising her skirts as he rubbed himself against her.

At the encampment in Independence, she had caught a glimpse of a frantic coupling when she returned from the latrine in the dark. They were pressed against a tree, and the man's naked buttocks were furiously pumping with the woman's legs wrapped around his waist. Rebecca had averted her eyes and hurried on. In their passion, they had not noticed her.

Perhaps her worry was unjustified; Ben's attentions appeared to be focused on Nellie Bingham – and Willie was competing with him to gain Nellie's attention in return.

On the far side of the circle around the fire, she spotted Joe and Bert furtively edging away into the shadows, then hurriedly disappearing behind the wagons. Rebecca feared they might have some prank in mind that could get them shot by a nervous picket, so quickly moved to cut them off.

'We was just going over to the LaForces' wagon,' Joe explained.

'Were you invited?'

'No, Ma'am, but we don't bother them none. We just listen to Semple.'

'Who on God's green earth is Semple?'

'That Negro belongs to Mr LaForce. He plays the concertina and sings, too.' Joe flashed a smile. 'It's real pretty music.'

He and Willie had both been born knowing the best course of action was to be agreeable to one and all. The trait didn't appear to run in Sarah.

Rebecca was so amazed Joe could find an interest in something that didn't include blazing arrows and a scalp or two, she let the boys go. She lingered behind the wagons, straining to hear the concertina. The night was dry and not too cold, and the moon was just past full, with no clouds about; a congenial atmosphere to take a stroll while John was occupied splicing whiplashes by the fire.

The wagon circle was drawn up each night in the same order and the LaForces' wagon lay to her far right. Rebecca used a tall tree close to their wagon as a guidepost; it would also provide a convenient shelter. As she quietly crept closer, she thought she saw movement next to the tree. She hoped it wasn't an Indian.

It was Mrs Prescott. She turned at Rebecca's approach, then smiled, and, without a word, made room for her in the shadow of the tree.

Rebecca did not know how to explain her presence, so also said nothing, becoming aware of a deep male voice singing of the Lord and His blessing.

Cora LaForce was propped up on her feather bed in the back of the wagon, wearing a frilly dressing gown and looking like a china doll. Kitty sat with Early LaForce on the tailgate, quite as if she were part of the family. And Semple stood by the campfire, his eyes closed and his face lifted to heaven, completely given over to song.

'It's a rare gift to be able to listen to something so lovely out here on the prairie,' Mrs Prescott whispered to Rebecca.

Her smile was so open. Rebecca felt guilty she had yet to pay her a call, allowing her own prejudices to hold sway. But she scarcely knew what conversation she could make with Margaret Prescott, aside from agreeing on the beauty of Semple's singing.

The Journal of Rebecca Springer

April 26, 1846

Made only six miles and we are still in Missouri. Today we came across two chairs on the trail. They are not matching, but nice, one with a spindle back. John says he will hook them to the side of the wagon (I am down to only one hen coop so there is ample room). It'll be a blessing to not have to squat on a flour sack at nooning. Also found part of a Webster Dictionary. It starts with 'M', but there are still enough words to learn a new one each day, with plenty left over for Oregon. It will help fill the time and will be useful when I undertake my child's education.

MALIGN – to speak evil; entertain malice, plot, contrive against.

Lord, close my ears to unkind thoughts and words. I pray that fifteen women will be enough to keep up standards, and I ask You to give all of us guidance and allow us to live in harmony.

May 4, 1846

Made only six miles today because we got stopped by the Kansas River. Our way lies north of it, so there is nothing to do but cross over. It is running high and a Shawnee Indian named Charles Fish runs the only ferry around. He charges a dollar a wagon. He will surely make himself rich, as there was already more than one train waiting for a turn when we arrived. Those guidebooks claimed the water would be low enough to wade across. I wonder what other lies they hold?

MUTABLE – changeable; inconstant.

John came up from the riverbank wearing a

sly look and carrying a small basket stuffed with straw. 'I know women who are expecting get their cravings,' he told Rebecca, 'and it seems all you talk about is eggs these days.'

'It is only because the chickens are proving worthless except for the stewpot and I had counted on eggs for some of my receipts.' It was true she dreamed of eggs. She hoped it wasn't a bad sign for the baby.

'No matter. I was able to buy two dozen at a good price off a man waiting to cross. He said they'd get broken for sure.'

John pushed aside the straw to reveal the speckled brown eggs. Rebecca was touched by his thoughtfulness.

'I will start you a cake right away.'

John shook his head. 'We will be delayed here for at least another day, Rebecca. Have yourself a rest.'

Rebecca was too used to activity to consider 'a rest' as something taken in a prone position. She regarded the gentle hill behind the camp. It was called the Blue Mound and she had heard one could see miles around from the top. Quite a few people had already taken in the view while they waited to cross; it seemed more a walk than a climb, so Rebecca decided to give it a try. Letty could start the biscuits.

Walking beside the wagon for so many days, she was in good condition and scarcely felt the effort. It was a fine day, the sun shining and the air still smelling sweet from the last rain. When she reached the top of the hill, the prairie stretched out below far into the distance, covered with wildflowers – pink mallow and blue phlox shading in and out of lavender shadows as lazy clouds drifted across the sun. It was raining in the distance, but nearer, a rainbow arched over the flat plain. She found a flat boulder and sat down to enjoy the luxury of letting her mind drift while her eyes feasted on God's beautiful creation.

But her good mood was broken when Sarah came over the crest, allowing her horse to lazily graze, while chatting with Ben Cooper. He leaned over on his saddle close to her ear to tell her something to which she reacted with a quick laugh.

Sarah couldn't pretend not to hear Rebecca's hail, since Ben returned it with a wave. She dismounted and took her time leading her horse across the summit to Rebecca, while Ben turned his back downhill.

'I wasn't doing nothing wrong. Just talking. You didn't have to come spying on me.'

'I came on my own accord to admire the view, and it is well worth the trip.' It was the first time since their confrontation that they had been alone together.

Sarah shrugged and played with the lacing on her bridle, not looking at Rebecca.

'I'd like to pick some flowers for the table.

Will you help me?'

She shrugged again. 'Might as well.'

Meaning, Rebecca assumed, since she had ruined any chance for Sarah to gain any pleasure from the day. But Sarah let her horse graze free and the two of them spent some time quietly picking the wildflowers that were blooming in profusion all around, the fresh pastels lovely against the pale green of the new grass. There was more mallow and phlox, and johnny-jump-up, violet and a kind of vetch a bit different from back home. Wild parsley and dandelion made splashes of yellow here and there as well.

Performing this pleasant and perfumed task seemed to loosen the tension that lay between them. First one, then the other, would point out particularly beautiful or unusual flowers – star of Bethlehem, white as snow, or purple ground cherry – exclaiming appreciation of each new discovery.

On the way back down the hill, their arms full of flowers, Sarah spied a small grave. She pushed aside the grass that had grown over the wooden marker so they could read it. From the dates, they realized it was a child: Becky Smith was her name and she had been buried a year.

'What do you think of that?' Sarah exclaimed. 'Right in the middle of nowhere.'

'Maybe she was put here because her parents wanted her to rest in a pretty place,'

Rebecca said. She helped Sarah pull out the tufts of grass so the marker could remain clear, at least for a little while. Sarah put some of her flowers on the tiny grave.

The Journal of Rebecca Springer

May 5, 1846

We have made it across the Kansas River, the crossing taking up most of the day. We had to ferry our goods separately as too much weight would have sunk the barge. The thought of getting on that rickety ferry made me shy, but I could see that others had made it safely so I told myself we would be all right.

The ferry was pulled across by ropes and it did not make for a smooth ride, with jerks and starts and the current to contend with as well. The poor oxen had to swim for it. The men put the lead animals on long tethers and guided them across, whipping the rest behind them. Their eyes bulged with terror and they bellowed something fierce. I was feeling much the same. And they tell me there are worse crossings to come.

We were all in a state by the time we pulled ourselves up the far bank. The men's clothes were filthy and even tucking up our skirts, we women hadn't escaped all the churned-up mud. Now we must load everything up again.

NEOTERISM – the use of new words or phrases.

Lord, rest the tiny soul of Becky Smith. Look after my baby and Elizabeth's.

When Rebecca rose to start the coffee in the morning, she was surprised to find Margaret Prescott waiting outside the tent, her son in her arms.

'Please forgive my intrusion, but Laurie has suffered the whole night from earache and I am at my wits' end. I was hoping you might have something to help him.'

Rebecca urged her to take a seat close to the coals, which were still smoldering from the previous night. It took but a minute to kindle them to full flame. When Sarah emerged sleepily from her tent, Rebecca asked her to place her mattress near the fire for the boy before she went off to do the milking.

Once the water was boiling, Rebecca consulted her medicine chest while Elizabeth fried the ham. She kept eardrops in a Mason jar and it didn't take long to warm them in a pan of water. Laurie protested for a moment, but the drops took effect almost immediately. Rebecca brushed off Mrs Prescott's thanks; it was just a common remedy.

'Not common to me. May I prevail upon

you to share it?'

There was bread to be fried (no sign of Letty) and John and Daniel coming from the corral, so Rebecca suggested they get together that evening after they had both finished their chores.

'I hope you don't consider me rude for cutting our visit short,' she added.

'Not at all! It seems to me every minute of the day is occupied with meals: the preparation, the consumption, and then the cleaning up afterwards.'

'And then it's time to start all over again,' Rebecca agreed.

She brought her chest to the fire that night, and dictated the ingredients of each remedy. Mrs Prescott carefully wrote them down in a leatherbound journal, her son sleeping across her lap. The earache had not returned, and before nodding off he had played with Betsy. Like most five year olds, he was delighted to find a child even smaller than himself to baby.

'It appears whiskey is quite a miraculous liquid,' Margaret Prescott noted, 'as it can cure snakebites, sore throats, burns, colds and rheumatism.'

'I have seen it cure some of these ailments,' Rebecca replied, 'and it certainly seems to ease the pain of others, if taken in sufficient quantities.'

'I am lost without a chemist's to run to.

You're kind to educate me.'

'We all have something to learn from our neighbors.'

'I doubt there is anything I could offer you in return, Mrs Springer.'

'That is nice for you to say, but I am sure you are possessed of real knowledge, not just receipts that are easy to come by. And if it is not too forward of me to ask, you should call me Rebecca. If you speak to Mrs Springer, there are three of us here that could answer.'

Elizabeth insisted on no less for herself, and Mrs Prescott requested they call her Margaret in return.

'I have found it difficult to break the ice with most of our fellow travelers, but I felt easy in approaching you, Rebecca, after sharing such an enjoyable evening at the LaForces' wagon.'

'They seem nice people,' Rebecca said uncomfortably, not having told Elizabeth about her eavesdropping.

'The only vice I have observed in them,' Margaret continued, 'is the odious one of possessing slaves, but I own they know no better, having generations behind them...' She stopped. 'I fear I am speaking out of turn.' She would have to be more careful with her tongue if she was to forge any friendships. Her husband called her 'a soapbox orator'.

'I am pleased you have shared your thoughts on the matter,' Rebecca reassured her, 'as I have been troubled: does the Lord consider it a sin for us to listen to Semple sing, when his singing is at the wish of his master and mistress?'

'I believe Semple takes joy in sharing his gift with others. In my observation, I believe he is singing to Kitty as much as to her mistress.'

'That must be some comfort to each of them.'

'That is surely taking the positive view.'

'Well, there's not much use complaining about the things in life you cannot change. Politics are beyond me; that's up to the men to decide.'

'I think women need to be concerned with politics,' Margaret said, 'if decisions are made that send their sons off to war.'

'That gives me pause in hoping for a boy,' Elizabeth said, putting a protective hand on her belly. 'There seem to be so many pains a mother must endure. I reckon she has her fears from the moment her child is born.'

'I think even before,' Rebecca added.

'It cannot be easy for either of you in your condition,' Margaret said, 'but how fortunate you are to have each other to rely upon.'

'There is little else to be done about it,' Elizabeth said with more than a trace of bitterness.

Margaret Prescott's Notebook

Remedy for earache: insert leaves of tobacco between an equal number of onion slices and cook slowly until the juices have been extracted. Drain off the juice through a cloth sieve. Squeeze quite warm, but not overly hot, drops into the afflicted ear.

Remedy for fevers: bind the sufferer's head in a cold cloth and his feet in cabbage leaves. The diet should be confined to sage tea, rhubarb and soda.

Remedy for bleeding: lay on cobwebs, or a mixture of flour and salt tied on with a cloth.

Remedy for insect bites: apply wet earth to the bite. A poultice can also be made with the scrapings from fresh vegetables and bread and milk.

Remedy for rheumatism: soak sunflower seeds in a pint of spirits for twelve hours, then take internally.

Note: diarrhea? vomiting? Must ask.

With all this practical knowledge, surely these farm women must know how to avoid conception!

The Journal of Rebecca Springer

May 17, 1846

Today being the Lord's Day, we did not

travel. Reverend Bingham has turned out not to be much of a preacher, but since we have John's family Bible with us, we can do our own readings, though it seems to me the stop for the Lord's Day in our train has become largely an excuse to catch up on all the business left undone during the week.

The men have been resetting iron tires and tightening wheel locks, and mending the bits of our gear that have broken down, as well as cobbling together replacements for what has been damaged beyond repair – not much, I am happy to record.

MULTIFARIOUS – having many parts or forms.

May 18, 1846

Got through the entire basket of mending.

The cock managed to get into the wagon and made a picnic of the flower seeds I spent the better part of a year collecting from just about every flower in our part of Indiana. I wasn't about to have them wind up in his gullet, so straightway wrung his neck. The seeds spilled out when I slit his throat, and the family had a laugh seeing me down on my hands and knees collecting them while the cock was still around. He made a passable stew. Side dish of dandelion greens fresh picked. Cobbler for dessert from dried apples.

Joe found another grave nearby. Indians or animals had been at it and a foot was sticking out. John set it right again. There was a marker: Joseph Weston, of Rushville, Illinois, deceased only five days ago. There was no birth date. I offered a prayer for his soul at evening service.

OCCIDENTAL – of or in the west, or belonging to or found in western countries or regions of the earth. I can't call these new words my own until I have occasion to use them, but there seems little opportunity to fit them edgewise into a conversation. Margaret would understand them, but would also know they were not natural to me.

Margaret Prescott's Notebook

My heart sinks at the sight of a river! We have crossed the Kansas, the Big Blue, the Little Blue next, and it's days before we get to the Platte, which is rumored to be even bigger. The scouts lead us miles out of our way to avoid a difficult crossing, only to end up at a ford that couldn't be any easier. The creeks and streams are the size of rivers and the rivers have to be crossed and recrossed; they are like snakes that slither around to meet and trip us up again and again.

We are encountering more and more Indians. The ones today are the Oto and the

Ponca. Their clothes are a hodge-podge: buckskin leggings with a calico shirt or beaded moccasins next to worsted trousers. These tribes have been tamed, but they are still far from being civilized. The only English they know is 'swap' and 'no swap'. They have no idea of specie and they trade buffalo hides for blankets and buttons, or mirrors and beads. They would like to trade for guns and bullets as well, but that sort of barter is frowned upon.

The civilized ways of the white man: a boon or a blight? Our missionaries assume that the word of God solves all. I wonder.

Margaret had told Rebecca that her father was a man of the cloth, which made her feel they had at least one thing in common because of her own grandfather's calling. But Margaret felt she would have been better off being born the daughter of a farmer than a Connecticut theologian. At Mount Holyoke, she had learned more than to merely paint and play musical instruments, but in practical matters, she was woefully ignorant.

It took all her energy to produce a loaf of bread that was neither leaden nor spotted with grit from the campfire. She was bruised from flying pots she had failed to secure in the wagon, the bottoms of all her skirts were filthy and she could barely keep Phillip in clean shirts.

He and Early LaForce had recently led a hunt. Most of the men were terrible marksmen, but they were both expert, doing themselves proud by bringing down a deer as well as several brace of birds. Phillip was a fine shot from a horse, which was quite a feat, and Margaret hoped this had helped his standing in the company.

She was all too aware what some others thought of them. There had been grumbling that the Prescotts slowed down the train at the crossings. Their wagon was cumbersome and heavy, and Philip and his bachelor, Tom Miller, had to take extra caution fording the horses; they were their future and their fortune.

Margaret often drove the wagon while Phillip and Tom tended their small herd. Since it was so slow, the other wagons soon pulled ahead and out of sight, leaving her feeling quite alone on the trail.

It came as a surprise to spy Emily Walker, equally alone, walking ahead of her. She had been intrigued by the concept of Miss Walker – a single woman and a schoolteacher – but had had no chance to attempt to engage her in conversation. Mrs Stokes worked her every minute to earn her keep. She had not as yet even appeared around the campfire at night. For that matter, neither had the Stokeses' daughter, Nancy, who appeared to be kept as much a drone as Miss Walker.

She didn't even need to stop the team to ask Miss Walker to join her. They were at such a slow pace, it would be simple to board. But Miss Walker shook her head and continued marching.

Margaret's curiosity made her persistent. 'The rest of the train must be some distance ahead.'

'I will surely catch up when they stop for nooning.'

'As will I, and admittedly you would probably make no better time with me, but you might be more comfortable and I would enjoy the company.'

Miss Walker might've stubbornly continued to refuse her, if she hadn't turned her ankle on a stone hidden in the grass and stumbled, scratching her face and hands on the sharp spears. Margaret insisted she at least climb aboard long enough to freshen herself. Once there, she was determined not to let go of her until she'd learned her full story.

'I understand you are from Massachusetts?'

Miss Walker nodded affirmatively.

'I myself am from Connecticut, but I have often travelled through Massachusetts. Where is your home?'

'Lowell.'

Lowell was best known for its cloth mills, and Margaret made connections in her mind. Catherine Beecher, the great proponent of female education from her own state of Connecticut, had taken as one of her causes the overworked and underpaid girls at the eastern mills. If her hunch was correct, no wonder Miss Walker was so taciturn! There was little use for the conversational art in a noisy mill. Margaret had visited one with her father; the conditions had been horrible.

'Might I ask if you are familiar with the name of Catherine Beecher, Miss Walker?'

Finally Margaret received a response: her hunch had been correct. Miss Walker had been trained to be a teacher by the great Catherine Beecher herself. 'Women like yourself will be much needed in the West,' Margaret told her warmly.

Miss Walker snorted. 'And I hope better treated than on the way there!' Filled with bottled anger, she was ready to pull the cork.

'I paid for my bed and board on the same terms as the Stokeses' bachelors, but they've treated me far less than equal. The men were provided two blankets apiece, but I received nothing. I am not even allowed to sleep in the Stokeses' wagons with the other women.'

'Mrs Stokes can be difficult,' Margaret agreed, 'but surely Captain Stokes' mother...'

'She is terrorized by her daughter-in-law, and senile as well,' Emily interrupted. 'Mrs Stokes doesn't consider the teaching profession proper for a woman, therefore I am not proper, and forced to sleep under the wagon in the rain and mud, with only a board

151

beneath me! I am walking to Oregon rather than spend a minute more than is necessary with that woman.'

Rebecca was in good humor as she set up their campsite. A story had spread through the wagons as one by one they rolled into camp: Ben Cooper had been on picket duty the night before and the Indian he thought he heard turned out to be a skunk! Ben had had to strip buck-naked and bury all his clothes and had not been seen since.

When her new friend approached her campsite, Rebecca started to pass along the story, but Margaret was too filled with outrage over Emily Walker's treatment to listen.

'Rebecca! We must do something.'

'I don't think it's up to us to upset the order of things, Margaret, or interfere in the business of others. It would not be taken kindly.'

'Your husband carries a great deal of weight with Captain Stokes.'

'I reckon he does, but his stock would go down if he concerned himself with something like this. I cannot ask him to do so.'

Margaret found it hard to believe Rebecca would take such a position. Rebecca had to speak in plainer words.

'Margaret, I cannot see using up my credit with my husband on someone who must have known what she bargained for by putting herself in such a position.'

'Wanting to better herself?'

'Going off on her own without a husband or any close kin to look after her. It isn't natural, Margaret. Maybe you look at things differently where you come from, but that woman does not put me at ease.'

Both women felt badly let down. It was human nature to think your friends shared your convictions and a disappointment to learn this was not always the case.

The Journal of Rebecca Springer

May 19, 1846

A good fifteen miles today and almost to the Platte. After unloading the wagon a dozen times, I begin to wonder if all our household goods are necessary, but I remind myself how much I will enjoy nice things when we get to Oregon. Those less determined to stick it through have abandoned much of value – today I saw a fine pine bureau, a decent tin washtub and even a whole set of dishes. I also found one more chair.

PERTINACIOUS – stubborn in holding to one's own view. I hope I was not too pertinacious with Margaret, but she was as well.

Lord, I hope our disagreement has not caused an end when our friendship was just beginning.

Rebecca's conscience pricked her. On an impulse, she offered Emily Walker the slicker Joe'd outgrown, but Miss Walker turned her down cold, saying she didn't need charity.

Ben Cooper returned to their campsite at the end of the day, decked out like an Indian brave. He had bartered a hunting knife for a yellow deerskin shirt and trousers and strutted about like a barnyard rooster for the pleasure of Nellie and Sarah – and even Nancy Stokes, who had miraculously found a moment away from under her mother's thumb. Rebecca was pleased to see the poor girl smile for once, even if it was at Ben. While Sarah had too much time for flirtation, Rebecca didn't want to keep her under lock and key as Mrs Bingham kept Nellie, or belabor her as Mrs Stokes did Nancy. She felt she might learn a thing or two through bad example.

Sarah

All hell broke loose that evening! The wind rose to a fierce level and the sky turned black as ink. Then rain commenced to pelt down in a fury, with thunder and lightning almost continuous – and if it wasn't for the lightning, none of us would have been able to see our hands before our faces it got so dark.

It came upon us so sudden, it was impossible to prepare for it. The piercing wind found ways to force the rain into the wagons and soon everything inside was soaked. We were scrabbling about on our hands and knees trying to cover up our goods with oilcloth while the wagons rocked and shivered and the wind threatened to fill up the canvas covers and carry them off like kites.

The men worked with all their might to chain the wagons together, only able to see clearly what they were doing when the lightning flashed, and then they were in danger of being struck by handling the metal chains.

There was noise everywhere: yelling and cussing from the men when they were cut and bruised by the wagons crashing together, a woman screaming (I couldn't make out who), and the neighing and bellowing of the animals, which were even more scared than the humans. All of a sudden, we stopped hearing the animals, so we figgered they had broken out of the corral and stampeded. Rebecca said it seemed like the judgment day was at hand and God was pouring out his vengeance on us for hanging Harold McAdam. She was always saying Biblical things, and I didn't like hearing this as she might be right.

That black night seemed to go on forever,

but by morning the storm had dropped, leaving only a steady drizzle behind. Several wagon covers did get blown off, but the ground was still underfoot, even if it was one big puddle. There wasn't any use crying over it, so we all pitched in to get a cook-fire going so the men might have something hot in their stomachs before they started looking for the stock. The wood was so wet there was more smoke than fire, and some of the men wound up eating raw bacon – but not ours, as I made it my duty to keep at it until that fire was good and warm, even though I smelt of smoke for days after.

There was so much to do, no one noticed Letty wasn't alongside us. Elizabeth and Rebecca relied on her almost as little as they did on me, so that wasn't unusual. But then Matthew turned up wearing a long face – just like when Letty left him in the lurch back home.

'Letty wants to go home,' he announced. 'She was hollering all night and it's taken me half the morning to get her calmed down.'

'You want me to go talk to her?' Rebecca asked.

'Meaning no disrespect, Rebecca, but if nothing I say makes a difference, I don't see how you're going to sway her mind.'

'She's that stubborn, you just tell her to go ahead,' Daniel said. 'You have called her bluff before.'

Matthew looked ashamed. 'She will not have it called again, and if she's bent on going home, I'll be going with her, Daniel. I couldn't be happy in Oregon without her.'

'Well, that's about the d***dest thing I ever heard!' Daniel said, and Papa warned him to watch his language.

'I'm sorry, Papa, but a man needs to control his wife.'

A couple of the other men were listening in, it being hard to hold a conversation privately under the conditions.

'A fine man, letting a woman make his decisions!' said one.

'A good switching'll put her head back where it belongs,' said the other.

'Don't be putting your noses where they weren't invited,' Daniel told them, and he was right: this was family business.

Papa stayed calm. 'I am not going to advise you, as you are a married man now and must make your own decisions. You have to do what's best for your family.'

'I am sorry, Papa, but I must choose my new family over the old.'

'It is only right,' Papa said, but I didn't agree with him.

Letty wouldn't even come out of the wagon to say goodbye. I reckon she was just too humiliated over being a quitter. Of course she wasn't reared to stand up to hard times, but I am still too mad at her to make excuses.

Willie and Joe weren't above giving Matthew a hug along with me, and even Daniel gave him a thump on the back.

'We'll know where to find you; and we'll make certain you know where to find us,' Daniel said.

'We'll send you letters whenever a go-back crosses our trail,' I told him.

Papa figgered out how much of our supplies would be fair to turn over so Matthew could make a new start back in Indiana. Along with a horse and a cow, he gave him a full share of gold pieces, which Matthew wrapped up in a handkerchief and put inside his shirt.

'None of us think the less of you, son,' Papa said. 'You keep that in mind when you get to feeling low.'

We all watched the honeymoon wagon turn around and go back the way we had come until it got lost in the misty rain. Then we had to finish the cleaning up.

The storm left some folks bad off. Grammy Stokes was fading fast from pneumonia. And that bachelor chum of mine that played the fiddle, Jake, broke his arm in the storm and the bone came through the skin. Everyone told him it would soon be right again, but he was powerful worried he wouldn't be able to touch a bow as lightly as he had before.

Every wagon in the train had become waterlogged. The fact that the Prescotts' was no exception was scant consolation to Margaret. Her own treasure was a complete set of Shakespeare. Though some volumes were dry and others merely damp around the edges, a few would have to be carefully dried, two pages at a time.

She spread them out on a dry blanket, hoping that revealing she had brought a library wouldn't cause resentment; the only other books she had seen in their train were Bibles.

One of Phillip's horses had broken a leg and had to be shot. Another horse was still missing. Other men were also missing livestock and it was assumed Indians had made off with them. They took their losses stoically; their animals represented an investment, but weren't intended to bankroll their future.

Phillip was in a defensive mood and she had to treat him with tact. He had recently badly misstepped with Captain Stokes, who had warned him their wagon'd be too heavy for horses to pull over a mountain range.

'If you don't mind me suggesting, you'd be better off with either a lighter load or a team of oxen. I've got an extra team I'd be willing to sell.'

'I might be a Yankee,' Phillip replied, 'but I am not so easily parted from my money.'

Phillip seemed to bear a perpetual chip on his shoulder. It had been embedded there before he and Margaret had ever met and there was little she could do other than try to bolster his confidence.

Her father had had reservations about Phillip's character when they began their courtship, but she was as hot to have him as he to have her, and she had to have her way. Now she knew much more about the source of that chip: Philip had not come close to his father's achievement at Yale, and trying to practice law in Albany in the shadow of the great man had further diminished his sense of his own value.

The military had seemed an answer. Margaret, a new bride, had encouraged him, but although Phillip had talent, taking orders from the chain of command had only increased his desire to be his own person.

Everything they had had gone into this new venture, which would take Phillip a continent away from all the devils that beleaguered him. She was still hot to have him – that mad attraction compelled her to continue supporting him; as his wife, she was bound to see him through.

Margaret Prescott's Notebook

Our last crossing is of the south fork of the Platte River. The Platte looks shallow, but it is filled with quicksand and the current runs fast. Beyond lies a straight trail following the southerly side of the North Platte River all the way past Fort Laramie, which is near where the Laramie and North Platte Rivers come together, two hundred miles away. Most of this land has been bought from the Pawnees by the government and under the Missouri Compromise will be non-slave.

Method of River Crossing

1. The scouts patiently pick their way across the river, marking a safe way with sticks.
2. One of the scouts then rides over on a tall horse, carrying a guide rope. When the line is secured, a second rope is pulled across to create a loop.
3. The wagons are pulled across: The men tie the wheels together to ease them down the bank, then knock the wagons off their axles so the beds can be used as ferries.

Sarah

I remember every detail of the last crossing of the Platte. The river was full of driftwood, some pieces big enough to jar or even tip a raft. Papa devoted considerable time to balancing the loads stacked on the wagon beds, and as he kept shifting hampers and bags, Daniel grew more and more impatient.

'They are lining up for the ferry and we'll be last in line, Papa.'

'It won't make much difference once we're all on the other side.'

'But it will make a difference in making a good campsite the end of the day.'

'And it will make a difference if we lose a wagonload.'

'At least allow me to get one of our wagons in line, Papa. That justifies holding a place for the other two.'

Papa had a lot on his mind so he agreed, and Daniel found us a place well ahead of most of the train, which meant Papa and Pink had to hurry to bring up the other wagons.

I got on the wagon bed with Rebecca and Elizabeth. They held on to each other for dear life as our raft bobbed and jerked while Papa hauled us along on the rope. I was sure-footed, though, and turned around to watch Pink launch the next wagon bed. It got into the water all right, and Pink was pulling it along on the rope when a drifting log jammed into it and began to tip it over. The load commenced to slide, straining the lashings, and then some sacks broke free and spilled into the river, followed by two chests. Pink managed to push the log away and right the raft before any further damage was done.

I worried about what Papa would say to Daniel about not securing the load, but when we got to the other side, Papa just gave him a look and said, 'There is too much work to be done to be laying blame.' Then they both set to snagging our things out of the river. A flour sack had got caught on a rock and ripped open, but the bacon and salted beef were none the worse for wear.

One trunk had sprung and lost some of its contents. What was left was soaked through, so Rebecca and Elizabeth spread the contents out to dry while the men started to put the wagons back together. I went off a way to sit with Nellie Bingham to watch the bachelors drive the stock across. Nellie was going on about how scared she was of the water and how she couldn't imagine learning how to swim and I was thinking I could just see her mama allowing her to do such a thing anyway.

Willie was working with the bachelors. We both waved and I hollered, but with all the commotion, he didn't look up. Nellie started talking about Willie and how she hoped he was being careful. I wasn't paying too much attention, because Nellie talked about Willie a lot around me since I was his sister and she kind of thought that being with me was a way of getting close to him. I didn't like that idea much – I had nothing particular against Nellie, it not being her fault her mama kept her all trussed up like a Christmas turkey – but I didn't want Willie ending up like Matthew and leaving me for some silly girl.

So I just said to Nellie that Willie was not only a fine horseman but he was a tip-top swimmer too, and started bragging about myself a bit, saying that I could have swum that river myself if I'd had a mind to.

Then I saw that Willie's horse had got itself into quicksand. The horse was starting to sink and Willie tried to pull him back into the shallows, but he spooked and reared up and threw Willie, who never would have lost his seat if it hadn't been so wet and slippery. I'm not too sure what happened next, because I was already running down the bank toward the river and Nellie was screaming. I think Willie hit his head on a rock, because when I saw the horse kick him, his head was already in the water.

He started to slip away into the current. Papa and Daniel didn't even see him, they were so occupied. It seemed like it was only me and Willie in the world and the space between us didn't seem to be getting any closer no matter how hard I ran. I plunged into the river, kicking off my shoes, but I got pulled down by the weight of my skirts. I thrashed and screamed, trying to get to where Willie had last been, and then I started swallowing water and choking. I don't know who grabbed ahold of me, but I kept trying to push them off, raging and battling to go after Willie. I think it took more than one man to wrestle me to the bank, where I couldn't fight any longer as I started to vomit.

The men searched downriver a long while, but they never found Willie. I couldn't accept that he could just disappear like that. I was sure he'd pop up any minute, turning it all into a joke – a bad one that had upset us all, but still not something real.

As soon as I got my breath back, I ran after the search party. I didn't want to stop looking even when it got dark and Daniel came to drag me back to the wagons. I knew my eyes were better than anybody else's and I hated the idea of Willie out all alone in the dark.

The train had to go on, but our family stayed an extra day to search, all of us going back and forth along the banks of the river. Papa had given me some whiskey the night before and wrapped me up in a blanket and I guess I slept some. My heart wasn't racing any more, but it was stuck up in my throat and my stomach was tied in knots.

I couldn't believe I'd never be seeing Willie again, and I still can't. Even now, it's not real, just another nightmare. Why can't I have a dream where Willie doesn't float away down that river? Why can't I have a dream where I am able to reach him? In my whole life, I will never have a better friend nor find a better person. I know he was only seventeen, but with some people, their character is formed that early. Willie was who he was right from the start. Folks just took one look at him and felt better. He was that kind of person.

Finally, I stopped going up and down the river. There didn't seem to be any more use in it. But still I couldn't stop moving; if I did not do something, the aching in my heart took over every part of me. I started to pile up stones on the bank where I was sitting the last time I saw Willie. Joe seemed to know what was on my mind and started to help me. Rebecca and Elizabeth got the idea and brought more stones. Papa and Daniel and Pink pitched in and brought some big boulders until we'd a monument standing almost as tall as me. We didn't have Willie to set to rest properly but there wasn't anybody in the future going to come this way wouldn't know that someone important was marked here.

On our own, we could move fast, and it only took us another day to catch up with the wagon train.

It turned into a whole different trip for me after that.

Part 4

The Great American Desert

The Journal of Rebecca Springer

May 23, 1846

Not having his body to pay our last respects to, it doesn't feel we have put Willie's soul truly to rest. We didn't even have a Bible to read from as it was in the trunk that opened in the river. But I know a great deal of scripture by heart and at least was able to recite the 23rd Psalm, which always brings some comfort. Although Willie has not been led to still waters in life, he has surely found them in Heaven, along with the green pastures of the Lord and will dwell in His house.

We sang 'Rock of Ages'. My grandfather told me it had been composed during a terrific storm, so I think it was fitting. I will note Willie's dates until we can get a new Bible: August 11, 1828–May 22, 1846. Generations of my family going back to before the Revolution were marked in the one I lost; who married who and where they came from, so one would always know their kin. My name was in that Bible too, with the date of my marriage. I had hoped to note the birth of my child.

I do not have a new word for today. The

dictionary has also gone.

Lord, I will try to look on the bright side of things: my husband still has three children by his side and another gone back home. He has a grandchild and another on the way to bring him comfort, as well as the child I carry. No one child can be expected to make up for the loss of another, but I pray You will allow time to at least dull the pain.

Grammy Stokes quietly died during the night. She had always took her ease in her rocker and now it was broken up and the good hardwood used to put a marker atop her grave.

Gangrene set in with Jake's arm and no one dared to tell him it would have to come off. He lay on his mattress clutching his fiddle.

There was a hard climb up Windlass Hill to a high plain, then a drop down Ash Hollow's slope with wheels locked to reach the northern branch of the Platte. The river was a moving mass of sand and unpleasant to drink, but Ash Hollow provided a good campsite, with a spring, dry wood and good grass for the stock. The first buffalo were sighted just across the river.

A fur trader stopped at the camp on his way back to St Joseph, Missouri, reporting that beaver was gone around Fort Laramie, so now it was overlanders that kept trade going. The Springers sent letters home with him, reporting Willie's death to Matthew.

Margaret Prescott's Notebook

This far side of the Platte has been called 'The Great American Desert', because it is so empty of habitation or even trees. It might just as easily be termed an ocean, as a sea of grass undulates in the breeze as far as I can see – above my knees where it hasn't been trampled down by the buffalo.

These great animals are everywhere and not at all shy of us. They are slow-moving and it is easy to keep well clear of them, though the scouts warn that they can cause great destruction if they stampede. I am frightened of beasts so huge, much larger than the oxen. Indians bring buffalo hides to trade, and Philip is talking to the council about the prospect of staging a hunt. Fresh meat is much desired.

In the absence of wood, dry buffalo dung has become our fuel. It is not easy to light, but the distasteful matter produces a hot, clear and <u>odorless</u> flame, though I worry about the ashes getting into our food.

Sarah blamed herself for not rescuing Willie, and no amount of talk could shake her of that conviction. She slipped away each day early in the morning, not returning

171

until well after camp had been made. Rebecca worried that one day she would fail to come back. Sarah seemed to have lost all zest for life.

She would be sixteen in a few days; of age as a woman. For weeks before her last year birthday, she had given constant reminders and hints as to what she would like as celebration, but now she didn't even seem aware it was imminent.

John would not talk of Willie. Rebecca could only offer the comfort of her body at night, which he seemed to crave more than ever. Although they rarely talked afterward, she hoped now they might, but he remained silent. It wasn't good for him to bottle up his grief. Part of him had slipped away like Sarah.

Joe was different. He talked constantly of Willie, trying to remember each funny thing he had said or brave deed he had performed; Willie had been his hero.

Joe spent more and more time at the Hansen wagon, and Rebecca did not discourage him; to hear him talk so much about his brother must be bringing John even more pain. But it meant he was also drifting away from the family circle, when it had grown so much smaller already.

Night after night, Rebecca still lay awake after John had fallen asleep. It had become her habit now to get up and sit by the fire until she was too exhausted for her worries to continue to torment her mind. Usually a few men stopped for coffee on their way to and from picket duty, but they paid her little attention. She would have welcomed the distraction of conversation, but it wouldn't have been seemly for her without her husband present. She had only her nagging thoughts for company.

Margaret's own concerns forced her from her bed. When she saw Rebecca perched on a log by the fire, she dragged over a feed sack and sat next to her.

'You have no remedy for sleeplessness among your receipts?'

'None that has worked for me.' Rebecca poked at the fire with a stick. Preoccupied with day-to-day chores, the two women had scarcely spoken since their disagreement over Miss Walker. She didn't know if that obstacle could be overcome, but, she longed for conversation.

'I find myself dwelling on things that cannot be changed.'

'It was a sad thing to lose someone so young,' Margaret said sympathetically. 'His father must miss him grievously.'

'He bears it. But I worry for Sarah – Joe has found himself a friend, but she has no one to turn to.'

'She has you.'

'She considers me her enemy,' Rebecca

admitted bitterly.

Margaret was surprised. 'Surely not! "Enemy" is far too strong a word for a young girl's emotions.'

'Sarah has not been reared like other girls. She is fierce about guarding her freedom – and I am in the position of trying to take it away.'

'How?'

'These days by setting her to domestic tasks. But our biggest set-to was over my desire to see her better educated.'

'How much schooling has she had?'

'Enough to read a little, but she scarcely writes. Joe is worse than Sarah – she has to read to him. It is a shame.'

'I think learning has to become a natural habit. But it is never too late to learn,' Margaret assured her.

'I hope you are right, Margaret. I have always believed in order in all things, but now everything is in such disarray. I don't even have the Good Book to guide me any longer. Sarah and Joe are wild and ignorant, and as we go farther and farther away from civilization, I feel in danger of slipping into ignorance myself.'

Margaret shook her head. 'Rebecca, you are far from ignorant. From the little I know of you, I think you have taken on far too much of the weight of sorrow in your family. Please allow me to help you bear the burden.'

Friends find one another by instinct, no matter how unlike they might seem. Both women were able to return to their beds feeling their personal loads had lightened.

Margaret Prescott's Notebook

Before Rebecca, I was lonely for female companionship; the trading of receipts, small talk, knitting patterns and speculations – all the threads of understanding and reliance that weave us together as a sex.

When we gather around the campfire at night, the men discuss how far the train has traveled or the state of the livestock. Women reminisce about what we have left behind and how we hope to replicate it in its entirety once we have reached our destination.

It is as if the men have embarked on one journey, while we women make a parallel but separate way.

Rebecca felt some gesture of consideration should be made of Sarah's birthday, even if no one's mood welcomed a proper celebration. A yellow cake could mark the occasion as special, but not overly festive. The eggs would have to be from a turtle, but extra butter and sugar might make up for it, along with currants and cream. The cows were producing very well with such good grass.

There was no problem keeping the cake a surprise as Sarah did not appear until well after supper had started. While the men wolfed down their food, she picked at her own plate, pushing greens around and crumbling cornbread to bits.

Finally the table was cleared and Rebecca produced the cake, covering it with her apron until the last moment.

'Just to let you know we have not forgotten, Sarah,' she said as she set it down in front of her – presented on her best platter, which she had taken from the trunk for the occasion.

Sarah jumped up angrily, almost upturning the table.

'How can you want to be celebrating?' she yelled at Rebecca.

'Sarah! Sit down!' John warned her.

'I am not spending one more minute with a person who has no feelings in them!'

She dashed off into the tall grass.

John started to follow her. 'Sarah! Willie is gone! You can't change that!'

Rebecca ran after him, grabbing his shirtsleeve. 'Let her go, John. I was mistaken in trying to mark her birthday.'

'I have had to face up to Willie not coming back and she must do the same,' he said. 'Her suffering is no excuse for her rudeness.'

Rebecca looked at him sharply. 'Have you faced up to it, John?'

John seemed to shrink. He shook his head. 'No … not really. I have tried to think of Willie the same way I think of Matthew… "Right about now, Matthew will be getting back to Vermilion County", or, "I reckon Matthew must have bought those acres over by the Mumfords". I've just put Willie with Matthew and picture them both doing some late planting together and going on with life. It is not the truth, Rebecca, but it is what keeps me going.'

The Journal of Rebecca Springer

June 8, 1846

Everybody has their own way of handling death. Sarah's way is to be angry about what can't be changed, and John's to pretend nothing has changed.

But he has been able to express this and I thank You, Lord, for giving him his voice. I pray You make his life more bearable from now on and allow him to continue to unburden himself to his wife, who is a foolish woman, given to making foolish gestures. Help me to find the way.

Sarah

Turning sixteen took me unawares. It wasn't until Rebecca brought it up I even thought about it – and the only difference I could find from being fifteen was not having Willie anymore. I didn't want people acting like it was all right to be doing ordinary things like marking birthdays. I couldn't bear other folks acting natural, particularly my own family.

I spent my time by myself out on the prairie, which is a lonesome place to begin with, and it made me feel even more lonesome, which was fine because that was how I wanted to feel. Sometimes I went so far off, I couldn't see the wagons. The prairie was so big and empty, I started feeling smaller and smaller until I felt I might just disappear entirely. Like Willie, with nothing left to remember me by. Part of me thought that would be all right.

One day, I laid myself down on the ground and folded my arms across my chest and decided I would just look at the clouds until – well, I don't know what. But then I felt the ground start to rumble under me. It had to be buffalo running somewhere near, so I jumped up, near to panic – I may have felt like disappearing, but I wasn't ready to be trampled to bits.

That cleared my head. I began to go around in circles, not able to see the train and not knowing from which direction the buffalo were coming. There was nothing to stand on to see over the grass.

I was getting more and more flustered and I kept saying to myself that folks were always getting themselves lost when they went off looking for a private place to relieve themselves, and they got an unmerciful teasing over it. But there was nothing humorous about it and I was a fool trying to get myself lost on purpose.

I wasn't quite ready to never see my family again, even though the sight of Rebecca made me think that if her baby was a boy, everybody would say that he would take the place of Willie, which I just couldn't abide.

That was the way it was: I couldn't bear being with my family and I couldn't bear being without them.

Margaret felt she must fill her days more constructively than with the production of burnt biscuits and badly ironed shirts, along with constant worry about the future. Rebecca's sorrow at Joe and Sarah's lack of education had given birth to a possibility: it was one area in which she might claim some expertise – and might also offer an opportunity to kill two birds with one stone.

She invited Emily Walker for dessert. Miss Walker was suspicious of the invitation, but since Harriet Stokes kept her on short rations, her sweet tooth got the better of her.

Since Miss Walker appeared devoid of social graces, Margaret thought it best to come to the point. 'I am planning to give lessons to the young people in the train. It isn't right they should be so long without schooling.'

'That is your affair, not mine. I have no children.'

'But you are planning to teach the children of emigrants. These children are emigrants-on-the-way and will give you some practice.'

'I don't even have a grammar,' Miss Walker said. 'Everything is to be set up by the mission.'

'I plan to use Shakespeare as a text. I own a complete set of his plays, as well as the sonnets. It is not enough that men know how to farm and women to spin. If this new land is going to be civilized, it's going to require education as well.'

Miss Walker started to say something, but Margaret would not be held back. 'I suggest an hour during nooning and another hour at supper. To make schooling part of mealtimes is only practical. And for convenience sake, I trust you will be sharing our meals?'

'I am not a beggar any more than a servant, Mrs Prescott.'

Margaret was exasperated with her contrariness. 'Oh, for goodness' sakes! We both loathe Harriet Stokes and you are on the verge of starvation!' She glared at the schoolteacher until she saw she was not going to receive additional argument. 'And you must call me Margaret.'

After summarily dealing with Emily, it didn't take long in convincing Harriet Stokes to 'volunteer' her charge, who had become no use to her anyway, but she pretended it was a gesture of largesse on her part.

Rebecca, though excited for the opportunity the school might offer herself, was less confident of her stepchildren's response.

'We will sugar-coat it, except for the youngest,' Margaret explained. 'We'll masquerade knowledge as competition or games – reading stories and finding clues, or solving mathematical puzzles to unlock a mystery. There is so little to break the monotony of the days.'

Rebecca could not be a naysayer in the face of Margaret's enthusiasm. 'I will leave the matter in your hands, Margaret; my own will be best occupied providing the nooning meal for both our families.'

They gathered beneath a cottonwood the following day. Some of the younger bachelors had been invited, along with Sarah and

Joe, Bert and his sister Sally, and Nellie Bingham. Nancy Stokes had been asked as well, but her mother felt the release of Miss Walker had been quite enough sacrifice. Nancy was required to pick up the slack left by Emily's rebellion.

While Emily helped Laurie and Sally trace their letters, Margaret suggested conundrums to the older group. Everyone had already worn out their personal stock around the campfire, but she posed a fresh one:

'What goes forth on four legs in the morning, two in the afternoon, and three in the evening?'

'A horse's got four legs!' Bert called out.

'So's an ox!' Joe added.

'And so do a dog or a cat for that matter,' Nellie pointed out. 'But it has to have two legs in the afternoon and three in the evening, isn't that right, Mrs Prescott?'

Already, Nellie was angling to be teacher's pet, Sarah thought. She had decided to assume an air of disdain for the proceedings, but secretly found comfort at being in the midst of humanity again.

When all proclaimed to have given up, Margaret supplied the answer: 'It is a man: he goes forth on four legs crawling in the morning of his life; then on two when he learns to walk in the afternoon of his life; finally, in the night of his years, on three as an old man with a cane.'

The bachelors whistled in appreciation.

Margaret shook her head. 'I can't take the credit for it. It is part of a play written almost two thousand years ago, if you can imagine. Have any of you ever seen a play?'

Their faces were blank. 'A play is a story performed,' Margaret explained. 'It can be great fun to read them out loud.'

Rebecca wasn't surprised when Margaret showed the group a large leatherbound volume, trimmed in gold. She had spied her drying one just like it in the sun.

'I could read a bit to see if you find it of interest. It is called *Macbeth* and takes place a long time ago in Scotland where some of your ancestors might have lived. It has conundrums as well, but it is known mostly for bloodshed and witches.'

She smiled at their reaction; she had thought this observation would capture their attention. Nellie wasn't certain talk of witches was suitable for a minister's daughter. Sarah suggested she could leave if she wanted, and she fell silent.

'The language is somewhat old-fashioned,' Margaret continued, 'but I will try to interpret whatever you don't understand.'

She knew the play well enough to read easily and with emotion. Even though there were several pauses for explanations, it came as a surprise to her audience to hear the call to yoke up for the afternoon.

The Journal of Rebecca Springer

June 12, 1846

Margaret claims women are natural-born teachers as the rearing of children is in their natures. Emily Walker is childless and of a sour disposition, but she does not seem to be doing a bad job teaching Laurie and Sally their ABCs.

The mission where Emily is going is run by a missionary couple named Whitman who have become famous in the East as Mrs Whitman was the first woman to cross the Rocky Mountains.

Lord, there are still so few of us coming after her.

Sarah

I had heard Miz Prescott talking to Rebecca once about how their bachelor Tom would come into their wagon at night to listen to Laurie's bedtime stories because he was an orphan and he'd never had a mama to read to him. Well, I hadn't neither. Papa never thought of the idea, it not being a man's work, and Daniel and Matthew scarcely liked to read themselves.

About the only reading out loud that went on at our place was *Nick of the Woods*, but that was so we'd get a good scare over injuns scalping folks, but the scare got taken away because we had to stop all the time to figger out the words and sometimes we figgered them wrong and it didn't make sense.

When Rebecca came, she encouraged reading, and would have each of us read a passage from the Bible on the Lord's Day, but I looked on it as a chore. Rebecca tended toward the praying parts, not the story parts.

Being read to by Miz Prescott, without having to think about it being improving, took my mind off things. I was impatient when Rebecca or Nellie asked what some word or another meant. I didn't think it mattered to understand every last word to figure out what was going on. Nellie was showing off and Rebecca was just pernickety.

Macbeth sure wasn't a happy story but neither was mine, and those folks had even worse trouble so it kind of made me feel less sad and angry.

It also set me thinking in some new directions. William Shakespeare had a lot to say on a lot of different subjects and Margaret (she told me to call her that as I was not a child) said that no matter what talking point might come up, she would wager Shakespeare had said something about it. He had put it in an old-fashioned way that needed some sweat to work through, but once you figgered out what he meant, the sense of it was right modern.

She said that whenever something he said particularly struck my fancy, I should commit it to paper and by and by I'd have a right good collection of wise things to say. That notion sounded good to me and got me to working on my penmanship so I would be able to read all those wise things I had written down. I started to pay more attention to my spelling, too, as I mostly didn't always spell things the same way twice.

Margaret promised me it wouldn't be an ordinary school with rules and regulations; we would try one thing, and if that was not to our liking, we would go on to another. She said she would try not to bore me and I must catch her at it if she did. I agreed this was fair.

The men had been itching for a buffalo hunt and Captain Stokes felt their pace had been quick enough to take a day to stage one. The scouts picked a herd more than two miles from the train in case a stampede might occur, and an early start was warranted.

Stokes appointed Philip Prescott and Early LaForce to lead the hunt, electing himself to remain in camp. Jake was his bachelor, and there hadn't been much more of him that could be amputated to stop the gangrene without killing him, so the Captain had put him on opium and whiskey until the end had finally come.

Jake's best chums stayed behind for the funeral, but most of the other men went on the hunt. Jake was buried with his fiddle. After Reverend Bingham said a few words, Captain Stokes hitched up a team to drive back and forth over the grave to prevent it from being easily dug up by animals.

John was among those who stayed behind, planning to spend the day rebracing the oxen's yokes.

'There aren't but two or three of the company that might be of real use on a buffalo hunt and the rest will just be spectators,' he grumbled. 'I have better things to do with my time.'

Daniel was too eager for the hunt for the remark to sting him.

But John was distracted from his task when he spotted another wagon train slowly moving across the prairie in the distance. It didn't seem its path would cross their own, so he and Curt Hansen decided to ride over to see if they had any news that was not as stale as their own.

After the funeral, the women took their leisure in the shade of a thin grove of cotton-woods near the water's edge. Except near water, it was becoming rare to encounter the cooling canopy of trees, so it was a welcome retreat. Conversation was intermittent and drowsy; it was a luxury to simply enjoy a few idle moments.

Suddenly a child screamed. Every woman knows the sound of her own, and Margaret immediately leapt up.

Captain Stokes had left his oxen in their yokes, and it had presented too much of a temptation for a small boy like Laurie – Joe and Bert often balanced themselves on the wagon tongues to hitch a ride and he wanted to try the stunt himself. The stationary oxen had seemed an easy opportunity but when they decided to try a new patch of grass, he had lost his balance and fallen under a wheel.

Margaret couldn't see him at first, as the tall grass almost covered him, hidden behind the huge wheel. She scrambled under the wagon, following the sound of his whimpering.

Captain Stokes unhitched the team and took care in rolling the wagon backward. Margaret hovered over her son protectively until it cleared. Laurie moaned in pain when Captain Stokes picked him up to carry him to the Prescotts' wagon. Margaret stumbled along beside, her skirt torn and stained with grass and her hair fallen out of its pins.

It wasn't until he was lain on a mattress that it became evident that Laurie's leg was twisted at an odd angle. When Margaret tried to undress him, he screamed, so she left him as he was, kissing and caressing his face, her tears mingling with the sweat in his hair.

Captain Stokes carefully slit Laurie's pant leg with his hunting knife to get a closer look. There was no break in the skin which he told Margaret was encouraging.

Rebecca brought laudanum, with honey to soften the taste. Margaret forced Laurie to drink it and he was numb when Captain Stokes straightened his leg and bound it to a board.

John returned in the late afternoon, filled with news from the other train, but Laurie's accident took priority.

'He could be crippled for life, John,' Rebecca worried.

'It seems to have been a simple break.'

'We buried a man this afternoon who had a simple break.'

'Rebecca, there is a doctor in the other train. I will fetch him for a consultation if it will give you and the boy's mother some reassurance.'

The look on Rebecca's face told him what he should do.

The other men had still not returned from the buffalo hunt, so Rebecca sat with Margaret, while Laurie lay in a drugged slumber.

As their own fires were lit, they were mirrored in the distant camp. 'They are beacons to guide John and the doctor,' Rebecca reassured Margaret. Elizabeth and Sarah quietly prepared supper.

Margaret nodded off from exhaustion and Rebecca continued to keep watch. She wasn't aware she had fallen asleep herself until she was startled awake by the sudden appearance of a massive bearded face poking through the canvas of the tent. The lantern light glinted off thin gold-rimmed glasses. A mass of shaggy hair tinged with gray was barely contained by a shiny black felt hat.

The hat was tipped to Rebecca. 'I apologize for startling you, my lady.' The words were heavily accented. 'I am Dr Hugo Weiss.'

Margaret stirred, awakened by his voice.

'It's the doctor,' Rebecca whispered, and moved the lamp while she and Margaret made room for him next to Laurie's pallet. Since Dr Weiss was dressed entirely in black, he seemed even more bear-like as he crawled into the wagon. Setting down a battered black satchel, he gently unwrapped Laurie's bandage. The boy didn't awaken until Dr Weiss attempted to manipulate his leg; then he thrashed and cried. Margaret held him tightly, whispering comforting words into his ear.

'It does not feel like a fracture,' Dr Weiss concluded, 'but still he must remain immobile.' He consulted the contents of his satchel. 'I will give you a salve, and com-

190

presses will also be beneficial, first hot and then cold. I will know more in a day.'

After accepting a mug of stew from Rebecca, Dr Weiss made a bed for himself under the Prescott wagon, curling up like a grizzly settling into hibernation.

Rebecca pressed John for more information.

'He speaks strangely.'

'He's Swiss, but studied medicine in Vienna. His entire party emigrated to the United States together. Their religion prohibits taking up arms and they did not want their young men proscripted by the Austrians.'

'What is their religion?'

'They are Mennonites.'

Rebecca was alarmed; she had misheard him to say 'Mormons'.

John reassured her. 'The Mennonites are hard-working people. They're all farmers and will do well in the West.'

Dr Weiss agreed to join their train for a few days. Since his own train was also stopping at Fort Laramie, he could meet them again there.

The hunting party finally appeared early the following morning, announcing they had to return with a wagon to collect their kill. John was not in a good mood over this report and directed his displeasure toward Daniel.

'One or two buffalo would have been sufficient. They could have been dragged home behind the horses on a rig like the Indians use. Shooting more animals than you can carry was wasteful.'

'I was not in charge.'

'A man doesn't have to be in charge to show common sense. If he does, then maybe he'll be the one in charge the next time.'

'I don't lay claim to leading a buffalo hunt.'

'Well, you thought you were equipped to go tearing off with the rest of them when we had work to be done.'

'If there was work, you should have said so.'

'There is always work.'

They continued to argue until Rebecca felt like pouring her dirty wash water over both their heads. It was disloyal to her husband, but even though he was in the right, he was wrong to hector Daniel. The other boys had never held an opinion opposite to their father's, and John seemed to think that was the way things should be in the world. Daniel thought he was entitled to his own opinions, and Rebecca supposed he was, as long as he was not in his father's household.

It was a good thing Daniel planned to put up his own house in Oregon. She just hoped it wouldn't be too far away for Elizabeth and her babies to play every day.

The Journal of Rebecca Springer

June 18, 1846

When the men returned to their kill, Indians or animals had gotten to the carcasses and most of the remaining meat was spoiled. They were only able to save a few of the hides.

We covered sixteen miles today. The ride gave Laurie pain, but Margaret says he has not developed a fever, which Dr Weiss claims is a good sign, though I have always maintained a good sweat is the best thing. Her husband is most attentive, never leaving his son's side, which has given Margaret a rest she richly deserves. I have more respect for him now that I can see how fine a father he is. That is surely a better measure of a man than how well he sits a horse – or chooses his wagon, for that matter.

The land about us has become strange. We have entered a broad valley with fantastic shapes along its rim. They have been carved by generations of wind and rain, I reckon, or maybe they have been here since Noah's Flood.

We are told to watch out for rattlesnakes. At least they announce their presence. I wonder what You had in mind, Lord, when you created all of this. It is surely not fit for human habitation, but it is a wonder.

Margaret Prescott's Notebook

We have now left behind what was purchased from the Indians and come into unorganized territory, though I suspect that not even the cartographers in Washington, DC, know for certain where one territory ends and another starts. So much land came with the Louisiana Purchase, they are still organizing the material brought by Mr Lewis and Mr Clark.

We are camped at Chimney Rock. Some of the men took a side trip to Courthouse Rock, but Chimney Rock is the wonder: five hundred feet high and so like a chimney straight up into the sky in the middle of the prairie, one can almost imagine it smoking when wisps of clouds drift by.

Hailstones came down the size of snowballs last night. I set a bucket to catch them and had a very cold wash of hands and face before breakfast. My preference would have been to effect a more thorough wash with such crystal-clear water, but it required too much organization with the land offering so little shelter. The men proclaim these plains make them feel open and free, but none of us women are pleased; there is no privacy and there is a feeling that one can be spied upon from miles away.

The urge to comply with the call of nature has caused even those less congenial women, Harriet Stokes and Ivy Bingham, to grow closer out of necessity. We all become human trees, forming a circle around our sisters, spreading our skirts to create a shield of modesty. A quorum of four is necessary: three to create the circle and the fourth to do their business.

Joe and Bert were all for finding a way to climb Chimney Rock, but there didn't seem to be any way to gain a foothold, and the whole thing looked as if it might come tumbling down in the first stiff breeze.

Sarah and Rebecca stood looking at it in wonder. 'I sure wish Willie could see this!' Sarah exclaimed.

'He would have appreciated it more than anyone,' Rebecca agreed.

Some of the pain of Willie's memory seemed to have eased.

'I'd like to ask your opinion about something, Sarah,' Rebecca asked.

Sarah gave her a guarded look; there was a truce, but not complete amity.

Rebecca hastened to explain. 'Do you think it would be acceptable to finish reading *Macbeth* on our own while Margaret is occupied with nursing Laurie? I for one am anxious to know how it all turns out.'

Sarah shrugged, trying not to appear

eager. 'Might as well.'

Rebecca tentatively took charge, carefully passing the beautiful volume around, after making sure all hands were well washed. Rebecca and Nellie were the best readers, but all agreed that even the slowest must have a go, at least for a page or two.

Emily Walker was not averse to resuming the routine, as having burned her bridges with the Stokeses, there was no other place for her in the train; she hadn't had a decent meal since the schooling had been interrupted.

In return for financing her journey, the Oregon Provisional society of Methodist ministers had insisted Emily remain unmarried, reasoning that a married woman had no business dealing with any children but her own, not to mention ministering to her husband. That seemed a large price to pay to Rebecca, but Emily soon made clear her opinion of men, taking offense when Rebecca didn't offer the women cobbler so John and Daniel could have seconds. She seemed to prefer a sweet to a sweetheart.

Sarah

Mr Prescott took the failure of the buffalo hunt as his personal fault, though I think there was plenty of blame to go around for the waste of all that meat. When the first opportunity arose, he went off on his own and brought down a buffalo with a single shot. The other animals didn't know enough to be afraid and just kept on grazing. It was in clear view of the train, so the accomplishment somewhat quieted the general grumbling against him, particularly since all of us were concerned about Laurie. Rebecca said Mr Prescott was taking the blame for what happened to Laurie too, but I think that was more the fault of Captain Stokes for being careless.

We weren't the only ones after buffalo, because that same day a Sioux party came riding into view, one after the other like in parade, with their banners flapping in the light breeze. Their backs were straight as ramrods and only their knees moved to steer their ponies, which they rode bareback. They seemed almost like they were part of their mounts.

When they came closer, I could see scalps

hanging from their belts – these were the first I had seen and it was frightening to think how they had gotten them. The hair was long and black and not likely to have come from white heads, but that didn't make me feel better.

The party didn't wear much else but the paint on their faces, and their bare bodies were lean and hard, muscles glistening with sweat. Miz Bingham hid herself and Nellie in the wagon, but the rest of us women couldn't stop staring, never having seen such a thing. I felt sort of funny inside, scared, but at the same time excited. All of us had heard tales of white women being carried off by wild injuns, and the thought of it made me weak at the knees, and something else as well, which I can't explain.

Captain Stokes and the council ordered us to stay well back and the men to line up in a show of strength as we were more than equal in numbers to the injuns.

Both sides sent out parlay parties. They had to do their talking with signing, which Captain Stokes was good at, as the Sioux didn't know any English. Papa was one of the men Captain Stokes asked to be in our party. He was so tall, he cut quite a figure, which is the truth and not just bragging.

'I don't think they're hostile,' Margaret said, shading her eyes to see from where we were bunched together by the wagons.

'They seem to be offering buffalo hides and buckskin clothing in exchange for coffee and tobacco.'

I was impressed. 'How'd you learn injun signs?'

'They are not dissimilar to what my father taught me. He preached at the Connecticut state school for the deaf.'

Margaret could figger out a lot of what was going on, even though back in Connecticut I reckon they didn't have signs for such things as buffalo. An important chief was part of the injun party, and that called for a pipe-sharing ceremony. The chief had a pipe decked out in feathers and Captain Stokes took out a pouch of his best tobacco and filled up the bowl to the brim.

Once the smoking was done with, things sort of got easier on both sides. The chief signed that his braves would show us what good shots they were, and it was quite a show. Those injuns were so sharp-eyed, they could split a biscuit propped up on the side of a barrel.

After the braves had emptied their quivers, there was a pause so they could gather up their arrows, which was practical as they didn't want any to be wasted. I saw Joe sneak one when they weren't looking, and I think he was lucky none of them caught him. He and Bert were beside themselves being surrounded by real savages.

I reckoned they were going to shoot at something else now, maybe something smaller like peppercorns, but the chief signed that now it was our turn.

It didn't take much figgering to pick our best at firearms, which was Philip Prescott and Early LaForce. Ben was tacked on as well, along with two of the scouts. My papa was best in a lot of things, but he had never had much time for firearms except to know what he had to know, so I didn't mind that he wasn't included.

Our men did real good, but the best was Mr Prescott shooting a three-cent piece out of the air with a pistol. That man had his talents; he just couldn't put them all together to work out right.

By now everybody was the best of friends and the injuns joined in digging a huge firepit so we could have a feast off the buffalo Mr Prescott killed. Injuns are partial to mush, so a whole mess of it was cooked up, using just about every kettle in the train. The Indians sat cross-legged on the ground and a lot of the men imitated them, even eating with their fingers in the same way, which Rebecca didn't like and wouldn't let Joe do, but he did anyway when she wasn't looking.

Captain Stokes was kept so busy he could hardly eat, the way the injuns kept signing and he had to sign back. 'The chief's saying the meat from the cow buffalo is the best ...

and the best parts are the tongue, the hump and the marrow bones...' he told us.

I almost choked trying to keep from laughing, since the injuns signed the buffalo parts by pointing to the same parts on their own bodies, and some of the parts would have been downright unfit for female ears if they had been talking in real English words. It appeared there wasn't a part of a buffalo that didn't get used in some way by the Sioux, including the private ones.

'He says the buffalo run many miles and Indian ponies are better than white men's since they don't get winded,' Captain Stokes said.

'We ought to be getting ourselves some of them,' one man said, and some of the others felt the same.

The injuns were quick to pick up their interest and Papa said he suspected they were hiding the fact they knew at least a little English.

'The chief says he might be willing to part with a couple for four rifles apiece,' Captain Stokes said, being honest and saying exactly what they were signing, even though there was no question he might allow it. Some of the men would have been willing, but we had a disciplined camp, so our men just went back to the business of sucking their marrow bones.

The Sioux didn't leave until dusk, so we

couldn't make any further progress that day – but to cut the proceedings short would have been insulting and maybe caused those arrows to be used for more than splitting biscuits. The moon was just a sliver and it seemed like the injuns were swallowed up by the darkness the minute they left us.

Captain Stokes said the conditions were perfect for them to sneak back for the stock, so the animals were brought inside the circle early and the wagons chained in case the Sioux tried to stampede them. He set extra pickets, too. Once all was safe around the fire, the men were in the mood to swap injun stories, each trying to outdo all the others.

'I knew a man had an Indian steal a blanket right off him while he was sleeping,' Pink said.

Ben had to top him. 'I heard of one feller suddenly woke up to see the business end of a tomahawk slashing through the canvas, of his wagon. Cool as can be, he grabbed that tomahawk and turned it around to do in its owner.'

That kind of talk stirred everyone up, and when one of the men got up in the night to relieve himself and fell in the dark over a chain, a picket thought he was a Sioux and shot him dead. Rebecca said it was real important to make a note of the feller's name and where he came from, so I asked around, as he was not more than a nodding acquaintance, and learned that his name was Edward O'Brien and he was not long come over from Ireland, which was all anyone knew about him. Reverend Bingham read him a service. Rebecca said she reckoned he was Roman Catholic as most of the Irish are. But she didn't see as how the Lord would turn down our prayers on those grounds.

Dr Weiss' foreign manner elicited wariness, but also curiosity. His bulging satchel held more than medical supplies. First, he pulled a clever traveling watercolorist's kit from its depths and did a good rendering of Chimney Rock. He also ran off some quick sketches of the Sioux, but was disappointed with the results. 'I do better with things that stand still like the rock,' he professed.

A few nights later, a chess set was magically produced, the box that held it hinging open to make a board. Both Prescotts could play, and the board was set up each night while the three took turns caring for Laurie.

Mrs Bingham was scandalized. 'Playing chess is no different from any other form of gambling; it is a step on the road to iniquity.'

Rebecca was uneasy. The Prescotts couldn't seem to keep in harmony with the company. Mr LaForce at least knew about planting, which provided a topic for conversation, but farming was not Mr Prescott's interest, and unlike Cora LaForce, who was the picture of feminine charm, Margaret acted sometimes as if she felt the equal to a man. Rebecca thought to turn her friend's attention to less controversial activities.

'I would appreciate it if you could teach me a few signs. It would be helpful to be able to converse with the squaws about which of the new plants we are finding might be fit to eat or have some use in healing. Even the grass is different than in Indiana and I do not want to be poisoning my family. Was it difficult to learn your signing?'

'Not at all,' Margaret said. 'Most of it has a real logic.'

'I surely hope so, as I am out of the habit of learning.'

'Do not make so little of yourself, Rebecca. You have done so well with Shakespeare without me, I am hardly needed.'

'Now that is not the truth, Margaret, and you know it.'

'I would also be interested in communicating with these red Indians,' Dr Weiss said. He had grown bored with waiting for Phillip to decide his next move.

'Can I get in on this too?' Sarah asked. Careful not to directly cross Rebecca by openly asking for chess lessons, she had been closely observing the play. 'Being able to talk to injuns would be something!'

They practiced whenever Indians appeared seeking to swap. They had discovered that hair clips were considered choice merchandise by both male and female, and soon ran out of spares, but Cora LaForce was able to provide an ample resupply. Though she remained content to lie in her feather bed, stroking her swollen stomach, she enjoyed hearing of the other women's doings.

When the women met with one or two Indians, they felt no fear. There was no need for women to exhibit postures of bravery the way the men did, and the Indians didn't expect much from them.

The Springer women were washing the Sunday dinner dishes when several squaws appeared, some with papooses strapped to their backs.

'I wonder how old they are,' Elizabeth pondered. 'One looks more to be the grandmother of her papoose.'

'That's what comes from working "hard as a squaw",' Rebecca joshed. This was an expression the women often used when faced with a difficult day.

'The Indians treat their women better than the men of our company do theirs,' Emily Walker remarked in displeasure.

She had joined the Springers for dinner, even though it wasn't a school day; Rebecca wouldn't allow anything but scripture to be contemplated on the Lord's Day.

The squaws were presented with some of Cora's hair clips and other baubles, and

Rebecca signed that she wanted nothing more in return than some knowledge. The women giggled, apparently thinking Rebecca was a foolish bargainer, but nodded their agreement to the proposition.

Sarah ran to fetch Margaret, who was still the best signer, and volunteered to carry Betsy for Elizabeth, whose advancing pregnancy was causing her difficulties. Counting the Indians, there must have been a dozen women and children trooping across the prairie, looking quite like a ladies' auxiliary out for a Sunday School picnic, to Rebecca's mind.

As they walked, Rebecca searched for new plants outside her experience – sometimes something small in the grass, sometimes a bright flower, or occasionally a shrub that looked promising. She had known the properties of quite a few plants in Indiana, but a great deal of what grew on the prairie was as strange as Chimney Rock.

She pointed to a plant, then to her mouth. The squaws replied with a headshake and a frown, or nodded and smacked their lips to show a plant was tasty to eat. One or two plants they dug up with sticks to show it was the roots that were important. If the plants were medicinal, they mimed headaches or stomach pain.

When Sarah took the initiative, pointing at a plant and then to her mouth, the squaws doubled up with laughter. She gathered that if she ate it, she would no doubt die on the spot.

After a while, Sarah announced that Betsy was in need of a change and they stopped by the side of a small stream.

The squaws watched Sarah give the dirty napkin a rinse with fascination. She never liked this part of tending Betsy, but Elizabeth was too heavy to squat on the slippery slope.

Judging by their tittering, the squaws apparently thought it ridiculous the way white women cared for their infants. They kept their own babies tightly wrapped in soft skins and lashed to boards – far easier than shifting a squirming child from hip to hip. They slipped out of the shoulder straps that held those neat packages on their backs and unwrapped the babies' swaddling. To the white women's wonder, instead of napkins, moss had been packed between the papooses' legs! The mothers threw away the soiled moss and gathered fresh near the side of the stream.

Elizabeth was impressed. 'If I could be sure there was no insects living inside that moss, I'd try the same.'

'It would sure save a heap of work, especially when Betsy makes a real mess,' Sarah agreed.

Then one of the squaws lifted her buckskin skirt and quite matter-of-factly took advantage of having such an abundance of moss available to use for her menstrual flow. Rebecca was embarrassed and tried to look away.

Margaret was impressed. 'Now that is a considerable improvement over trying to find some privacy to wash out monthly rags.'

Something came over Elizabeth and Rebecca and they started to giggle.

'Can you imagine going on a picking expedition of this nature?' Rebecca managed to say.

'How would we explain it to our husbands?' Elizabeth squealed.

The squaws joined in the laughter, as if they had understood the joke, then kindly offered their white companions dried berries from the deerskin pouches they wore at their waists. In return, Rebecca presented some cornbread she had brought tied up in a napkin.

'Well, I am feeling confident now that I can prepare a nice salad for supper,' she said. 'And I had best go tend to it now.' She didn't comment that the squaws had failed to return the napkin.

The Journal of Rebecca Springer

June 21, 1846

Fourteen miles today to Scott's Bluff, which is a line of cliffs rising up out of the buffalo grass. The land behind us is so flat I can still see the outline of Chimney Rock in the distance. We have come about 600 miles so far and completed a third of our journey.

I reckon we will have another three or four days before we finally get to Fort Laramie and some civilization again.

The prairie sage is in bloom everywhere. We are all getting sick of the smell.

We have finished *Macbeth* now and started on *Much Ado About Nothing*, which is a comedy, Margaret says, according to Mr Shakespeare's use of the word. A comedy means nobody dies, at least nobody important.

They read at night and mixed poetry, signing and science, compliments of Dr Weiss, at nooning. Margaret wanted Tom to be part of the reading group.

Rebecca cautioned her not to pay too much attention to her bachelor.

'I think he is sweet on you.'

Margaret looked shocked. 'You are imagining things, Rebecca; I think he looks to me as the mother he has been denied.'

'You are just about the same age.'

'I am sure you are mistaken. He is merely grateful to have a woman cook his meals, mend his clothes, and lend a comforting moral tone to his life. Do you think I am being too sentimental? You take your role seriously as the keeper of your home and family.'

'Well, it is true that with women around, the men pay more attention to cleanliness and sanitation,' Rebecca said thoughtfully. 'I think they also become more alert to any hazard, feeling they have to provide us protection. Of course, we provide them well-cooked meals at regular times, which prevents much sickness and waste of food.'

'Let no one say the members of our sex do not make their contribution,' Margaret agreed. 'Tom is such a wonder helping Philip with the horses, I wish I had a distaff version of him to help me. I would love to have a day when Laurie did not complain of my "black bread". Philip and Tom are both complimentary, but Philip is accustomed to a much higher standard of cuisine.'

Rebecca knew Margaret would do as she pleased with respect to Tom, but she was certain he was smitten. She also had her concerns about Dr Weiss. She had asked him if he was married and he was not. It was not natural at his age.

The Journal of Rebecca Springer

June 22, 1846

Bright stepped into a hole today and went lame. John had to shoot him. It was like losing a companion. I can't help but think Buck will miss his yokemate.

John has put a lariat around our mattress at night to keep away the rattlesnakes. I hope it works.

Lord, I guess it is Your way to mix the good and the bad to keep us humble; we have had some good days lately, so I guess it was about time to have a bit of the other so we won't forget our lives are in Your hands.

For days the buffalo had been in the corner of their eyes, thousands peacefully grazing as the train slowly passed. Hunting fever had died and the animals scarcely merited a glance unless fresh meat was needed; then it was a simple matter for Phillip Prescott or Early LaForce to bring down single animals on the fringes of a herd.

Even before the first buffalo had been sighted, Captain Stokes lectured the train on the danger of a stampede. But with accustomization, fear had faded, so nothing ominous registered when what sounded like distant thunder was heard. But then, across the far prairie, billowing clouds of dust rose in a line far too straight for nature.

Rebecca was walking beside the wagon as the ground began to shake beneath her feet. It suddenly dawned on her that the thunder was in the hooves of the buffalo. She had a moment of panic, then assured herself it was misplaced: the spare stock, which would have been difficult to control un-tethered, were far behind with the bach-elors, and the wagons were strung out with wide spaces separating them. A stampeding herd should be able to gallop between them.

The men had been drilled well and hurried to turn the wagons so if the buffalo did cross their path, they would not meet any vehicle broadside. After setting the brakes, John, Daniel and Pink each took one of the Springer wagons, positioning them-selves between the lead pairs of oxen to hold them steady. The other men in the train did the same.

'I don't know which would be best for you,' John said to his family, 'inside the wagons or under them.'

'I reckon we might be better off under than in if one of them toppled,' Sarah concluded, and the others agreed, even though it was difficult for Elizabeth to crawl beneath the floorboards. Rebecca stayed close to her and Betsy, while Sarah and Joe crawled under another wagon.

Lying on the ground, Rebecca felt the

vibration even more strongly. It continued to mount, along with the sound of approaching hooves, which soon became a deafening roar. The dust cloud rushed forward like an explosion, completely blocking out the light. She had to close her eyes to not be blinded by flying grit.

Elizabeth tried to protect Betsy, who cried and choked on her muddy tears.

With her eyes shut, Rebecca was only dimly aware of flashes rushing by, but she could smell the buffalo and hear their panting breath in rhythm with their pounding hooves. The wagon shook with the force of it all. At one point, it gave a sudden lurch and started to move. Rebecca felt they had come to their end, but miraculously it steadied, though it continued to shudder from the buffet of the stampede. It was a time spent in hell.

Finally, the flashing shapes began to recede, taking the noise and vibration with them. When all was quiet, Rebecca finally opened her eyes. Elizabeth and Betsy were so coated with dust they were all of the same ocher color, except where Betsy's tears had left darker streaks down her cheeks. Rebecca knew she must look the same. The baby had been gripping Elizabeth's bodice so tightly, she had ripped it down the front.

'Lizzie, I think you and Betsy best stay here just for the moment,' Rebecca advised her, seeing how shaken she was. 'I will check on the others.'

When she crawled out from under the wagon, she couldn't find her bearings for a moment; nothing seemed the same as before the stampede: the ground was stripped bare of grass and the wagons lay zigzagged haphazardly, one tipped on its side with its canvas shredded. Several dead oxen lay in their own blood, mangled by the hooves of the buffalo.

Her heart was in her throat until she saw John standing between a yoke of their oxen – filthy, but a joy to behold, and she rushed to embrace him. It was several moments before he could collect himself enough to finally release his grip on the yoke and put his arms around her.

Daniel and Pink had stood fast by the other wagons. After a few moments, Joe and Sarah emerged from beneath one. Other dust-covered members of the company also slowly crawled out, as if from deep beneath the earth, slapping each other on the back to see the dust rise.

The Prescotts' wagon was still standing, but the lead horses had broken their traces and disappeared. The back four stood shivering in their traces and the remaining pair were dead – with Philip Prescott's body lying beneath them.

Emily Walker wandered about, a dazed look on her face.

Rebecca took her arm. 'Where is Margaret?'

'Still in the wagon with Laurie. He was jostled badly and Dr Weiss thinks it has undone all the healing.'

'Does she know about her husband?'

Emily nodded. 'But she says the living need her more now.'

For once, Emily's face held compassion.

The Journal of Rebecca Springer

June 23, 1846

Phillip Prescott was the only member of our company lost in the stampede. He has been buried on the prairie. Laurie is back on laudanum and does not know his father is in heaven. Dr Weiss dosed Margaret as well.

When she awakens, I will try to be of comfort, but no friend can replace a husband. I rely on John totally and hold an all-abiding trust in him. I wonder if Laurie will even remember his father in a few years?

Lord, look after the soul of Phillip Prescott. He was a man with his faults, but he died protecting his family.

Dear Lord, protect us from further tragedy and look after Margaret. This is no journey for a woman alone.

Margaret Prescott's Notebook

The Indians of the plains perform a ritual dance to honor the spirit of the buffalo they slay. I wonder if Philip's failure to do the same brought vengeance? Foolish thought.

To lie in his arms one more time. His body on mine.

No more.

Part 5

The Parting of the Ways

Margaret was in no state to discuss her future rationally for the next several days, but those in the train with her interests at heart did so at some length. Captain Stokes recommended he find a military train to accompany her back to Independence or, failing that, some trustworthy trapper to serve as escort. Rebecca was in favor of this option, as Margaret had family in the East to turn to.

Dr Weiss said she was welcome to join his party, but this suggestion was rejected as tactfully as possible. Rebecca believed he had a personal interest in mind with his offer, but the Captain and John simply took the practical view that someone like Margaret would not fit in with a group of Mennonite farmers.

Emily Walker suggested Margaret join her at the Whitman Mission. From what had been heard of Narcissa Whitman, she was a formidable person and not fond of other women. It would be Emily's lot to continue to serve under someone much like Harriet Stokes, but no one wished the same for Margaret.

When she collected herself, Margaret asked Emily to join her in her wagon. She said it wasn't seemly for a woman to be traveling alone with a man not her husband, but she told Rebecca she was only using Dr Weiss as an excuse, as, with Emily's pride, she might have otherwise rejected the offer as an act of charity. Excuse or not, Rebecca was pleased.

Sarah

The train had to go on, even with Laurie in so much pain, but we would be stopping again soon at Fort Laramie. We spied another train heading in the same direction, so we'd be having company there. The other folks kept a respectful distance to maintain sanitation and ample feed for the teams, which Papa said was a sign of a well-run outfit. The scouts said they were from Ohio.

We laid out strings of buffalo meat to dry across the wagon covers for jerky. It was getting hotter and some of our food was spoiling.

'I am growing tired of the sameness of our meals,' Rebecca said mostly to Elizabeth as I was not one she ever consulted when it came to cooking. 'Maybe they have something new in that Ohio train. There must be women there keeping up cooking standards.'

'What I would really like is an Indian to come by and offer us a nice fresh fish,' Elizabeth wished.

'You love fish so much your baby's going to be born with a scaly tail,' I teased her.

'This kind of talk brings bad luck,' Rebecca scolded. For a religious woman, she sure had her superstitions.

I was in a good mood. 'I will catch you a fish, Elizabeth,' I said.

'You are supposed to be stirring the grits,' Rebecca reminded me. 'They will get lumpy.'

'You said yourself you wanted something different,' I told her. 'You just don't think I can do it.'

'I didn't say that...'

'I used to catch fish all the time back home, didn't I, Elizabeth?'

'You did seem to have the knack,' Elizabeth agreed. She didn't want to be getting caught in the middle of anything that might be starting up between me and Rebecca.

'The thing about fishing is it takes time,' I explained to Rebecca, 'and I only have that kind of time when we make camp, but then you keep me occupied doing some chore any fool could do, like stirring grits.'

'Now that is a tall tale. You barely lift a finger to help.'

'I am offering to lift all ten of them right now to catch our dinner,' I said and I felt I had won. Elizabeth was trying not to smile.

Even though Rebecca was her best friend, her and me got along fine and I took care of Betsy for her a lot.

So I accidentally on purpose let the grits drip off my spoon and get into the other food that was on the fire and Rebecca gave up and took the spoon to give the grits a proper stir. 'If you can come home with a fish that can feed this family, then I will not give you any chores for a week. But if you don't, you will do what I say for the same week without complaint.'

I found a stick that could be turned into a pole and commenced to rummage through the sewing box for a bit of string and a bent pin.

'Don't be leaving that box in a mess,' Rebecca scolded, peeved, I reckon, that she had made a fool's bargain.

I grabbed a rasher of bacon and made for the river, but not without hollering over my shoulder, 'And your baby will cluck instead of coo, you love eggs so much!' I didn't say it meanly and I think she knew I was just joshing.

The Platte was sluggish there, wide with sandbars in the middle and broken brush in the water, which caught what little drift-wood there was and created pools where a fish might hide. It was mostly shallow, so the few deeper places were the best fishing spots for trout or perch or crappie or bass.

Three young fellers from the other train were already lined up on the riverbank when I got there. They had staked out the best spot, where a broken-down wagon was making a dam with the water spilling over to where fish would be waiting to snap up whatever came their way. It was also one of the few places where there was some shade from a couple of cottonwoods, and shade was important when you had to sit for some time waiting for a fish to bite. I couldn't tell what bait they were using as their poles were in the water.

I didn't pay them much attention, taking off my shoes and hitching my skirt so I could wade out to a sandbar that curved almost like a horseshoe, making an eddy in the water that reckoned to be a good place to fish.

But out of the corner of my eye, I could see those fellers – scarce more than boys – nudge each other and snicker. They commenced to whisper a bit, and then I guess they decided what the smartest thing to say was, because one of them hollered:

'Hey! Don't you know girls ain't allowed to go fishing?'

'I don't see any sign says this is your river and you make the rules.' I settled down and got my line in the water, not even bothering to turn my back on them.

They didn't like it that I wasn't whimpering and running back home, which set them behaving like children, mad because they hadn't got their own way.

'We was here first,' they said.

'And you ain't caught nothing,' I said back.

''Cause you scairt away the fish!'

'Ain't me doing the hollering,' I told them.

That seemed to stump them for an answer. After a couple of minutes, one of them said, kind of giving up, 'Ain't nothing biting anyways.'

'Wait and see,' I said, confident, and we continued to sit there, waiting each other out.

After about fifteen minutes of ignoring their whispering and snickering, I suddenly felt a weight on my line. 'Well, I got me one,' I said, getting up. 'Feels big, too!'

'She's just faking!' one of them said to his friends.

I made a face at them and pulled on my pole. 'Pretty hard to fake a fish this big,' I said.

I wrestled with the pole, taking a step or two back for leverage, and then gave a jerk. A tree limb rose up to the surface of the water, hooked fast to my line.

Well, you should have heard the way those fellers hooted, slapping each other on the back and making quite a show. I could feel my face getting redder and I wanted nothing more than to shut them all up.

'Just you wait and see!' one of them aped

me. 'Well, we did wait and we saw quite a sight!'

'Pretty hard to fake a fish this big,' another said, pretending to talk in a girl's voice.

'Gotta hand it to her: she's a good faker!' another one said, which set his friends off to laughing again.

By that time, I had thrown down my pole and splashed back across the river. I marched straight up to those jokers and gave the nearest one a good punch in the stomach, taking him in complete surprise and doubling him over.

Now the joke was on him as his friends commenced to tease him for having been taken down by a girl, and that was so much fun they paid me no more mind and I got out of their sight as fast as I could.

I wasn't about to come back to camp and have Rebecca lord it over me, asking where her fish dinner was, so I snuck a horse and rode back to where Ben and the other bachelors were camping and shared some salt beef and didn't come home until everybody had gone to bed.

When it was time to stop for nooning the following day, Rebecca and John's wagon was the first in the family to make camp. They had just begun to unyoke the oxen when a young man rode up. His stomach was still sore from the blow Sarah had delivered the previous afternoon. He politely removed his hat.

'Morning, Ma'am, Sir. My name's George Black from the train over yonder. I hope you don't mind, but I have done some asking about in your train and figgered out who you were and where to find you.' His next words he addressed only to John. 'I would like to have a talk to you, man to man.'

Rebecca stepped away and pretended not to listen while she measured out cornmeal.

'Yesterday I had the opportunity to meet who I find out is your daughter,' George said. 'Her name is Sarah, if I am correct?'

'That it is.'

'I also understand there is a preacher in your party.'

'That is so.'

'Then it is a very good time for me and your daughter to get hitched. A man's going to need a wife in Oregon and she seems to be right strong and sturdy, judging from the wallop she gave me. I'm hoping the next time we get together, I'll get a kiss instead of a punch.'

'How old are you, Son?'

'I am nineteen and know a great deal about farming, and what I don't know, I know enough to ask.'

This seemed to impress John and he went on to ask George for more details about his family.

'I have got five sisters so I am used to dealing with difficult women, and as I am the only son, the acres my daddy gets in Oregon will be coming to me once he has passed, though I hope that is not for a good long while.'

'You sound like a man with a bright future,' John complimented him, 'but this is weighty business and I'm sure you'll understand that I can't make a decision on the spot.'

They shook hands and agreed to meet again in a day or so, as their trains were following the same line to Fort Laramie.

After George left, Rebecca behaved as if she had not heard every word.

'What business on earth would a boy that age have with you, John?'

'You know full well what business, Rebecca, as you were eavesdropping.'

Rebecca was no longer so shy as to blush and stammer. 'Very well, John, you have caught me out, and I apologize.'

'And you have your piece to say on the subject, I imagine.'

'No, John, you have good judgment and can probably pick out a husband better than Sarah. But I am surprised you would consider marriage at her age.'

'Some men might be wondering what was wrong with her if she wasn't married by the time she was sixteen.'

'These days, sixteen is still a young age,

John. Letty was too young to be marrying Matthew at seventeen.'

'Sarah's made stronger than Letty.'

'In many ways, but she's still feeling for Willie. I reckon you didn't give that George an answer because you thought it better to keep her with the family a while longer.'

'I want to see Sarah happy again.'

'It is not my decision to make, but I scarce see that to remove her from the remainder of her family will lift her mood.'

John shook his head. 'Sarah is so pig-headed, she wouldn't have made the poor boy much of a bargain anyhow.'

The Journal of Rebecca Springer

June 26, 1846

I wonder if John really intended to marry Sarah off, or just to consider the pros and cons of it as he does with most things? Could he manage a marriage if Sarah didn't want it? She adores her father, but has a will of her own.

Sarah may have had her birthday already, but today was the real beginning of her womanhood. I can see why George has gotten a bee in his bonnet over her, even if her hair is a mess and her face is dirty. Her mother must have been a pretty woman.

Fort Laramie tomorrow. Thank You, Lord, for bringing us some civilization for a change.

Fort Laramie gave the train their first news from the outside world for some time. A military detachment had recently arrived from Fort Leavenworth. Beaver had been trapped out, and the government was considering converting some of the trading posts into forts, since there was public clamor to provide protection for overlanders.

There was also uneasiness over Mexico. The army men reported that the first blood had been shed over the disagreement with Mexico about California. The previous month, a band of Mexican troops had crossed to the eastern side of the Rio Grande and fought a company of American soldiers. No doubt war had already been officially declared and General Fremont in California had engaged the enemy.

The feeling was strong that California would soon become a US possession, and argument continued over the Missouri compromise. Some would replace it with popular sovereignty, but even so, the movement was strong to preserve both Oregon and California as free territories. There was no escaping politics.

Fort Laramie was not much to shout about, even though it represented civilization: just an old trapper post looking out over the

Platte, mostly built of mud bricks with only one or two buildings of wood, it being more scarce than mud. But it also served as a secondary jumping-off place. There was a long haul ahead before the next outpost, and everyone who passed through assessed what they could add to their supplies. Even though stocks were sparse, there was a lot of abandoned gear lying about for the taking: bar-iron and axes and spades, along with plows and baking ovens and cooking stoves and any number of broken-down wagons, some with parts that were still good if a man had a sharp eye and some ability.

Dr Weiss found his company waiting for him, so no longer resided with Margaret and Emily, although Rebecca noted he continued to spend time at their wagon. It was much too soon for a man to be pressing suit on Margaret; Rebecca had hoped for better from him.

The Journal of Rebecca Springer

June 27, 1846

I bought moccasins from an Indian woman for fifty cents. I will save my boots for walking and use these for camp.

Prices here are a disgrace. After finding lucifers and bacon, it took about all I had left to buy seersucker and a bit of muslin. Most else of what is on offer here is of too bright a color to be proper. Elizabeth gave no thought as to how her figure would be enlarging on the way and it was certainly not on my mind. There is only so much an apron can cover. I have to add pieces to all my waistbands, no matter the fabric won't match.

Sarah has done a job on her everyday dress getting off a horse, and she has been wearing her palm leaf muslin, which is really supposed to be preserved for special occasions. It is high time we get all our situations corrected. I don't think much of fashion, but I am getting tired of praying what I am wearing will not just give up and fall off my back.

Thank the Lord we still have two milch cows. The price of a good milk producer is such here that you would think it was the same cow jumped over the moon. I guess I will not acquire any more laying hens until Oregon either.

More trains have arrived, some heading for California, convinced that the bounty that lies there is superior to Oregon. Daniel has been much impressed, I am afraid, so now he and John have a new topic to argue over.

June 28, 1846

There is to be a wedding in our company.

The bride is Nancy Stokes and it is no surprise that she has taken the first opportunity to remove herself from her mother, and the groom is that same boy George who came asking John for Sarah's hand. I guess he was determined to get himself a wife.

After Sunday service, Reverend Bingham performed the ceremony. Harriet Stokes was not generous, but George's family made up for it with a fine spread. There were several preachers in Dr Weiss' company, as well as one or two in the other trains that had gathered, but they were outnumbered by those celebrants who didn't care much about what was considered a sin in civilization, and had their way and rigged up a dance floor.

Ivy Bingham would not allow Nellie to take part, which meant Sarah had more of Ben Cooper's attention. Rebecca chose not to interfere; with George's proposal (of which Sarah had been kept ignorant), she felt she should allow the girl to develop her skills at flirtation – a luxury she herself had never been allowed. Even though she was not her own blood, it gave her pride to see that quite a few men had their eyes on Sarah.

When it grew late, the young people put on a chivaree, banging skillets together, beating on cans with spoons, or picking up whatever else they could find that could make noise. Some of the men had been taking a nip or two and were in particularly high spirits.

They shot off their guns and dragged the newlyweds' wagon out on to the prairie almost a mile, with many others trailing behind hollering and banging. They kept at it until almost midnight, but still got up the next day to cheer Nancy and George when they walked back into camp. They left with his train the same day.

'Do you reckon we will see them again?' Elizabeth wondered. 'They are going to Oregon as well.'

Rebecca shrugged. 'It's a big territory.'

If Nancy's marriage wasn't enough excitement, Sarah reported that she had learned there would soon be one more.

'With so many preachers around, there's a regular wedding fever going on,' Rebecca commented.

'Want to know who's caught the fever?' Sarah asked, grinning mischievously.

'I can't imagine,' Elizabeth said. 'Someone we know?'

'None other than Emily Walker.'

Sarah was pleased to see how Rebecca and Elizabeth's jaws dropped, as she always liked to be the first with any new bit of news.

'But she doesn't like men!' Elizabeth cried with astonishment.

'She told me the ones that took after her the devil himself wouldn't have,' Rebecca remembered.

'Well, Dr Weiss has sure took after her and she's accepted him.'

Rebecca was sure Sarah was pulling their legs. 'Emily told me that she'd had just about enough of the Bible to last her for a lifetime, which is a mighty peculiar thing for someone to say who is going to teach at a mission, and Dr Weiss is part of a most religious community.'

'Who told you?' Elizabeth asked, also sure Sarah was pulling a prank.

'Well, I don't remember exactly,' Sarah said, so both women gathered she had been eavesdropping again, 'but Margaret says Dr Weiss is being expedient – that means since Dr Weiss is a widower and Emily is on her own, it makes sense.'

'Well, don't that beat all,' Elizabeth said, forgetting her grammar.

'I guess he saw something in Emily no one else had the patience to discover,' Rebecca said, still trying to digest the news. 'Or maybe he's seen enough in life not to expect much.'

The Journal of Rebecca Springer

June 29, 1846

There isn't much time for preparation, but I can provide some quick bread for the celebration and John will donate a whole ham. Margaret is still in a delicate state and we are the closest to family Emily has. With so many trains, a decent group of musicians can be assembled and the party should be well attended, as this is the last one before most of us depart.

Bless this most surprising union, Lord, and forgive me for suspecting Dr Weiss had designs on Margaret.

Rebecca's legs and feet swelled during the day. Propping them up at night gave her some comfort, so she left the wedding celebration early and took a short cut to her wagon across an open field. It was dark as pitch taking this route, but her boots were pinching. It had been vain to wear them, but it was a special occasion and she had wanted to look her best.

Halfway across the field, something white stood out. It looked at first like a sheep or perhaps a big rock, but when she drew nearer, she could hear a woman crying.

'Do you need any help?' she called out.

She was surprised to hear Margaret's voice in reply. 'I am quite all right, thank you.'

Margaret had gone to the ceremony; Rebecca knew it had been an effort for her. She had not seen her at the party afterward, and had no idea how long she'd been alone in the dark.

When she drew closer, she saw Margaret's face was streaked with tears. It was hard enough to find the privacy to take a wash, let alone have a cry, so Rebecca backed away. 'I am sorry to have intruded on you.'

Margaret got up, brushing bits of grass and twigs from her skirt. 'It is all right, Rebecca. Let me walk along with you. I have been alone with myself for some time and I am growing bored with the company.'

'They say there is nothing better than a good cry, but I think that only applies to small things, nothing so big as what you are carrying.'

'Philip was not an easy man, Rebecca.'

'He seemed a devoted husband and father, which is the most any woman could want.'

'He was all that, but ... he had his demons.'

Rebecca remained quiet, as a good friend should, ready to hear whatever Margaret wanted to say. It would go no further.

'He was so driven to prove himself, Rebecca ... for my sake as much as for himself, though it didn't matter to me. In a new place, we thought he could be his own man.'

'Now that he is gone, there is no shame in returning to your own home.'

'But would returning be of my own will, or because there seems no alternative? I do not feel entirely helpless.'

Rebecca was shocked. 'Surely you are not planning to continue to California?'

'I know no one there. California was Philip's dream. I've been considering Oregon.'

'Have you acquaintances there?'

'I would be acquainted with you.' She took Rebecca's hand. 'I have spent a great deal of time this evening feeling sorry for my predicament and even more time avoiding making any decisions about it. But you are right about a good cry, Rebecca. I think it cleared my head.'

'Then I am happy at least for that.'

'I have become so accustomed to looking toward a new life, I cannot envision returning to the old, particularly as it will be filled with such memories of Philip.'

'No woman can manage on her own.'

'In a new land, there will have to be new ways of thinking. If I can sell what remains of the horses and our merchandise, I will have money enough to found a business suitable to a woman. With so many men alone, there will be a need for decent meals and laundering ... perhaps even a boarding house.'

'I do not see you in those lines of trade.'

'Then suggest another.'

'I could see you starting a proper school.'

'Then you don't disagree I might find a place for myself?'

Rebecca had no argument in return except the biggest one: that Margaret was on her own. But that was not what was needed. There was too much already to discourage her. 'I will try to be a friend in whatever you decide, Margaret.'

'I have decided to make for Oregon.'

Margaret didn't tell Rebecca how she had come to be alone in the dark field. Her friend had been right and she had been wrong, hurtfully wrong.

She had been in no mood for the wedding festivities and had accepted Tom's suggestion to take a walk. Once the darkness could cover his shyness, he had stopped and shifted his feet awkwardly. 'I wonder if you would mind marrying me?'

'Mind?' Margaret was completely taken by surprise. 'Tom,' she said carefully, 'I am flattered by your suggestion but I am far from ready to take on another husband.'

'You wouldn't exactly be taking me on. I can take care of myself, and you and Laurie too. I am very fond of him.'

'And good to him as well – as you are to me. But I am still grieving, Tom, and not prepared to cast my lot with any other man, no matter how admirable he might be.'

'I am sorry to have added to your grief. If you want to see the back of me now, I will understand.'

'Of course I don't! I rely upon you and value your friendship and support. But I can't place an obligation on you, when I can promise you only that same friendship and support in return.'

Tom was silent for a long time. 'That will be enough,' he finally decided. 'It's still a long way to Oregon and you're going to need help.'

'Thank you, Tom,' she said quietly.

He offered to escort her home, but by then, her tears had started to flow. He couldn't see them in the dark, so was not alarmed when she said she wanted a few quiet moments to herself. When his footsteps had faded away; when she was completely alone without Laurie to be brave for; and with the music of the fiddles drowning out all else; she rocked and wailed and loudly mourned Philip, along with her own foolishness.

Margaret Prescott's Notebook

Cash on hand: $275
9 horses sold @ $1,300
2 oxens purchased @ $250 each = $500
Supplies: $75
Net assets: $1,000

The Journal of Rebecca Springer

July 1, 1846

We finally left Fort Laramie today, and I

miss all the company we found there. Two of the wagons in our train have chosen to give up and return to their homes with a group of go-backs who passed through. One man said he would rather starve among the people he knew than have a life of abundance in a strange country. We all sent letters with them. Sarah's hand is much improved, thanks to Margaret. She says she is ready to undertake schooling again. Maybe Sarah can work with the younger children now that Emily has gone off as Mrs Weiss.

Both John and Captain Stokes have both lent Margaret their spare oxen. She is much better off without horses.

I cannot help but feel glad that Your wish has led Margaret to continue to be with us, Lord. Don't think the less of me for taking that pleasure.

They nooned at what was called Register Cliff. Daniel took a pot and tar brush and saw that the Springers' names were properly set down with all the others who had passed by.

The company had gained two wagons of men in Fort Laramie, but lost the company of the Hansens. They had broken an axle on one of their wagons just as the train headed out. They had already used their spare, so the fort smithy would try to make repairs, but he was pressed with other urgent jobs and it could take several days, perhaps weeks. Martha Hansen and her daughter-in-law were good company who never caused any dissension and were missed by the few women remaining in the company.

They had hoped that Cora LaForce's child would have been born at Fort Laramie where at least she could have had a semblance of civilization. On this fresh leg of the journey, it was a wonder the rough ride didn't send her into labor. The trail had taken to higher ground and the soil was so thin in places that the wagons which had passed through before had carved deep ruts in the sandstone.

Sarah

Since Joe had found Bert for company and I had found interest in Shakespeare, him and me weren't so much together. He was always darting in to grab a biscuit or to have a sock darned, then darting out again: visiting Bert, exploring, or sometimes spending the night with Pink and the other bachelors minding the stock.

Rebecca didn't like the way he ran around, but the only time she really put her foot down about it was on the Sabbath when she insisted the whole family sit down together for a proper dinner. But the next Lord's Day when we sat down for the blessing, Joe's place at the table stayed empty.

Papa said we might as well eat as the meal would get cold. But as time went on and Joe still didn't appear, it dawned on us that he had not been seen since we left Fort Laramie.

After that, we lost our appetite and fanned out through the camp, asking other folks when last they had seen Joe. Daniel rode out to where Pink was on watch, and I crossed my fingers that Joe was with him, but Daniel came back alone. The last time anyone remembered seeing Joe was back at the fort eating cake with Bert at Emily Walker and Dr Weiss' wedding.

'Maybe Joe was so plumb tuckered out from all the partying going on, he and Bert were still sleeping in the Hansens' wagon when the train left, so didn't know we had gone on without him,' I said, feeling awful I had not missed Joe right off; he had always been so good at taking care of himself, I hadn't thought twice about not seeing him.

'At our pace, he could have caught us up on a good horse,' Daniel said.

'I doubt he could find anyone to lend him one,' Papa considered. 'Horses are too valuable out here to be given to a twelve-year-old boy.'

'Well, I would think Luke Hansen would have done the favor as Joe was his responsibility,' Daniel said.

'Luke has responsibilities enough of his own. I bear responsibility for my own son and should have paid better attention.'

Papa looked so upset, Daniel didn't argue. 'Now don't start blaming yourself, Papa; Joe was just thoughtless.'

'It wasn't Joe's fault the Hansens' wagon threw an axle!' I said hotly.

'I don't think it is of much use placing the blame on anyone's shoulders,' Rebecca pointed out. 'What are you going to do, John?'

'I am going to talk to Captain Stokes,' Papa said. 'If he can spare me a bachelor, I will send Pink back to Fort Laramie. Whether he meets Joe and the Hansens on the way, or if they are still tied up in Fort Laramie, he and Joe can ride back here double. It makes more sense than turning around our wagons.'

'I could ride back to the Register Cliff,' I volunteered, wanting to do something myself. 'I will leave a note for Joe. He is sure to pass that way with the Hansens and there isn't nobody that doesn't stop there.'

'I think that would be a good idea, but you can't go back there by yourself,' Papa said.

'I will do it, Papa,' Daniel said. 'It's one more way to make sure we don't miss Joe.'

'Please take me with you,' I pleaded to Daniel. 'I have been working on my hand-writing. Don't take it wrong, Daniel, but I

243

think I could write a message better than you, and you know Pink can only put down an X.'

Papa saw how I was hurting and gave his permission, allowing me my own horse. Elizabeth and Rebecca packed us something to eat and Daniel rolled some blankets so him and me and Pink could sleep at the Register Cliff overnight.

I had never been so long by myself with Daniel and tried to show him I could keep up and not be a nuisance. Of course Pink was along too, but I was used to doing things with Pink. None of us had much to say, as we concentrated on looking about the landscape just to make sure Joe hadn't had some mishap and was out on the prairie on his own. I was mostly convinced he was with the Hansens like I'd first figgered, but there was still a little bit inside of me that worried he wasn't, because of what happened to Willie.

We had the advantage now of longer days, so we made Register Cliff just as it was growing dark. There was another train camped there, but they didn't know who the Hansens were, much less Joe. When they heard our story, they offered us hospitality, so we didn't have to have a cold supper.

First thing in the morning, I wrote Joe a message in big letters right where I was sure he couldn't miss it. We got offered breakfast, then said our goodbyes to Pink. He headed off to Fort Laramie, and when we made it back to the train, they hadn't made that much time on us. We only had to ride in the dark for an hour or so and we had their cook-fires to guide us. Daniel told me I'd been good company.

It created much excitement in the camp when a famous 'mountain man' passed by and stopped for the night. James Bridger had been trapping beaver, trading furs and fighting Indians for almost thirty years in the territory. He'd discovered a huge lake that was nowhere near the ocean but was even saltier, as well as hot springs that spouted water into the air like fountains.

He had recently founded a trading post a few hundred miles west, and suggested the trail that led to Fort Bridger was easy and would allow the train to make up some of the time it was losing.

'What about Joe and Pink?' Sarah asked. 'They won't know we've taken a cutoff.'

Daniel also had concerns. 'Seems to me Bridger might have said his way's easier to get a few dollars from us at his trading post.'

'The council has voted,' John told them both. 'I have pledged our family to Captain Stokes' leadership and won't be undermining it. If we each start going our own way, there will be no discipline or direction.'

But he didn't look too pleased over the

council's decision either. He made a pile of rocks as a marker for Pink and Joe in the middle of the trail, wrapping an explanatory note in oilskin, and tying it to a tall stick which he thrust into the top of the rockpile.

Soon after taking the new trail, the train took their last fording of the Platte – the river was turning north and their way lay south. The weather grew warmer and the land drier as they approached the Continental Divide.

The Journal of Rebecca Springer

July 3, 1846

On the far bank of the Platte, we came upon a grave that had been dug up by either wolves or Indians. I knew it was a white person, because the skull still had some yellow hair attached, but I couldn't tell if it was a man or a woman and I had no desire to go closer to make sure. Some of the bachelors made jokes, but they did right by the remains. There wasn't any marker, which upset me as I always note the name and dates of whatever poor soul has died along the way.

No sign of Joe and Pink. Look after them, Lord, and bring them to us soon.

The Fourth of July dawned, and even if they

hadn't reached Independence Rock yet, a proper celebration of the nation's independence was called for. Everyone raided their trunks for red, white and blue, mixing up their best with their everyday to gain an effect. Margaret had had the foresight to buy some red calico in Fort Laramie for a song, as no one would touch the gaudy stuff. She cut it into streamers to wave as the company marched in parade. Sarah begged Rebecca for a few blank pages from her journal and carefully wrote out patriotic slogans for the men to display on their hats. Their neckerchiefs were all red or white or blue, adding to the colorful show.

With Jake gone to meet his maker, there wasn't much in the way of musical instruments, except for Jake's chum Mike and his mouth organ, but patriotic songs were sung a cappella as the parade wound around the wagons, Captain Stokes leading the way and carrying a large flag.

Daniel had been given a bottle of liquor by his friends back home. They had made themselves an agreement: at dusk on the Fourth, they would look west and he would look east, and they would share a toast. John joined him in the ceremony and the bottle was carefully hidden away afterwards, so as not to cause talk.

'Well, even though we are still shy of Independence Rock, I think we have done right by the day,' Daniel said with satisfaction.

'I sure wish Joe could have been with us,' Sarah said, 'but I reckon the Hansens are celebrating too. Maybe they are all at the Register Cliff and looking at that note I left them. And Matthew and Letty will be having a good time too, if they've got home by now.'

'It's really something to think that all over America people are having the same celebrations,' Daniel mused.

'Remember how we all used to go to see the drum and bugle corps back home?' Elizabeth recalled.

'And there was always a big picnic with the first of the watermelon,' Sarah added.

'It seemed like summer didn't really start until then,' Rebecca said, looking wistful.

'And when the speeches got too long, some boys always set off gunpowder to cut 'em short,' John recalled.

Sarah smiled in remembrance; once, she had been one of those 'boys'.

It took until July 7 to finally reach Independence Rock. It looked like a giant turtle and was covered with travelers' messages. With so little in the landscape to use for milestones, such oddities as this gave overlanders a goal to strive for and some sense of satisfaction once they had attained it. Oregon still lay far off, but small successes provided some reward for the sweat and fatigue.

Snow-capped peaks stretched as far north

as one could see, but the way to Fort Bridger lay across easier hills to the south. The company bedded down in anticipation of what lay ahead; several men swore they could smell the mountains.

It was still dark when a soft voice outside the tent awakened Rebecca. She didn't know how long Kitty had been calling, but her mistress had been in labor since before sundown the night before.

'I know how birthings is supposed to go, Miz Springer,' she said, her voice trembling. 'But I just feel in my bones that things ain't right.'

John agreed that Rebecca should go to Cora at once.

'But I have never given birth,' she objected as she hastily dressed.

'The other women look up to you, Rebecca.'

This came as a surprise, but did not make her feel more adequate as she hurried to the LaForce wagon.

Semple stood vigil outside and helped her mount the step. 'Mr Early is inside.'

The hours of pain had taken their toll on Cora. Her beautiful face was pasty and glistening with sweat and her eyes were sunken and rimmed with black. She clutched her husband's handkerchief to her mouth in an effort to stifle her screams, though she was so weakened, no more than a kitten's mew escaped. Early bathed her forehead, but it seemed to bring her little comfort.

Kitty climbed into the wagon after Rebecca. She pulled down Cora's bedclothes and started to lift her gown.

'Perhaps you could leave us for a minute, Mr LaForce?' Rebecca asked, feeling awkward.

Cora grasped his hand. 'Don't leave me,' she beseeched in a tiny voice.

'I will turn my head,' he told Rebecca, covering Cora's hand with his own.

The bulge of Cora's stomach was enormous compared to her small frame. With no shyness now, Kitty guided Rebecca's hands over the mound, then looked at her purposefully. Even with her lack of experience, Rebecca could tell the baby was breech – she had heard tales of women doomed because their child had not turned.

She managed to smile at Cora. 'You are doing well, but I think you could use some help.'

Mrs Stokes had had so many children, Rebecca reasoned, perhaps one of them had been breech. She excused herself and hastened to her wagon. Harriet Stokes was bent over her cookpot, stirring her morning grits. She regarded Rebecca's approach sourly, but when she was told the circumstances, donned a fresh apron and accompanied her back to the LaForce wagon.

By this time, the entire camp had arisen and it took only moments for the word to spread. The rest of the women soon joined Harriet and Rebecca at the LaForces' wagon. Kitty stood outside, openly weeping. As Harriet ducked inside, Rebecca impulsively gave Kitty an embrace, shocking Ivy Bingham.

It wasn't long before Harriet emerged, looking grim.

'Both the mother and the baby will be lost unless the child can be turned.'

She banished Early from the wagon. 'There is little use for a man at a birthing, and no room for you anyway.'

With Kitty and Rebecca holding Cora, Harriet kneaded her stomach. Cora groaned and panted, but was too weak to scream.

'Well, that's no use,' Harriet announced, wiping the sweat from her head. 'We'll have to go at it from the inside. Hold out your hands,' she demanded of the women.

She was too much in command for them to question the order. After a quick inspection, Harriet nodded to Kitty. 'You've got right small hands for a nigra. Let's see if you can get 'em up inside of her.'

Kitty shrank back, appalled.

'She is not a cow!' Rebecca objected.

Harriet shrugged. 'We don't have any instruments.'

'I will do anything to help Miz Cora,' Kitty said softly, wiping her hands on her apron.

251

Harriet nodded approvingly, then instructed Kitty to cover her hands with lard to make the job easier. 'Look for the head,' she told Kitty, 'but if you meet up with a leg, follow it to the body and try to turn it.'

Kitty tried to do as she was bade, but Cora screamed in agony.

'She ain't opened up proper,' Harriet judged, then beckoned Rebecca outside, though Cora seemed past comprehending anything she might say.

'There ain't no way to save her,' she announced to the assembled women, 'but I've seen a baby come out alive if the woman was cut.'

Rebecca started to object, but Harriet waved her quiet, continuing matter-of-factly, 'It's a matter of losing them both or mebbe saving the one.'

'Would you take it upon yourself to make such a decision?' Margaret asked.

'I reckon it's not mine to be making – it's up to her husband.'

'It means asking him to kill his wife,' Rebecca pointed out.

'She's going to die. That baby's ready to live, but it ain't coming out the natural way. You don't want to put it to him, I will.'

Rebecca didn't want Harriet to be the one to speak to Early; she would be far too blunt. She didn't want such an awful decision put before him at all, but if there was an opportunity to save one life, it must be done. The other women were looking at her: John was right. Without a vote, she had been elected.

Early LaForce sat on a rock with his head in his hands. Semple was by his side, his arm around his shoulder in comfort. Rebecca tried to be calm as she explained the awful choices he had before him.

'I will need to talk to my wife.' There was no expression on his face.

He called Kitty out of the wagon, then disappeared inside. Semple led Kitty away, whispering what Rebecca had told Early.

Sarah brought fresh water. 'I told Elizabeth she should stay with Betsy. This has got her mighty scared.'

'That was wise of you. Give the water to Kitty. Early will call if he needs it.'

'Is anything to be done for her?'

'We can offer our prayers.'

The men occupied themselves with various tasks as the women held vigil and prayed. Perhaps Early and Cora had to wrestle over making a decision, or perhaps it was made right away, but after two or three hours, Early came out of the wagon to announce that his wife and unborn baby were dead.

Kitty dressed Cora one last time, picking out her best finery. Early wanted his wife to wear her diamond earrings and necklace. No one had the heart to try to talk him out of it, though they knew the jewelry stood a good chance of winding up on the arm of an Indian brave.

Most of the men volunteered to dig Cora's grave, as she had given them all joy with her beauty. Semple worked alongside them and no word was said against sharing the task with a slave. Early broke a spare wagon wheel in two and set a half at each end of Cora's grave as markers after Semple had spent some time burning out her name and dates on one of these arches.

'I didn't know a slave was allowed to do letters,' Rebecca whispered to Margaret.

'Some people feel such knowledge is dangerous,' Margaret said. 'That is *real* ignorance.'

Sarah

When Cora LaForce died trying to bring her baby into the world, I felt almost as scared as Elizabeth and Rebecca must have been. It struck me that those two must have been feeling scared even before – I mean right from the very beginning when they first knew they were in the family way. And that was a pity, as they sure didn't have a choice in the matter. It gave me some shame that I had looked upon their condition as not much more than a nuisance and I vowed to myself that I would do better by them from now on.

About the only good thing that happened at Independence Rock was coming across the Sweetwater River, which was a name that fit. There was good grass along the banks and the stock had time to fill their bellies before we started climbing up to the South Pass over the Continental Divide. We were going eight thousand feet up, according to Captain Stokes, and that meant grass would be scarce for at least fifty miles. The plain was so wide and the slope so gradual, the climb didn't present much of an effort, but it seemed to get hotter the higher we went. Margaret said it was because the air was thinner, and I did have some trouble catching my breath before I got used to it.

'I think I will fetch us some snow to cool us down,' Ben Cooper announced. Those snow-covered peaks didn't seem so far away now.

'Ain't no way to get it,' another bachelor said.

'Bet you that silver piece in your belt buckle I can,' Ben said back.

Some of the other boys joined in the lark, and I was all for going along too, but then I decided against it, meaning to follow through with my vow to be more mindful of Elizabeth and Rebecca. Anything might happen, especially with all the bending and stooping

255

they had to do with their chores. Elizabeth's belly had swoll up so much, it was a wonder she could walk without toppling over.

So I washed the dishes without any nagging, then sat in the wagon concentrating on darning my socks, which was the devil with all the bouncing, but the surprise on Rebecca's face to see me doing such work was almost worth the effort.

We did have an enjoyable hour at nooning with *Much Ado About Nothing,* and not too much work with the cold dinner we had decided upon in the heat. But it hurt when Ben and the others came back in time for supper with canvas buckets of snow hanging from their saddles and a pile of stories. I tried to ignore them and keep the beans from burning, and I felt a whole sight better when I had a taste of their 'ice cream' sweetened with molasses.

'I haven't ate something so sweet since way back when Matthew got married and I got a sore arm from cranking up the ice cream,' I said.

'That was the best party ever,' Daniel agreed.

'Maybe because we all knew it was the last one,' Rebecca put in, and she looked so sad I wanted to give her a hug, but I didn't as that was not the way her and me was.

'When we go over the Continental Divide,' Papa said to Rebecca, 'you will just have to put all that homesickness aside and start looking toward where the sun is setting instead of where it is rising.'

She put away her long face then and started talking about how nice it was to be seeing trees again and how the smell of the pines was downright medicinal, but I knew that was just a show for Papa's sake.

We decided we had reached the top of the Continental Divide as the slope looked downhill toward the west. The men shot off their guns, as they considered it a great accomplishment.

'I hope all this hullabaloo doesn't bring on a war party,' Rebecca said.

Margaret Prescott's Notebook

We have taken our last look at the waters that flow eastward to mingle with the streams where our lives have been spent before. When we go down through the pass, the waters will flow westward toward our new home.

We are halfway to that home.

Although the descending grade was as gradual as it had been in ascending, the train had to pick its way down through a narrow canyon with little room to maneuver the wagons around the rocks. Heat built up between the walls of the canyon during the day, but the streams ran icy cold with pure melted snow. The company walked beside their wagons, easing the wheels over the worst sections.

This side of the South Pass, the land was still largely unknown and said to have the deepest canyons and the shaggiest mountains. The Wind River Range had been explored by Kit Carson himself, the greatest mountain man of all, who had traveled the entire route to Oregon and mapped most of it for General Fremont. The range rose to the north, covered with snow. Many obstacles still lay ahead on the way to Oregon, and many earlier overlanders who had passed had forged alternate trails. First they found a map nailed to a tree pointing in one direction. Then, soon after, an arrow painted on a rock appeared, pointing the direct opposite. Another cutoff proclaimed a superior route to California.

This country was tagged 'the parting of the ways' for good reason. On Captain Stokes' first journey, there had been but one way, and he was still for sticking with the tried and true. But many of the other men considered the various options offered around the campfire at night. The train was falling even further behind the schedule Captain Stokes had set, in spite of all Jim Bridger had promised. They itched to make better progress.

The Journal of Rebecca Springer

July 15, 1846

We have come down out of the trees, and
the trail to Fort Bridger offers very little for
man or beast. What water there is has
become brackish with alkali, and the stock
has developed the scours, their stomachs
rumbling and growling like thunder, and
the smell of escaping gas and runny patties
is almost impossible to tolerate with no
fresh breeze to clear the air.

The men pitched in with us women to fry
up all the bacon we could find and pour the
lard down the oxen's throats to settle them.
One of our milch cows has had to be put
down, leaving only one still producing. She is
down to a trickle with all the walking she has
done, and Elizabeth worries that Betsy will
go hungry. But at least we now have beef-
steak for dinner instead of smoked buffalo
jerky.

Margaret has set Tom whittling a chess set
to replace the one that belonged to Dr
Weiss. She sketched out how the pieces
looked and he has already turned out most
of the pawns. The knights he considers will
be his biggest challenge. The plan is to soak
half the pieces in red dye when they are
done. The set won't be black and white, but
it will do. Ivy Bingham won't approve when

the game is taken up again, but this time I intend to learn.

Thank You, Lord, for small pleasures.

This evening it felt like a feather was tickling my belly from the inside. And I thank You many times over for this sign of growing life.

Fort Bridger offered no relief except for a pretty view of the Uinta Mountains to the south. The buildings were mostly made of stone, as there was a shortage of lumber in such arid territory, and all were low, dark and desolate. Jim Bridger was nowhere to be seen. What meager goods that were on offer were highly priced. Even the news from the outside world was stingy: only word that war with Mexico was going well and California was sure to become a free state. John wondered if that wasn't just a rumor spread by the California boosters, whose leaflets extolling its wonders had been posted along the trail.

But there was another five hundred miles to go through rough country before any other settlement, so John decided to make the best of things. He bought hay from a Frenchman who seemed to be running things in Bridger's absence. It wasn't fresh, but the dry weather kept it from rotting, and keeping up the animals' energy was critical.

The Frenchman's wife did not like the life

there. 'I have fear to leave the fort because of Indians,' Madame LaLonde moaned. 'If it were not for my religion, which holds the vow of marriage sacred, I would go with the first people who return to the East.'

She made pin money selling eggs (at far too high a price) and she also possessed two massive laundry tubs which she used to launder for overlanders with no women to care for them.

'The money is safe under the hen coop. I will need it if I can escape from here!' she confided to anyone who would listen.

'I am certain her husband will hear of the scheme,' Rebecca observed.

'It will no doubt come to a head soon, but we won't be here to see what happens,' Elizabeth said sadly. 'If only I could will myself to have my child at Fort Bridger! At least there are buildings with four walls in them.' It had been four months since she had slept in a bed.

'Elizabeth, everything is so filthy here, that baby would come out scratching with bedbugs,' Sarah told her.

She had to smile. 'Well, I could have the baby in the wagon, which I know is clean, and just have the pleasure of looking at a real building during the process. And I am worried my milk won't come in, with us traveling through such rough country.'

'We will have to buy ourselves a new milch

cow,' Rebecca said, but everything was so expensive.

Two other trains were already camped at Fort Bridger, one heading for California and the other with their own destination. Both of them contained some women, and Rebecca suggested a bit of trading might be arranged.

'I guess we have all learned a bit from the Indians,' she told the other women. 'You want to swap?'

They were just as hot, tired and dirty, and also starved for a bit of pleasure, so they took Rebecca up on her offer, everyone shouting out 'Swap!' and 'No swap!' One woman was growing tired of rice and another felt the same of beans, so both sides were satisfied. Extra needles were traded for extra thread and unneeded shirts for unneeded trousers. Bleached flour sacks were offered to turn into aprons and waists, but everyone had quite enough sacks of their own. And no one would part with any scrap of lace or linen they had in their possession, though both were much in demand.

A man bound for California was widely respected for his ability at dentistry and a long line of patients formed at his wagon. Generally, a tooth was left to rot until the pain became unbearable and then it was yanked out with a pair of pliers. It was not a pretty sight to see and Rebecca hoped it would serve Sarah as a reminder to clean her teeth daily.

Early LaForce had kept mostly to himself since his wife had died, but he sought out Rebecca, who was bickering with Madame LaLonde over the fee for using her washtubs.

'You have been kind to us, Mrs Springer, so I feel you might lend me a sympathetic ear.'

'I will certainly try to. I miss Cora sorely.'

'Thank you. It is Kitty and Semple I wish to discuss – I owe a great deal to them both and cannot continue as their master in either conscience or fact.'

'The Lord will bless you for that decision.'

'I feel strongly that California may well become a free territory, so I plan to join the train that is going there.'

'We will be sad to see you go, but you must do what is right.'

Early nodded. 'But there is more that needs to be done. I think it is no secret that Kitty and Semple are devoted to each other. It was a simple matter to grant them their freedom in writing; it has not been so simple to arrange for their marriage. Reverend Bingham told me the rite of marriage was sacred and not intended for ignorant savages.'

'It is useless to argue with someone who refuses to recognize that Kitty and Semple are human beings like any others,' Rebecca told him. 'The Lord will not frown if they make their vows in His presence. Later on, you might find a man of the cloth more noble in his aspect.'

When Margaret heard the news, she offered Kitty one of her handkerchiefs and Semple a pair of Phillip's gloves in congratulation, but they didn't want to take them.

'It is customary to bestow a gift on such a great occasion, as well as giving those who part a remembrance,' Margaret told them.

'In that case,' Semple said, 'please give these fine gloves to Mr Early. I wouldn't know what to do with them. Give me something that won't get ruint.'

She went through Philip's trunk and came up with a belt that fit Semple's waist perfectly.

The Springers ransacked their trunks as well, though Rebecca wasn't satisfied, saying they owned nothing she considered good enough to present as a gift.

'Why don't you bake something like you did for Emily's wedding?' Sarah suggested.

'The only eggs for miles around are in Madame LaLonde's coop, and she is mad for money.'

'Maybe I can come up with something.'

She told Rebecca the eggs were from a prairie hen nest, but Rebecca was no fool, though she pretended to act one and didn't say anything when Madame LaLonde ranted on about egg-sucking thieves.

The Journal of Rebecca Springer

July 20, 1846

Twenty miles out of Fort Bridger, and we are all worn out with the effort. This country is harsh. The council set a new schedule to help us deal with the heat. We started out before dawn and marched some six hours before the oxen started to flag. There was a trickle of a creek at nooning, but no shade. John rigged a ground cloth on the side of one of the wagons for shade and we had a cold dinner, none of us thinking to put anything hot into our bodies.

We spent the heat of the day under our makeshift awning, trying to nap, but I found it difficult with the sweat running into my eyes. It took us another four hours to get to more water and we had to make camp after it was dark.

We came across three men walking. They were on their way back to Fort Bridger after meeting up with a whole string of bad luck. A fourth man in their group had died when his horse stumbled in a prairie dog hole and tossed him on his head. The horse had to be shot and their other animals got stolen by Indians – this was after their wagon was tipped over into a gully and wrecked. They were still bent on Oregon, so have joined our train. Since Pink is still not back (and I don't like to consider what may have happened to him), we have been needing some help, so John signed up one of these unfortunates as our new bachelor. His name is Frank and I hope his bad luck does not rub off on us.

I had to start the cookfire with dry grass, then pile on sagebrush. I don't like this fuel as it burns far too quickly. Sarah was pulling up bushes and stoking the fire all through supper. Frank helped out, so maybe he will work out all right.

Some Indians rode up, saying they had fish to swap, but John said any water deep enough to grow a fish would be so far away the fish would be rotten and we would've smelled the stink. He said they were just taking our measure. The men made a point of cleaning their rifles, and after some signing that didn't come to much, the Indians rode off.

One of the scouts chopped his foot off with an axe. He was on his own for some time, with no fire to cauterize the stump. He bled to death before his companions got to him. His name was Joseph Allen and he was twenty-eight and an experienced man from Tennessee. It seems as if every mile of the trail is marked by some ill happening.

This is rough country, Lord, but it is Your creation and I know it must have its purpose, if only to steel our resolve. Lord, grant Early LaForce and his freed slaves a safe passage to

California and continue to guide our own steps along the way. Please send us some sign that Joe is on his way to join us.

After another twenty miles of hard going, they came into the Bear River Valley where hot springs sent up clouds of vapor. The water wasn't fit for drinking, but the women didn't want to miss the advantage of hot water without hauling and boiling it themselves. The men grumbled, but allowed a stop long enough to soak some dirty linen. The soda in the springs was an excellent spot remover, but harsh on the women's skin as they scrubbed.

Following the Bear River, they soon found fresh water for a rinse as well as all their other needs. There was no call to hurry from the men now: in their topsy-turvy day, it was time to make camp.

Another train appeared on the horizon, approaching from the east. This came as a surprise; they had no idea there was any other trail for miles around. Three men rode over to trade information. They had not come through Fort Bridger, but by way of the Sublette cutoff near the South Pass. Moreover, by comparing notes, it was concluded that the Captain's train had had a week's head start on them!

'We were wrong in not trying a new trail,' Daniel argued with John.

John disagreed. 'This party looks much the worse for wear by taking a short cut, and they have done in several animals.'

'Papa, I think you are just being stubborn.'

Rebecca had known for some time that John was uneasy over the short cut through Fort Bridger, but he would never admit it to Daniel now. She had to step in. 'Did anyone think to ask if they had seen any sight of Joe or the Hansens?'

Daniel apologized. 'I should have mentioned that first, Rebecca. I am sorry, but no one remembered whether they had or hadn't seen them.'

'What they actually said,' John added, still belligerent to mask his own mixed feelings, 'is they were more concerned with themselves than with what was happening with any other train and they'd just made a hard drive with very little water and were tuckered out.'

'Well, their excuses are of little matter,' Rebecca said sharply. 'Most folks only concern themselves with what is in front of their nose. Both of you better wash up for supper while there is still water to spare.'

The Journal of Rebecca Springer

July 22, 1846

The growing heat is wearing the company

down and everyone falls into bed early. It bothers Elizabeth the most in her advanced state. Sarah has taken Betsy into her own bed, which allows Lizzie some rest. I do believe that mothers have the worst of it in any train.

Dear Lord, these words do not mean I am regretting I will also soon become a mother. I was just saying that I think that's the way things are, but it is all part of Your plan.

While Rebecca wrote by the fire, John and Daniel had continued to argue until well after she had closed her journal and gone to bed.

John told his wife the news at breakfast; he had no stomach for the meal. 'Daniel has decided to take the trail to California with these other folks.'

Rebecca started to say something, but he stopped her. 'I know he changed his mind before, but he will not do it a second time; he has too much pride.'

The finality in John's tone frightened Rebecca. She stupidly continued to stir the beans, not wanting to believe things had finally come to a head.

'I'll have to be dividing our gold again,' John said, getting up with a sigh.

'Please, John! Make peace with Daniel so we can all continue together.'

'He has been making up his mind to do

this for some time and nothing will alter it now. Do you want me to change our plans for his, with no forethought to where we might wind up?'

'No...' She felt drained and hopeless. 'There is nothing you can do?'

John shook his head. 'I have come to the conclusion that the only way there can be peace between us is to go our separate ways.'

'You would each have your own farm in Oregon.'

'And he will be comparing his to mine and I will not be able to help myself from doing the same. Maybe I am at fault for things becoming the way they are between us, but there is no getting around it that we are like oil and water.'

'I think it is just the opposite, John. You are too much alike. Daniel has modelled himself after you since he was a child, and you should take it as a compliment, even though it leads him to challenge you.'

'That is hard to see, and will not change anything. I am going to see to dividing the stock.'

She had already said too much, but her husband's authority was crumbling as his family disintegrated. It frightened her to see him give up; she could not.

Daniel was already yoking his team.

'John has not put me up to it,' Rebecca told him, 'and I doubt if he would approve if he knew. Can't you stick with us a just a little longer? Elizabeth is almost due.'

'There are women in our new train who'll tend to her.'

'But they are not family, Daniel. Even if you are determined to leave us, you are bound to find another train and another cutoff after she is delivered. We have still got a long way to go to either place.'

'This Captain Donner is a man I trust.' He continued with his work. Rebecca had no more arguments to offer.

When she returned Betsy to her mother Sarah learned the news.

'Elizabeth is just sitting and rocking Betsy,' she reported to Rebecca. 'I can't get her to stop crying.'

'She will have to dry her tears and help the men divide the goods.'

'You're not going to try and stop them?'

'Sarah, I have gone so far as to beg Daniel to reconsider. No one can go any further.'

Sarah's eyes brimmed with tears. 'I know Daniel can be prickly, but he's been there for me as long as I have lived and he has been a fair brother and can be counted on. Damn me! It's hard feeling kindly toward him for doing such a thing to Elizabeth and Betsy!'

Rebecca couldn't call her for cursing; she felt the same. 'Sarah, there is nothing to do except keep busy and try not to dwell on our sorrows.'

It hurt her to do so, but she called Elizabeth out from her wagon. Demanding that she prepare for a departure she dreaded was preferable to allowing her to remain crying inside. It wouldn't change her husband's mind and might even harden him against her. A woman could not go against her husband's will. Along with Sarah, they silently divided the Springers' possessions and repackaged them.

John and Daniel avoided speaking to each other and Sarah became their go-between as supplies were sorted out. There was no occasion for argument, as John was more than fair, giving Daniel both a horse and the new cow that had been purchased at Fort Bridger, as well as half the spare team.

Rebecca decided she had had just about as much of silence as she could take.

'We are all going to be leaving within the hour and no one ate any breakfast. This family is not going to get another chance to break bread together and things need to be done right. Sarah, you set the table while I warm up the beans. And use the best cloth. Elizabeth, would you fry up the bacon?'

Rebecca prepared the meal as if she had something to celebrate. John scowled, and she returned his expression. He had had his will in the most important matter, so she felt entitled to have her own in such a small one. They would have a farewell meal even if there was more silence than speaking around the table.

When everyone was called to their places, Sarah surprisingly asked if she could say grace.

'Dear Lord, we thank You for all You have given us and hope You look kindly upon us sinners and give us Your blessing. We sure are going to need it because it'll be hard out there on the trail without the benefit of having family We've gotten used to doing things together and losing one part of our family is like losing an arm or a leg. Lord, we are just about run out of limbs now, but I am sure You want us all to make the best of things and that's what we're going to try to do, but that doesn't mean we're going to like it any. Amen.'

Not much was eaten as John and Daniel sat uncomfortably facing each other across the table. When Captain Stokes gave the call to move out, both men practically knocked over their seats, they were so eager to have an excuse to end the awkwardness. The Donner party wagons were also moving into line.

Betsy was still groggy with sleep when Sarah and Rebecca kissed her goodbye. The next time they saw her she might have grown out of recognition. If they ever saw her again.

'Trust in the Lord,' Rebecca said to Elizabeth as they embraced. 'He will watch over us both.'

'I wish I had your faith.'

'You will find it, I know.'

Rebecca sat in the back of the wagon and watched the Donner party move toward the west while the Stokes party turned to the north.

The Journal of Rebecca Springer

July 23, 1846

They say the way to California is easier than to Oregon. At least that will be of benefit to Elizabeth. But I cannot fool myself into making the best of such a bad thing. I cannot believe that after traveling so far together and being so dependent on each other in times of danger and accident I will be separated from my dear sister. I doubt that I can even be truly happy when my child is born when Elizabeth and her baby will not be at my side.

If women were allowed the decisions, they would never be separated from their families.

Lord, why have You chosen to rip us apart?

Part 6

The Devil's Country

The Journal of Rebecca Springer

July 24, 1846

Eighteen miles still along the Bear River, but the water is not sweet. My heart is not up to writing.

Forgive me, Lord, but I am not up to praying either.

As she lay on her sweat-soaked mattress, heat and heartache keeping her from sleeping even though she was exhausted, Rebecca tried to keep hope that one day she might be reunited with Elizabeth. Lizzie had needed constant reassurance and she had little initiative. But in friendship and reliability she had been a rock.

Wrapped up in loneliness and mourning, Rebecca feared she was drifting apart from her husband. Each concentrated on their daily chores and scarcely spoke. She had to pull herself together and find strength for her husband's sake. His heart bore a wound deeper than hers – he had lost his own flesh and blood.

When John spoke to his wife, he was filled with guilt over what he saw as his missteps.

'It seemed such a good plan to send Pink after Joe. I should have gone back to Fort Laramie myself. I have even begun to worry if Matthew has found his way home safely. It wasn't my plan to have my family scattered so ... Matthew back in Vermillion County I hope; Daniel gone to California; Joe the Lord knows where ... and Willie up in Heaven. I decided to go to Oregon so each of my sons could get a portion of land to call their own. Now I wonder why I'm going.'

This was the first time Rebecca had ever heard John express doubt, and it disturbed her. If Elizabeth had been her rock, he had been an entire mountain. She tried to give him some encouragement.

'I know Joe will be with us by and by, and there's the baby to consider as well. You may well have another son. And remember how you said there was talk of granting portions to women? We could be making Sarah's future too.'

'This is the first time I have heard you arguing in favor of Oregon,' he noted. 'I know it has been against your wishes from the beginning.'

'I am sorry I have not made you feel you had my full support, John. But we are more than halfway there now and I am not a quitter.'

She still felt like quitting right there and then, but if John did not find his way again,

278

what was left of their family would be without direction.

'You are right,' he conceded. 'All the reasons for going are still there. I am just getting too old to take change easily. I knew there would be risks, but I thought that with caution we would stay safe from harm. Rebecca, I will do all in my power to take good care of you and the baby, and to make you a fine home in Oregon. I promise you that.'

Rebecca lay awake again that night, trying to convince herself that John's promise was enough.

Sarah

We reached Fort Hall, another trappers' station, but nowhere as well known as Fort Laramie, or even Fort Bridger. Papa said we were into Oregon country now, but just at the very beginning of it, with still four hundred miles or more to go. The fort sat on the Snake River, which looked to be as treacherous as its name, with high steep walls, many rapids, and dangerous crossings.

There were tremendous cataracts on the Snake on both sides of Fort Hall. The local injuns were catching fish straight from the falls and I went to the very edge of the cliffs to watch. It was a long way down to the water, but still I could feel a fine spray misting my face, which was a welcome relief from the heat. Being up so high in what was probably a dangerous place gave me a thrill, but it wasn't long before I stepped back, thinking that I'd best not be looking for trouble as I had responsibilities to consider.

With Elizabeth no longer between us to keep the conversation going, I'd to figure out what to say to Rebecca that might make us more companionable. I was taking on all of Elizabeth's chores, but I could tell something more was called for, and that was the womanly chatter that Rebecca was so used to.

'There is nothing wrong in missing someone so fierce,' I said to her. 'I miss both Elizabeth and Betsy myself. And Daniel is one half my flesh and blood.'

'I know it is foolish to keep mourning what cannot be changed,' she said. 'I will try harder to put on a better face.'

'Now look, Rebecca, don't get me exasperated: I never called you for having a long face. I was just saying I understood why you are looking so sad. But there are some good things for us both to be thinking about. When we get to Oregon there will be a new sister or brother in the family – and I will be right happy to see our family grow again.'

'I do feel heartened to know you have decided a new baby is not such a bad thing after all.'

'Our family is down to you and me and Papa now, so we are going to have to work double sticking up for each other until Joe gets back with us, and then he'll make one more to share the load. There is a lot that needs doing, and Papa's just got that new man Frank and us to do it.'

'I reckon Frank is doing a good enough job.'

'Yep, but Pink was better. I wonder what happened to him. I sometimes think maybe he got homesick and took himself back to Vermillion County, but that doesn't account for Joe. I can't imagine Joe being homesick, as he makes himself at home wherever he might be – and I am hoping he is making himself at home with the Hansens.'

That was the most I'd said in one clip to Rebecca in months, but she didn't seem to notice. I guess she was just grateful to talk and didn't mind the way I don't know how to *stop* talking.

'I can go for days pushing my memories out of mind,' Rebecca said, 'but then someone says something and they all come back again. I thought I could get cured of homesickness just like the sickness from the baby, but it keeps coming back full force.'

'Just think of our family, Rebecca. That's more important, and I know what's left of us will get back together again one day.'

We sort of smiled at each other, but neither in a real happy way, though I guess happy enough that we had broken the silence.

Not to brag, but I had drawn the eye of one of the young fellers in another train that was passing through Fort Hall. I had learned to control my inclination to wallop anyone who paid me more than the usual attention by now, but I was not looking for any romancing from this feller, only his gift of a small bag of horehound drops. I intended them for Margaret, who had developed a fierce cough, and neither sweet treats nor medicines came cheap at Fort Hall. The horehounds only cost me a little hand-holding while on a walk to see the falls (which I had seen already, and far closer than that yellow-belly feller would go). I made sure no one in my own train saw me, but I did have a secret pride that it was me and not Nellie Bingham who had attracted an admirer, even if his hand was hot and sweaty.

'These are for your own personal use,' Sarah told Margaret. 'Maybe you could give Laurie one, but I want you getting better. Me and Rebecca and Nellie don't mind reading *Much Ado About Nothing* to each other ourselves, but you are, a far sight better, and we've got *Romeo and Juliet* to tackle next.'

'It's the constant dust,' Margaret claimed. 'It's made my throat raw. But now that we have fresh water, I am sure I will soon mend. Thank you for the favor of the drops, Sarah.'

'You could do me a favor as well.'

'I would be happy to.'

'I need to be having a womanly talk.'

Margaret was taken with a fit of coughing. 'About men and women?' she managed to gasp.

'Oh, I know all about how babies are made. What I don't know is how to bring them into the world. Rebecca was counting on Elizabeth to help her do the job, but now it's going to be up to me.'

'You know you can rely on me to help.'

'With all respect, you aren't family and it is my responsibility. Rebecca has been doing a furious amount of cleaning and rearranging things and such. I have heard women do this when it is just about their time. I keep thinking of Miz LaForce and how no one could do anything for her. Margaret, I don't want to be just standing around when it's Rebecca's time like I was then – I want to *do* something. Is it hard to learn?'

'My knowledge largely comes from having a child myself, but I will share it with you if you think it will help.'

'It will sure ease my mind.'

And it did a bit, though Sarah hoped she wouldn't have to put what she learned to use and that Rebecca would hold on until they were safe and sound in Oregon with more women around with real experience.

As wretched as Fort Hall was, it gave the train a chance to take a break from the trail and rest, which for Rebecca meant turning everything inside out and starting a major wash, with Sarah feeling duty-bound to help. It was still hot when the sun set, so they decided to throw in what they were wearing as well and work in their ragged petticoats – they'd been taken up so much they were almost at their knees. No one could see them with lines of wash tightly strung between their wagons.

They were still hard at work when John returned from a meeting of the council.

'I can add your shirt and trousers to the wash before we go to bed,' Rebecca told him. 'It's too dark for anyone to see you and too hot to be sleeping anywise but in the raw.'

'There is a full moon tonight. We have to be ready to leave within the hour to beat the heat.'

'I thought we were staying another day,' Rebecca said.

'Every day just gets hotter and dryer. Captain Stokes says the walls of the Snake River are a lot steeper than his last trip because the river's running low. He doesn't want to risk any crossings here and has been talking to a mountain man about another trail.'

Sarah was surprised. 'Papa, you are always saying how full of hot air most of those mountain men are.'

'I met this man, Fred Brenner, myself,' John explained, 'and he seems trustworthy. He says the banks go down to nothing a ways above the falls and he knows a good bypass from there that will get us all the way to Fort Boise. His fee is reasonable. We took a vote on it.'

Rebecca looked irritated. 'I wish you had done so before I started a washing.'

'It is not usually something you take up at night, Rebecca.'

Sarah started to gather up the wet laundry; its cool dampness felt delicious against her skin.

'I don't want you facing the hazards of a river crossing in your condition, Rebecca,' John continued. 'There was talk about abandoning the wagons and going on by mule, but I won't have you traveling another thousand miles by mule-back, either. This is the best way.'

'I thank you for thinking of me.'

'And I am sorry about your laundry.'

While Rebecca and Sarah packed, the men stockpiled every keg they could find, as once they forded the Snake, the bypass would be dry. The baker was roused and paid to create a store of crude bread for the stock; there would also be no grass.

'We will either have to put on wet clothes or go on the trail like two Eves in Paradise,'

Rebecca told Sarah, but the night was so warm it didn't take long for the clothes to dry on their backs.

It wasn't hard finding their way in the moonlight as they travelled close to the Snake, watching for the steep banks to fall away to something more reasonable.

When daylight came, the two women saw that the dust they'd kicked up on their way had settled on their wet dresses, leaving them caked with dried mud and dirtier than ever.

The sun was high before they finally found the ford, but it was easy enough for the wagons to make their way down the bank without braking ropes and the water was shallow. They took a break to give the animals a good watering to prepare them for what still lay ahead.

The company followed a dry and rough streambed the rest of the day, the way twisting and turning as much as the Snake, and filled with rocks.

Sarah

After two days of it, I began to hate the heat and dust and dryness just as much as Rebecca did. The soil was either fine alkali dust that got into every crack of wagon and body, or sand, which made the wheels grip. It wasn't good for nothing except those d***ed prickly pears.

When we first saw cactus, it was quite the novelty and the bachelors thought it great fun to put it in another feller's bedding. But it wasn't long until even Ben was in bad humor from the heat and far too tired to plan one of his pranks.

I felt real sorry for our oxen. Their eyes got red and crusted and weepy from alkali. Of course us human members of the train suffered equally, but at least we were allowed a damp washrag to clear our eyes. We weren't carrying enough water for anything more.

The country was strange, with twisted shapes to what little vegetation managed to grow. Even the animals were different. One of the men shot himself a jackrabbit for his supper, and it turned my stomach to see the odd shape of its scrawny body and oversized ears when he skinned it. Rebecca was still longing for eggs and I told her the only ones to be found in this country must belong to snakes.

We had to keep moving, putting as much of that badland behind us as possible and not stopping until we found some water. I followed Mr Brenner up the dry creeks while he searched for water, poking the ground with a ram. A work party of men followed behind with shovels. Where the ram went down easy, the men dug. Sometimes it wasn't until the third try that they hit anything.

'The thing to do when you're in dry country,' Mr Brenner told me, 'is keep looking for animal tracks or flocks of birds. They all go for water.'

'Snakes too?'

'Snakes and centipedes as well – looky there: them's snake tracks. Course there's water to be found in some of these prickly pears, too.'

I guess it was the fourth day out that Buck, one of our lead oxen, began to fail. That big tongue of his hung out of his mouth, which was all spotted with dried foam. A little bit of water wasn't enough for him and he couldn't keep up the pace. Papa replaced him in the yoke to rest him. As interested as I was in all Mr Brenner had to say, I lagged behind, determined to keep him going until we could find good water and some grass; he was my favorite and I couldn't bear the thought of Papa having to shoot him, particularly after already losing his yoke-mate, Bright. The poor creature was so worn out, we lagged farther and farther behind.

I was clearing his eyes when I spied a Blackfoot injun on a pony, dropping into a ravine – maybe he was hoping to pick off one of our animals, even though ones so dried out as ours would never be able to travel far.

The injun and his pony both looked fresh

to me, so I mounted my horse, dug my heels into his sides, and made for the ravine. I couldn't do it quiet; it was so rocky I sent down a whole raft of stones in front of me. The Blackfoot was waiting at the bottom, sitting on his pony and looking ready for whatever might happen. I couldn't tell what was on his mind as injuns are that way, but I raised both my arms to show him I wasn't carrying a weapon, which was always the right way to start things.

The Blackfoot backed his horse while I tried to remember my signing. Finally I just gave him the one for water, which was the same for drinking.

The injun nodded that he understood, then held out his water bag. I was sorely tempted, but felt I shouldn't throw all caution to the wind by getting too close to him. He might have been as polite as a white man, but he was still an injun. I made the sign for a river – I knew none was to be found, but maybe the same sign could mean a stream or even a dirty puddle.

The Blackfoot pointed off to the west and raised two fingers. I couldn't figure out what he meant: two hours? Two days? I shook my head and just kept signing, trying to make him understand he should follow me and show the train the way. I don't know if he understood me, but when I turned my horse and started to pick my way back up the ravine, he followed.

We kept our distance from each other, and I kept looking back both to see if he was still following me, and that he wasn't getting any closer. Buck was still on his feet and trying to follow the trail, but I didn't know if he would go on much longer if he didn't get water. I sure felt good when we caught up to the train.

'Ain't he a wonder?' I hollered, showing off my injun. 'He just come right out of the desert in good health and good spirits. And he knows where there's water.'

The Blackfoot did a lot of signing with Mr Brenner and Captain Stokes, me hanging around since he was my prize.

'What is he chewing?' I asked Mr Brenner, when it looked that they were taking a breather. 'It can't be tobacco, because his spit is green.'

'It's leaves. The injuns chew them to keep from getting thirsty.'

'Can you ask him where he got them? I'd like to give that a try myself, as I am powerful thirsty!'

'We're asking him to take us to water, not bushes,' Captain Stokes said to me crossly.

'He signed that it's an easy ride – for him on a fresh pony, that is,' Mr Brenner said, more friendly.

'You didn't know about this hole, Brenner?' Captain Stokes asked, even more cross. 'I thought you knew this territory.'

Mr Brenner shrugged. 'Well, the holes come and go. There's no telling.'

It took until near midnight to reach the Blackfoot's watering hole. I grabbed a bucket and went to find Buck, but by then he was too far gone and Papa did have to shoot him. I was too tuckered out and too sad to go looking for greenery.

The Journal of Rebecca Springer

July 29, 1846

We went until well after dark searching for water, but when the oxen began to stumble, Captain Stokes called for a dry camp. I fried some tough steaks John took off poor Buck. We used whatever we could find to start a cookfire, but the land was so rocky, there wasn't much for anything to take root on, so we had our meat on the bloody side, which I reckon was all right for once as we needed some juice in our bodies. We had to be stingy with the water so we couldn't wash up after.

This will be the first night in all this time I have gone to bed leaving dirty dishes behind. Sarah says it is one fewer chore to do, and with a good excuse for not doing it, but it seems to me a sign of order breaking down.

That break in Fort Hall wasn't enough to

relieve Margaret of her congestion. At least there is enough water allowed for her to sip some tea.

Lord, give her health and help me retain my strength. Watch over our family, wherever they might be, in Your kingdom or on this earth.

As they had not made camp until well after dark, it came as a surprise when the sun rose the next morning to see a thick black line stretching across the horizon before them, the beginnings of an ancient lava field. Many in the party had no idea what lava was or how it had come into existence, and those who did have some idea – or thought they did – enlightened them on both scientific and Biblical grounds. Afterwards, there still remained skeptics who were certain their legs were being pulled: an exploding mountain? But the landscape was flat as far as one could see, only broken where some of the jumble of black rocks had created mounds.

Captain Stokes asked Brenner if there was some way around the field, but he swore its breadth was far more than its depth, so the train cut straight through.

Some lava chunks were larger than the wagons, while others had been pounded into dust by the elements. Though many appeared to have been purposefully stacked in great piles, there were still so many scattered on the ground there was scarcely an inch between them and they cut the oxen's feet and caused them to stumble.

A work party tried to clear some sort of trail through the rubble. The men made hide boots for the stock, lashing them on with strips from old lariats. But the animals still suffered, and the men stumbled as well, bruising and bloodying themselves.

Though progress was slow, the black landscape soon closed in around them and no sign of the yellow prairie could be seen. The sun blazed above, radiating heat from the rocks. Reverend Bingham proclaimed it the Devil's own country.

The men used hats and kerchiefs to keep the sun and dust off their faces and the women draped sun screens of gauze off their bonnets. It was difficult to see, but it was better than choking. The black dust seemed worse than the alkali and made Margaret cough harder than ever.

In spite of their efforts to protect themselves, the grit and the sun caused them to break out in sores, which oozed blood when they stumbled and bumped themselves. They didn't bother to wipe off the blood; there wasn't water to spare to clean up anyway. The smells of animal sweat and human sweat mixed with the metallic odor of blood, the slightly sweet aroma of infection and the stink of vomit.

Sarah had been lucky to encounter a friendly Blackfoot – the harsh environment had extracted whatever good humor the others they encountered might have possessed. One party appeared at the camp, claiming the train was using their watering hole without permission.

'Offer them some trinkets for the use of the place,' Brenner advised. Indians were in the habit of demanding payment for crossing their stream or grazing on their grass, and it was easier to agree with them and give them something than to argue.

They seemed to think what they had been offered was sufficient and invited themselves to supper, which largely consisted of a horse that had had to be put out of its misery.

Nellie Bingham had her share of dust on her despite her mother's precautions, but she still stood out with her golden hair, which created a sharp interest in the Indians; the only whites they had seen before had been dark French trappers. They openly stared at her and even tried to touch her hair, which made Nellie's parents remove her to their wagon.

Ben had an admiration for Indian gear and made an effort to befriend the Indians and to trade, using sign language. The one who seemed to be the leader asked him if he would like to swap something for Nellie. Ben told him coolly that such a wonder as

Nellie did not come cheap. The Indian seemed to agree, and asked Ben to name his price. Ben offhandedly indicated six Indian ponies, which was a price he figured was far beyond the ragtag band.

Finally the Indians left and the company was able to go to bed, setting double pickets. They only had a couple of hours of rest since they had to break camp well before dawn to beat the heat.

It was getting on to the hottest part of the day when the Indians suddenly reappeared – leading a string of six ponies! No one had any inkling of Ben's offer, and he was far in the rear with the spare stock. But Captain Stokes didn't like the looks of the situation: there was no turning around with the wagons hemmed in by giant lava boulders, and the Indian party blocked the way forward. It wouldn't be easy to make a defensive circle.

Captain Stokes signed for the Indians not to come any closer, and he, Brenner and a couple of the scouts went out to parlay. They came back almost immediately in confusion.

'Them injuns have gotten it into their heads we would swap your daughter for six ponies,' Captain Stokes told Reverend Bingham.

Ivy Bingham almost fainted when she heard this. She pushed Nellie into their wagon and covered her up with a blanket.

'They said they had made a bargain for Nellie, and since they came up with their side, they expect us to do the same,' Brenner added.

Bingham was so agitated he started to shout: 'How would they get such a ridiculous notion?'

Frightened the situation could turn ugly, one of the bachelors who had been with Ben confessed, 'I did hear Ben Cooper joking with them about such a thing.'

'Where is Cooper?' Captain Stokes asked angrily.

The bachelor was sent to fetch Ben. He told him he was wanted, but not why, and made himself scarce afterward. Ben innocently rode up to the wagons, but when he saw the Indians and the ponies, he immediately took responsibility.

'I reckon I said something I shouldn't have and I am right sorry about it.'

Reverend Bingham had to be restrained from physically attacking him.

Captain Stokes ordered Ben to accompany him to parlay further, since he had created the crisis.

With signs, and a few clarifying words from Brenner, Ben tried to explain he never expected them to take him seriously, as white people weren't in the custom of trading their women under any circumstances. The Indians insisted they had gone to considerable trouble rounding up ponies and they weren't going home empty-handed. Ben offered them his horse, his rifle and all his gear, including his buckskins and boots, in lieu of Nellie, but the Indians responded that they had enough of all of those things. The one thing they didn't have was a yellow-headed woman.

During the parlay, the rest of the company prepared for the worst, trying to make a circle in the tight quarters and piling heavy sacks inside the exposed sides of the wagon walls.

Not long after the parlay party returned without solving matters, the Indians began to ride in wide circles around the train, sometimes disappearing behind the massive boulders so they could only be pinpointed by their war cries.

'Maybe it is all for show to save their faces after being fooled,' John tried to reassure Rebecca, 'and they will go away after a time.'

Their circling grew closer, but Captain Stokes warned not to shoot unless they shot first.

The women lay down inside the wagons while the men crouched outside, sighting their rifles through the spokes of the wheels. Sarah couldn't resist peeking out the gate, and Rebecca jerked her back by her skirt so violently that the threadbare material ripped, leaving her backside bare, but neither one saw anything funny about it.

When the first arrows were released, Captain Stokes finally gave the word to fire and a ragged blast of gunshots lasted several minutes.

The Indians retreated out of range and the company assessed what damage had been done. Bob Hannah had taken an arrow in the shoulder, and an ox had been killed.

The Indians crept closer once again, initiating a new tactic: an arrow that had been set on fire landed on one of the Stokeses' wagons. Both canvas and wood were so dry, it immediately burst into flames. Luckily Harriet Stokes was no longer inside. The men tossed dirt on the flames; there was no water to spare.

Another arrow set a second wagon on fire. The scouts came out of the protection of the wagons, moving forward and firing, which drove the Indians far enough back that their arrows fell short. The other men quickly joined the scouts on the line; most had taken the precaution of packing extra bullets. The barrage seemed to finally convince the Indians they couldn't easily carry the day and they galloped away, still leading the six ponies.

The arrow was pulled from Bob Hannah's shoulder and Captain Stokes pronounced the wound clean, but Bob was angry, as were the three Watkins brothers who owned the second wagon that had been destroyed. Both Nellie and her mother were hysterical and Reverend Bingham still wanted to kill Ben – and now he wasn't alone in his sentiments.

Rebecca shook her head. 'I knew his hijinks would go too far one day.'

Sarah didn't say anything, though she knew Ben didn't have one friend in the camp except herself.

The council called a meeting of all the men.

'I say we string him up right now!' Reverend Bingham said, with no thought to Christian charity.

'I am not one to be sitting in judgment in such a permanent way,' Captain Stokes replied.

'If he stays in this train, I will kill him!' Reverend Bingham yelled.

'And we will help,' the Watkins brothers offered.

Finally the cooler heads prevailed and it was decided Ben would be banished from the train and would have to make his way on his own.

Rebecca was upset. 'This is the same as killing him, since he is hardly likely to survive in such a hostile desert, particularly with a pack of angry Indians around.'

'It was either that or be part of a lynching.'

'Not much of a choice,' Sarah said.

'Men seem to want things either one way or the other,' Rebecca told Margaret after

John had gone back to the council.

'It is women who try to find a middle way,' Margaret agreed. 'Our lives are mostly compromises.'

Sarah

I was in a rage and could scarce contain myself, no matter majority rules.

The council wanted to get moving again in the cool of the evening. I found Tom Miller hitching up Margaret's wagon.

'You see which way Ben went?'

Tom didn't say anything; he just pointed.

'You won't be telling on me if I follow him a bit, will you?'

'I feel real bad about it, Sarah, but I didn't have a vote. I am just a hired hand.'

'Well, you're different from the others, Tom, and that is why I knew I could count on you.'

Nobody saw me sneaking into our provision wagon where I snatched up what I thought Rebecca would not miss, but might be of benefit to Ben. It didn't amount to much – a little bit of dried fruit and some flour and lard for making pemmican. I wrapt it up in a big rag which could also serve Ben some purpose. I wanted to add some medicinal supplies, but we were running so short, I was sure they'd be missed.

Now it's a bad thing to be thieving from your own family. I had already gone pretty far, so I went even farther. I had kept my ears open and had a good notion of how low Mr Brenner's stock had fallen as a guide, so I told myself he had it coming. He was arguing with Captain Stokes, so it was a simple matter to go to where he stowed his gear and take his leather water sack. Ben could go quite a way with no food, but he wouldn't get far without water.

I was just creeping away from camp when Nellie popped out from behind one of those infernal black boulders, cutting me off just like an injun.

'You gave me a start,' I said, trying to act natural.

'I'm sorry. I saw you walking away from the train like, well, like you had something in mind to do that you didn't want folks to be finding out about.'

'You're imagining things, Nellie.'

'I reckoned you were going after Ben.'

'You sure do like to make things up.'

'All right, you don't have to 'fess up if you don't want to, but I'd be doing the same thing if my mama didn't keep such a sharp eye out.'

She held out a small package. 'It's biscuits. They're still tasty even if they're hard. Will you give them to Ben? I don't want him to be going off into the desert with nothing when it's all on my account.'

I took the package. 'All right.'

'I knew that was where you were going!' Nellie said triumphantly, then raced back before her mama would miss her.

I knew somebody would take notice if I went horseback; besides, walking over rocks was easier with two legs than a horse's four, even if there was a rip in my boots. It took less than an hour to catch up with Ben on his horse, and I was pleased to see he looked most delighted to see me.

'Looks like I still got one friend left in the world.'

'I am sure you got more than that, but they're scared of the council.'

'Well, I reckon they did the charitable thing, letting me have my neck.'

'You didn't know those injuns would take you serious.'

'I guess I'm old enough I should have had more sense. I am just going to have to change my ways, Sarah. That is if I get the opportunity.'

'You're every bit as good at finding your way as any of the scouts. And you've been picking up the injun ways too, Ben. You'll get back to Fort Hall all right. I know it.'

'I figger I'm just as well off trying to make Oregon than going back. I'm betting these rocks can't go on any further than they've gone already – and I've always been lucky, Sarah.'

'I'll be crossing my fingers for you, Ben.'

'I thank you kindly.'

He bent down from his horse and planted a kiss on my forehead. I got so flustered I didn't know what to say, so I just pushed the food at him, muttering something about not wanting him to starve himself. I forgot to say that part of it was from Nellie. Well, I am trying to be honest these days: I don't think I forgot. I just wanted that moment for myself.

I watched him pick his way through the rocks, but it was getting too dark to keep him in sight for more than a few minutes. I wasn't worried about finding my way back to the train; any sound carried far with no other living thing around.

I hadn't been able to help Willie, but maybe that small bundle of food and the water sack would make the difference between life and death for Ben.

The Journal of Rebecca Springer

August 10, 1846

Only two miles. Margaret's cough is drawing everything out of her. Her eyes have lost their sparkle and she doesn't even have interest in

303

reading. It is this Devil's country bringing her so low. We had to make dry camp again and the stock is bellowing something fierce. My lips are so chapped they are bleeding, but I am no worse off than anyone else.

As wary as I have always been of Ben Cooper, I never wanted anything so bad to happen to him. Lord, please preserve Ben as he wanders in the wilderness as You Yourself have done.

Rebecca had run out of paper. Margaret gave her most of what remained blank of her own notebook to sew a new one. Rebecca made a cover from an old sun bonnet.

'I am surprised I managed to fill up every page. There is something shameful in having rambled on so long; I will have to do some serious editing of my thoughts from now on. I don't want my grandchildren to think me a self-indulgent woman.'

'They will appreciate knowing more about their history,' Margaret said. 'I have been neglectful of my own notebook lately, but there seems little to write of. It is all rock and dust without change.'

'You will soon have it filled when you are feeling better,' Rebecca reassured her.

'I just jot down a few notes about things that catch my fancy... I should be writing about the lava...' She looked frustrated; she simply didn't have the energy.

Rebecca shook her head in wonder. 'The like of our journey has not been seen in this country before.'

'And no doubt will not be seen again unless some new Columbus comes along and discovers the United States doesn't stop at the Pacific Ocean. One day when we are both old and gray, we will sit around the fire with our grandchildren, telling them stories of our journey. And we will have your journal, Rebecca, as an aide-memoire, since our own memories will be gone.'

A hot wind began to blow. The dust was worse than Indians, storms, winds, mosquitoes or woodticks. Every member of the company had become weak and worn, with bleeding lips and clothes in rags. There was no custom to mark the passage of the hours, only dust and more dust and all effort put toward getting through the hours. Bonnets and kerchiefs were grimy with filth, and sweat ran into their mouths, the salt only making them more thirsty and stinging the festering sores their poor diet had created. Alkali had blotched and blistered their skin, and their faces were drawn from toil and hunger. Their hands were raw and their feet so swollen with walking, most boots had split and were tied on with rags or string.

Margaret suffered the worst. It was difficult for her to swallow, and she spit up blood when she coughed. Rebecca made

her a mush with what little milk the poor
cow could give.

The Journal of Rebecca Springer

August 14, 1846

We saw some bones scattered about, most
of them oxen, but someone had left a
message written on a human skull set on a
rock for all to see: 'No water here.' We didn't
need having human remains treated so dis-
respectfully to tell us so. I asked John if he
wouldn't mind covering that skull up again
and he kindly obliged me.

Lord, it looks like You are allowing the
Devil to have the upper hand for a while. I
am trying not to question Your infinite wisdom.

The stock finally smelled water and no one
could stop them. The loose animals began to
run as fast they could in their weakened condition, and then the yoked teams joined the
frenzy, the wagons swaying so violently, any
loose object caromed off the canvas walls.

The men raced to head off the animals. The
first to arrive at the spring used whips to try
to drive them back, as the pool was ringed
with the carcasses of dead animals and was
clearly poisonous. They only managed to

gain control after several animals had gorged themselves. Eight oxen and two horses died.

Sarah painted warnings: 'Danger: poison water.' There was no paper, so the bleached skulls of the previous victims were her placards. She and Tom rode back along the trail with a sackful of skulls, depositing them where a stampede by the next train might be avoided in time.

Rebecca was proud of her initiative, but Captain Stokes said sourly, 'Just hope whoever sees 'em knows how to read.'

He was not in good humor and seemed less sure of himself. Brenner was his choice, of which he had persuaded the council. Brenner knew something of the way since they were not all dead, but someone of his experience of the territory should have guided them well clear of a poisoned spring, let alone something so large as a massive lava field. John wouldn't talk of it to Rebecca, but the tension among the men didn't escape the women even though they were excluded from serious discussion, and their own unease deepened.

Captain Stokes announced they would have to share stock to balance the teams; not all wagons still had full teams. The men followed his directions without argument, which comforted the women; discipline was still in place.

In the mad race to the poisoned spring, a

wheel had fallen off the Springers' second wagon. They decided to set it aside and consolidate everything into one.

'Even if we don't have a wagon for you to drive any more, Frank,' John told their new bachelor, 'the damage was not your fault and you are welcome to continue sharing our food and hitching a ride on the wagon when your feet get sore.'

Rebecca thought some of Frank's bad luck *had* rubbed off on them. John didn't like the way the wagon was riding. The additional load was too heavy for the oxen and they would have to lighten up. She remembered how stubborn she had been about possessions before they started out and wanted to show her husband she had learned something along the way. She would find more to give up, even though she had given up so much already.

The Journal of Rebecca Springer

August 16, 1846

Our last milch cow is grunting in an odd way and I fear she got into the poison. I am concerned if she goes as I am scarcely eating proper for my child. Everyone is kind and offers to share what they feel might be beneficial, but I do not like to claim special privilege when there are sick folks among us.

Bob Hannah is doing poorly as that arrow wound is not as clean as we thought. And of course there is Margaret's worsening condition. She can no longer walk beside the wagon, and the jostling in the run to the poison spring did her no good, though Laurie came through without damaging his leg further. John assured me the meat from the dead animals was not poisonous, so I boiled up a little in Margaret's water ration to make a broth.

Lord, I have lost all my other friends. Please do not choose to take this one away from me. Forgive me for this selfish thought: instead, I ask You to preserve Margaret so her child will not grow up an orphan.

When next Rebecca went into Margaret's wagon, she was shocked to find she had taken the shears to her hair! She looked more a man than a woman.

'I am past having any vanity about my appearance,' Margaret explained. 'It is easier to stay cool without a great mass of hair that is supposed to be a woman's pride. Now I can feel what breeze there may be about my ears, as privileged as a man.'

There was some logic in what she said, and Rebecca had not come to scold a sick woman.

Margaret seemed to gain some energy

from the broth. After eating, she showed Rebecca how she had saved her magnificent red hair, bound together with a ribbon.

'Perhaps one day I will feel ready to resume my femininity and then I will have a matched switch on hand. Of course, that day will have to wait until we have an abundance of soap and water.'

'Well, I am glad your senses have not left you completely.'

'Rebecca, certain things don't seem to matter any longer. But your friendship: that will always matter.'

What would a woman do in a train comprised only of men? Rebecca wondered. She would be alone, even if she traveled with a husband.

Rebecca had a concern she wanted to share with Margaret. 'Captain Stokes says we can no longer waste an entire day, so he plans to travel tomorrow on the Sabbath.'

The plan made sense to Margaret. 'Reverend Beecher said, "If I were crossing the ocean I certainly would not consider jumping overboard on the seventh day in order to avoid the onus of Sunday travel."'

Rebecca was skeptical. 'I wonder if Reverend Beecher would have thought the few miles we will gain is worth the sin.'

But at least Reverend Bingham had agreed to say a few words 'on the fly', and Margaret said she felt well enough to accompany

Rebecca. She put on her sun bonnet, but it was impossible to hide her shorn head. Ivy Bingham gave her a disapproving look.

The Reverend chose to compare their plight with that of the children of Israel. Margaret was in no frame of mind for his continuous talk of doom.

'Reverend Bingham, Moses and Aaron wandered for forty years in the desert and, in the end, only traveled a few hundred miles. I trust we might accomplish far more in a much shorter span of time.'

He was offended. 'It is not enough to commit the unnatural act of cutting your hair,' he lectured her, 'but now you have taken it into that shaven head to engage in argument as if you were a man!'

Rebecca urged Margaret to return to her sickbed, feeling she had become delirious, but Margaret assured her she was in possession of her wits.

'I simply do not care to hold my tongue any longer in the presence of hypocrites.'

It would not be easy for the other women to shun her for her behaviour. With only six of them in the train now, she would sometimes have to be called upon, if only to protect their mutual modesty.

They knew they were back on the main trail when they saw fresh dung. A little later, they came across a small group of men camping at what was called Inscription Rock, though it was not much of a landmark. Still it was a chance to see if Joe and the Hansens had happened by and left some message. John climbed all over the rock, but there was nothing.

Captain Stokes suggested joining forces with the other party. Only twenty wagons were left out of the fifty with which he had started. The campers had left their own wagons behind at Fort Hall, they told the council, and were making good progress with ponies. John suspected they were Indian ponies and that the men had traded guns or whiskey for them. He didn't like the looks of them and fortunately his viewpoint prevailed with the council.

'Those fools have a load of whiskey,' he reported to Rebecca, 'and seem to be bound to stay in a state of drunkenness.'

'Were there any women in their party?' she asked.

'None.'

She might have known: without women in a train, there was no telling what might happen.

They decided to stay over a day to give the bad bunch a good head start.

The Journal of Rebecca Springer

August 24, 1846

Twelve miles, which is more like a usual day. We are all feeling better since we have put Mr Brenner's cutoff behind us. Not only are we rid of it, we are rid of him too, and good riddance. Sarah was always keen on his stories, most of which weren't true, I am sure.

There's a muddy spring and a bit of shriveled-up grass, but it seems like heaven after what we've been through. I have been able to turn to the mending that was put off when it was all we could do to just keep moving. No washing possible yet. Buffalo jerky stew for supper.

Bob Hannah died from the arrow he took. He told me once that he was carrying his mother's rolling pin all the way from Ohio. 'This is all I have to remember my mother by,' he said. 'She always used it to roll out her biscuits, and they were awful good biscuits.'

The men tossed the pin away when they divided up his gear and I rescued it from the side of the road. I will take it with me to Oregon so Bob Hannah's mother will be remembered along with him.

Lord, I know I am supposed to be eliminating rather than accumulating. Please give me the heart to cast off more of what little I have left in life. But I am grateful that I still possess the most valuable possessions: a loving husband and a baby that is kicking mightily now. And thank You for Sarah as well. She is coming along right nicely.

The air was clearer, but Margaret was no better. Sarah and Rebecca did her housekeeping as she could barely manage to mother her child. Sarah handled the heavy work for both households and constantly nagged Rebecca to rest.

They tried to maintain a routine. At nooning, Nellie, Sarah and Rebecca picked up *Much Ado About Nothing*. Margaret enjoyed listening, even though she didn't want to take a turn reading. Tom played tag with Laurie; he was always 'it', and allowed Laurie to escape until he was ready to be caught. Exercise was a good tonic for Laurie, even though his limp was pronounced. His leg had only recently been unbound and looked quite puny next to the other.

Margaret roused herself enough to engage Sarah in a game of chess, remarking that Sarah had a good memory for the game. Rebecca figured that patience was a part of it as well; if so, there was hope Sarah could also gain the patience to allow a kettle to come to a proper boil before she threw in the coffee.

After the evening's supper, Rebecca took Margaret a jug of soup, but she set it aside.

'I need to make preparations.'

'You need to be preparing yourself to set up your home in Oregon, and you would best do that by drinking some of this broth.'

'I will ... in a little while. May I have my notebook?'

Rebecca found it and brought it to her.

'I want you to have my Shakespeare.'

'Don't be saying that,' Rebecca told her firmly. 'Try to take a few sips.'

Margaret shook her head, as if it weren't worth arguing over. 'I would like to write while I am still able.'

'You will be writing whole volumes before you are through.'

'Dear Rebecca – you have been such a comfort; giving me so much, even without my asking. Now I must ask you for more.'

'You know I will do what you want.' She knew she was talking about Laurie.

'It is so much ... you will soon be having your own child.'

'Laurie will never be in some missionary orphanage.'

'I can provide you with something for his care.'

'We will get by fine.'

'Of that I am sure. God bless you, Rebecca.'

'And you, Margaret.'

'In spite of what I might have said to Reverend Bingham, I am a believer, Rebecca. Pray for me.'

'Every night. But do not give up hope.'

'No, my dear one. My lungs have not been strong since I was a child. I am done with fighting; the constant jostling in the wagon is agony and I am going no further.'

'Captain Stokes will not stand for it.'

'There is no man in charge of me, so I am free to make my own decision.'

'You cannot stay alone.'

'Tom has agreed to keep me company until the end.'

Rebecca couldn't hide her astonishment, and it made Margaret smile.

'What difference does it make now if we are unchaperoned? The books are yours, Rebecca. There are a few momentoes for Laurie – Phillip's pistol and watch and chain. In the morning, will you keep him in your wagon and see that he is amused until after the train has departed?'

She could not refuse the last wishes of a dying woman, though all her nature went against it. She kissed Margaret like a sister and quickly left before she dissolved into tears.

Part 7

The Blue Mountains

The Journal of Rebecca Springer

August 25, 1846

Dear Lord, grant Margaret the peaceful passing that was denied to her husband. Let her find him again in happiness in Heaven by Your side.

Captain Stokes forbade Margaret's request, but she refused to accept his command and Tom stood with her. The Captain told Tom that if he didn't change his mind, he would not allow him back in the train, but his words lacked conviction; Ben's banishment had been haunting his dreams.

Rebecca and Sarah entertained Laurie in the wagon while they argued. When Captain Stokes finally gave up and the train moved on, Laurie didn't question the absence of his mother; any child was the charge of the entire company, and he was used to being in other wagons. Sarah and Rebecca tried to present a cheerful face. Sharing their sorrow would wait until Laurie had fallen asleep after supper.

Tom turned the wagon to block the sun and strung spare canvas as an awning. He piled blankets on the ground where Margaret could lie as comfortably as possible and look out across the prairie toward the mountain range in the distance.

He strained stream water through muslin and coaxed Margaret to at least take a few sips.

When she coughed up blood mixed with more solid matter, he held her up so she wouldn't drown in her own fluids. When the spasm ended, he tried to lay her down on her side, but she clung to him.

'Tom ... just hold me ... please...'

It both broke his heart and satisfied it to keep her in his arms.

'Tom ... if there was only time...'

'You don't have to say anything, Mrs Prescott. Just rest.'

'You have never called me by my name. Will you now?'

It took effort. Even so thin and pale and wasted, her beauty overwhelmed him. 'Margaret ... you are the best thing that's ever happened to me.'

'And you are one of the better things that has happened in my life...'

But when the final moment came, she clutched at him and murmured, 'Phillip...'

Sarah

Then Tom caught up with the train three days later, Margaret's passing was writ all over his face and I just had to swallow the truth, as bitter as it was.

Tom didn't say much, though he told Rebecca he had taken proper care with her grave, breaking up a wagon wheel to mark it. She had left him the wagon and what remaining gear she had and had given him a letter to pass on to Laurie when he came of age.

Testament of Margaret Prescott

August 25, 1846

Dearest Laurie, it is not my desire to leave you at such a tender age; if it were my decision, I would never abandon you, only let you go with as much grace as I could muster when you were ready to fly on your own. I have placed you at peril and I ask your forgiveness. But all that was done was in hope of a brighter future for us all.

As young as you are, it is clear you have

inherited the best from both your parents – compassion and intelligence from your father; ambition and stubbornness from me. Yes, I am calling stubbornness a virtue. It will be needed when others attempt to turn you aside from your dreams. Do not give up on them! Your father, who loved you if possible even more than I, was a dreamer. We both felt certain the West would enable him to realize those dreams. Dreamers change the world; they make it a better place.

I am entrusting Rebecca Springer with responsibility for your upbringing. She and her husband John will be your new parents. I hope her child will become your close friend. You will have a further friend in Tom Miller. My dream is that you will live with love – one not difficult to attain for such a remarkable child as you.

I love you very much.

Tom also brought back her switch of hair. I think that was his own idea, not Margaret's. Rebecca wove us all remembrance bracelets from it and Tom was most grateful. I think he had strong feelings for Margaret.

Rebecca tried to tell Laurie that his mama was with his papa and the angels, but he had seen his papa lain in the ground, so it was hard. There was an unfinished feeling for me as well in not having been able to witness Margaret's burial.

'It is kind of like when we didn't have Willie to pray over,' I said to Rebecca.

'We can have a memorial service for her like we did for him.'

'She wouldn't like it if there was too much praying and carrying on.'

'Carrying on by us or Reverend Bingham?'

'Rebecca, I don't care if you get on me for not respecting the cloth, but Margaret had no use for him.'

'I will give you no argument. It is for Margaret's benefit, so we should devise a program to her liking.'

'We can do poems – and read some of the Shakespeare, too.'

'Those same words were on the tip of my tongue.'

After fits and starts, me and Rebecca were starting to settle down and get comfortable with each other. 'Margaret and you were real close,' I said to her, 'and now it is just us two, so we're going to have to make do with each other.'

'You have been doing your part, Sarah, and I will try to do mine. If I get to lecturing you, you must stop me.'

'You can be sure I will ... but I will try not to be sassy about it.'

'That would be most welcome.'

That same evening, we read the Shakespeare sonnets that Margaret had liked best, passing the book around. Nellie read with us and I had to admire her backbone in standing up to her folks, as they said using other than God's Book was wrong. We had a good turnout without them. Most of that poetry was beyond folks – I hadn't gotten a handle on all of it myself, and now I didn't have Margaret around to explain it – but the words still sounded real pretty and I reckon everybody found them fitting.

Afterwards, it was like it was official that Laurie was an orphan and I had a talk with Papa about the situation.

'Papa, you don't mind Laurie staying with us, do you? He won't be any trouble as he's learned his lesson now and knows how to be quiet as a mouse if he's asked. And Rebecca doesn't need to take any time away from her baby to tend him because that will be my job. Margaret trusted us with him and it would be a sin turning him over to someone else.'

'Have I spoken of turning him out?'

'No, but that would be the practical thought.'

'Well, I guess you are right about that, Sarah.'

'But sometimes being right is wrong, Papa. I mean...'

Papa waved me silent. 'I know what you mean, Sarah. Let's just see how things go for now. We can decide what is practical and what is right once we reach Oregon.'

'Well, I guess that is fair enough, Papa. And by the time we get to Oregon, I am sure Laurie will have grown on you right strong!'

Papa looked at me real stern. 'Sarah, I will see that no harm comes to Laurie Prescott. But he is not my flesh and blood. He can't take the place of Willie, Matthew, Joe or Daniel, if that is what you have in mind.'

I tried not to tear up. 'Papa, how can you think such a thing? No one can ever take any of their places...' I couldn't help it; I started to blubber, which isn't like me at all.

Papa was not a hugging type of man, but he put his arms around me and patted me on the back. 'I know, Sarah, and I am sorry to take out my bad humor on you. I promise I will not direct it at Laurie.'

Papa said he had to go take the file to one of the oxen's hooves before it got too dark. I wasn't sure, but I could have sworn I saw a glint in the corner of his eye, which made me feel not quite the fool for my tears.

The Journal of Rebecca Springer

September 2, 1846

Ten miles and good water. The grass is sweet and I found wild plums for a cobbler as a treat for Laurie. Crossed the Snake River at Three Island Crossing. Men from

Fort Boise have set up a ferry in partnership with the local Indians, so there was no need to take everything apart. They demanded a high price, but there is nothing much our money can buy around here but a bit of ease, so we went ahead and paid.

While waiting our turn, I faced up to lightening our load and discarded my half-bushel of peach pits. I reckon someone else will have managed to get some trees growing in Oregon and I can beg some pits off them. A woman in another train here said she heard of a man who brought a whole orchard over the mountains to Oregon, the trees wrapped up in burlap and carted by a double team. She admired my bonnet and I gave her the pattern.

I wonder if any of those pits will sprout up where I scattered them alongside the river. That would be a treat for whoever passes by in a couple of years. Maybe I will hear someone remark on it in Oregon and have a smile.

I also sorted through linens and discarded about half. Some have seen their best days after these months, but the rest will make do if I take good care of them. I gave one set, much mended, to Ivy Bingham, who declared she had nothing as nice herself (and this only my third best). I confess I was trying to buy a little goodwill from the Lord for thinking so unkindly of her. But she is hard to bear.

I had to discard some foodstuff. The dry air has kept down mold, but the flour is infested. I do not know where these bugs can come from. I trimmed the fat from the remaining bacon. If we stop long enough at Fort Boise, I will render it down, as we have run out of lard and also have no butter with the cow going down to poison. I am still thinking of eggs, but that is too much to hope for.

The Stokeses put off a considerable amount of furniture and reduced their own wagons by one. John is handy, and will make up furniture for our new home bit by bit – starting with a nice high bed. If there are peach pits in Oregon, no doubt there are geese as well so I can freshen up our pillows and comforters.

We still have many miles to go, but I am already setting up my household. I guess even with all the heartache and loss, I can at least look forward to the end.

Lord, rest Margaret's soul. Please let her know her child prays for her and his father every night.

Compared to Fort Bridger, Fort Boise was a paradise, with wooden buildings instead of grim stone. Spirits couldn't help but be lifted by the sight of human habitation again; it seemed the ability to put aside past pain was part of human nature. Rebecca had been told that was true with the physical pain of childbirth, so that mankind could keep going.

Onions, carrots and potatoes were available for purchase and there was saleratus for the taking right on the ground, so baking could continue. Though no cows were on offer, John was able to buy two nanny goats.

Sarah complained she did not care for the taste of goat's milk.

'You have suffered through worse hardships up to now and are still full of life,' Rebecca reminded her, but her chiding was with humor. Her relationship with Sarah seemed to have progressed as far as the miles they had traveled.

Fort Boise was not civilized enough to have a scrap of paper to purchase, and Rebecca was forced to continue her journal on the margins of Mr Hastings' traveler's journal, which had proven to be largely worthless as a guide.

'I will get a headache having to keep turning the book around to fill in all the edges,' she complained to Sarah.

'You have suffered through worse hardships before,' she responded, and they both laughed.

John reported that one of the men at Fort Boise had died. He had been suffering mightily from the cramps.

'From where his britches were,' John informed Rebecca, 'I would venture he was taken away in the middle of heeding the call of nature.'

'I do not wish for any more details, John,' Rebecca said primly.

'I think there is one detail that will interest you very much, Rebecca. They have just auctioned off his belongings.'

'I don't think some poor mountain man smelling of bear fat would possess much of interest to me.'

'Now you know you should not judge a book by its cover, Rebecca.'

John had been hiding something behind his back, which he now pressed into her hands. It was a leatherbound Bible, which had been carefully kept. She was astounded and had to riffle through the pages to be certain it was all there.

'You don't know how much this means to me, John.'

'I think I do.'

She entered both her family and the Springer family dates, as best they could be recalled, and put Margaret and Philip Prescott's down as well, as their child was now part of their family. None of the dead man's family's dates were in it. Perhaps he couldn't read or write much. Rebecca assumed that just having the Good Book about him must have been of great comfort, though it certainly had not brought him luck.

The Journal of Rebecca Springer

September 4, 1846

We left Fort Boise this morning. Frank has opted to continue by muleback with another party and we wished him well. Some of our men have come down with the stomach cramps, as has Nellie. Fort Boise was too crowded and open to contagion. I fear they may have partaken of tainted food, though Ivy Bingham swears it could not be true with Nellie as she prepares every bite she takes. A good purging should set them right.

Lord, thank You for presenting us with more hospitable country. I am praying You will allow us to make up some time now and be able to reach the Dalles and the Columbia River before the winter sets in and we have to sit and wait for months before we can reach Oregon City and the Willamette Valley. I promise you in return I will press for Sunday stoppings again to pay You proper honor.

Nellie and the others didn't improve. Ivy Bingham treated her daughter with flannel cloths as hot as bearable on her stomach. The men received much the same regimen, but a good sweat didn't seem to do any of them any good. The sickness ran the same with all of them: stomach cramps, cold sweats and high fevers back and forth, along with complaints of aches all over their bodies.

It wasn't long before they were all too weak to complain. In the space of two days, six graves were dug, including one for Nellie Bingham. It frightened the rest of the company to have so many taken away so quickly, and each feared they might be next.

John worried they shouldn't have left Fort Boise as they were so few now.

'It might be best to go back there and wait to hitch up with another train.'

Rebecca had her own thoughts on the subject. 'I suspect our numbers would have been even fewer if we remained behind. I think the source of this contagion lies in Fort Boise, and those that remain there may well fall victim themselves.'

'Rebecca, you have a good woman's intuition, but you also live in constant fear of disease.'

'And why not? We are helpless in the face of smallpox or mumps and a thousand other evils. We can only avoid mists and close air.'

'Fort Boise was both high and dry.'

'But not clean,' Rebecca said firmly. 'There was a smell of cess in the air. I have given all the vegetables I bought there a good scrubbing.'

'Well, no one else has taken a fever,' John said optimistically, 'so whatever it was, I think we have escaped its grasp.'

'I pray the Lord you are right.'

Sarah was feeling low, but not due to a contagion, she assured Rebecca. 'I was kind of jealous of Nellie while she was alive, but it was more than that – I saw Ben before he went and I kept back something about her feelings from him as he seemed to have a liking for her.'

'Well, there is nothing that can be done about it now, Sarah,' Rebecca said. 'They are both gone and it cannot make any difference. There isn't a soul alive that doesn't feel some guilt when a relative or acquaintance dies, thinking they could have been kinder or done more to show affection.'

'But Ben isn't dead,' Sarah insisted, wanting so much for it to be true.

'I shouldn't have said that. I am sorry.' Rebecca was trying to be nice, but Sarah knew she had written him off.

Sarah

'When my mother died,' Rebecca told me, 'I thought I was alone in feeling guilty about not doing right by her, and then one day my brothers confessed they had been holding the same feelings. We talked it over and agreed we had not stinted in showing our mother affection, even if we had all had our minor shortcomings. What good would it have done to allow guilty feelings to take hold of us when there was so much good to remember?'

Now this was good advice and I was grateful to Rebecca for telling me such a personal story in return for hearing my own. I have tried to apply her words when I lie awake at night, going over in my mind those minutes before Willie disappeared and how I couldn't do anything to help.

Reverend Bingham could scarcely speak the words for his daughter's service, and was too broke up after to say anything over the others that had passed. When the train was ready to leave, Miz Bingham wouldn't remove herself from Nellie's grave, determined to stand guard so no force of nature or man would disturb it.

'I don't want those injuns digging her up to cut off her beautiful hair,' she said, looking like a wild woman.

The men looked real embarrassed and seemed to expect us women to give Miz Bingham a good talking-to. But Rebecca and me just stood and watched and didn't speak a word. Miz Bingham had crossed us both, and we bore her a double grudge for the way she treated Margaret, but she had suffered a great loss. Even Miz Stokes went about her business, pretending not to be aware of the situation. Finally Rebecca tugged at my sleeve and we left to tend to our own packing.

I guess it was when all our backs was turned Miz Bingham saw her chance: not a minute went by before the Bingham wagon burst into flames. The men rushed to put out the fire with their water buckets (we had plenty of water now), but Miz Bingham tried to stop them, screaming and jumping up and down and even hitting at them and trying to scratch their faces.

Reverend Bingham finally had enough and started beating his wife with a stick. Most of the men nodded their approval, but I didn't think it was right as it wasn't Miz Bingham's fault if she was out of her mind. I wanted to do something, but Rebecca held me back.

'No woman can interfere with what goes on between a man and his wife without risking getting a beating herself.'

'You think that my papa would lay a hand on you?'

'I wasn't thinking of him; I was considering what some of the others might be of a mind to do. Of course John would step in if you or I tried to interfere, and that would be putting him on the wrong side of the other men, which I could not allow.'

There was a logic to what she said, but not one I enjoyed hearing.

At least the Reverend's stick was dry and soon snapped. He looked around a moment for another one, but his anger had burned itself out by then. His shoulders slumped and all the wind went out of him. The Bingham wagon was past saving, but there was a spare which had belonged to two of the dead men, and Miz Bingham got tossed into it along with what of their goods could be salvaged. With all the sickness, we were falling even more behind in our schedule and Captain Stokes was anxious to get going.

The whole day as we traveled along, we could hear Miz Bingham shrieking.

The Journal of Rebecca Springer

September 12, 1846

Ten miles today, an easy climb all the way. We are down to fifteen wagons and not more than two dozen men; I cannot be certain since some are always either out ahead or back with what remains of the stock.

These months have taken toll on man and beast, but it does no good to be looking at the dark side of things. To the positive, we will soon be high enough to escape most of the heat. It seems to me that fewer people pass on in cooler weather. I am not speaking of the cold of winter, of course. That is a whole other matter, but I am told the winter in Oregon country is mild.

We have turned away from the Snake River for the last time, and now follow the right side of another river called the Burnt. This land has much to offer and might tempt some to put down their roots without looking farther. But we are pushing on, as Captain Stokes says the valley of the Willamette River puts this one to shame. At least I am on the edge of the promised land, Lord, for which I thank You.

It seemed a miracle to once again see pines with their sweet-smelling sap. There were all types, and fir and spruce as well, as well as hardwoods such as birch and maple and aspen. The greenery was a feast for all the senses. On the practical side, it also meant it was easier to find privacy for personal business. The women had become less than a quorum with Ivy Bingham no longer in her right mind.

She allowed Rebecca to clean her wounds from the beating, but would not be comforted in any other way, refusing to budge from the wagon or perform any chores. Her entire person seemed concentrated on rebellion. The talk among the men was that she was just being stubborn and a few more knocks might straighten her out. Rebecca considered they would not suggest treating a stubborn animal in such a way and was gratified her husband did not participate in such talk.

Men seemed to care more about the loss of stock than human life. Rebecca noted each grave they passed, but they scarcely gave them a mention. This particular attitude did, unfortunately, include her husband.

The remaining women now had to take care of the Reverend as well as his demented wife. He seemed incapable of looking after himself and he had also lost his heart for preaching. Tom and Laurie made two more additional souls to cook and mend for.

Sarah still had not acquired a knack for cooking. The biscuits she made were no softer than the lava rocks they had endured.

'Miz Stokes says it isn't natural for a woman not to have a hand with a skillet,' Sarah said when Rebecca told her not to fret over it.

'Harriet Stokes is filled with opinions and some of them aren't worth listening to,' Rebecca replied.

'I figgered she rubbed you the wrong way.'

'It is just the end of the day and I am tired. It is wrong to be uncharitable.'

'I used to hear you and Margaret calling her names. You got off some good ones.'

'I didn't think anyone could hear.'

Impossible to keep anything from Sarah! But Rebecca needed to let off steam now and then, and receiving agreement with her sentiments always made her feel better. Elizabeth had always taken her side, and Margaret often did her one better. Sarah didn't possess Margaret's eloquence, but she certainly never withheld her opinions. There was enough steam in her for them both. Theirs was a different sort of feminine companionship, but satisfying.

The trail began to climb. Some of the peaks surrounding them were more than ten thousand feet high, Captain Stokes claimed, though he admitted he had no sure way of reckoning. There had been heavy snow in the previous winter, as the aftermath of avalanches was strewn all about. Earlier trains had cleared the landfalls, but it was still hard work maneuvering around the stumps they had left. Huge falls of scree had tumbled down the mountainsides. It was slow progress to create a level trail, as rocks mixed with smaller pebbles shifted beneath the oxen's feet and threatened to create their own avalanches. Beyond the rockfalls, the trees became so thick, sunlight scarcely got to the heart of the forest even in the height of the day.

On the steeper grades, the wagons had to be double-teamed. This made for even slower going, as the train was so short of animals, they had to haul up one wagon at a time. To lighten their load, Rebecca tossed out her chairs, along with one trunk. Most of what was inside had been worn to tatters anyway.

Tom carried Laurie up the sharper rises. Laurie resented it at first, feeling, with the aid of his crutch, he could scamper up and down just like one of the goats, who had quickly become his pets. But after a few minutes, he was all smiles, enjoying his piggyback ride.

On the downside of each crest, the wagon wheels had to be rough-locked and a tree cut to drag behind as a brake. Even though the wagons were slowly let down by ropes, the brake trees were cut to kindling by the time they reached bottom. But at least it meant they always had a ready supply of firewood. It was chilly now when the sun set, and Rebecca unpacked their heavier things.

The men worked as hard as the animals, growing so hot they stripped to the waist. Sarah ran mugs of soup or coffee to them in the early morning, and the water bucket later on. Rebecca could no longer attempt anything close to running.

When they crested a particularly difficult rise and saw before them a gradual descent into a broad valley, the men began to cheer.

The Journal of Rebecca Springer

September 16, 1846

The squaws in this valley are good farmers and I have been able to swap for corn, potatoes, pumpkins and onions. John has seen deer tracks and hopes to add to the variety of our diet in the next day or two.

Thank You, Lord, for bringing us this bounty. The goats are a nuisance – they ate John's gloves this morning – but I thank You for their milk.

I think pine trees are among Your best works.

Sarah

Rebecca and me started reading *Romeo and Juliet* by the fire. She found it romantical, but I had little patience with how the Montagues and Capulets were feuding with each other.

We had reached the summit of Flagstaff Hill, but all the work getting that high was nothing compared to what we would have to do to scale the heights of the Blue Mountains the other side of the valley. Papa said it looked to him as if we had to resign ourselves to wintering at The Dales, as the Barlow Trail to Oregon City closed down from the snows early and he wouldn't have Rebecca rafting on the Columbia River. Rebecca said if The Dales was a civilized place, she wouldn't mind having her baby

340

there and resting a spell, and anyways we were already in the Oregon country.

Some of the men managed to shoot two deer and shared them with the whole camp. Umatilla injuns heard the gunfire and demanded we pay them for the deer. Their eye was on the livestock, but they had to be satisfied with a knife, a bridle and Captain Stokes' shaving mirror, which was the last unbroken glass left in the company.

I never had any desire to be looking at my own reflection, but Rebecca set store on appearances. Papa's own shaving glass had got broken long ago and Rebecca was always fussing over how she might be appearing.

'Nobody's going to look good after all this time on the trail,' I said to her without thinking. 'Just look at the state of the rest of us and you can get a good idea of your own.'

She looked so sorry, it made me feel real bad as I had not meant to be unkind and didn't want to set us back after we had patched things up. 'Actions speak louder than words,' Papa always said, so during the next long wait at the bottom of a hill, I slipped off into the woods. Rebecca looked peeved when I came back, figgering I had gone back to my old wandering ways I suppose, but when she saw my apronful of bird's eggs, she like to broke them giving me a hug.

Pete Williams and Henry Spence went out looking for deer. They saw something moving in the bushes and took a shot. Much to their surprise a grizzly bear reared up! They had wounded it and it was roaring mad and took after them like a shot. They ran for their lives, but the bear was quicker and caught up with Pete and mauled him badly. After the bear was done, Pete wailed for Henry to come back and put him out of his misery, but it was some time before he felt the bear was far enough away that he could do so.

It was a mercy Henry shot Pete, but Henry didn't feel any the better for it. Everyone told him it was not his fault. The men wrapped Pete's body up in an old horse blanket so no one would have to look at it, then found a level spot to bury him.

Reverend Bingham had to be pushed to do the service. It was Rebecca made him do his duty. She said surely he knew that God would bring him trials.

When the company ran out of coffee, Rebecca felt responsible. 'I should have packed more, knowing we would be running into cooler weather again before the end.'

'Isn't everything around here your respon-sibility, Rebecca,' Sarah pointed out to her. 'Sometimes you act like if the morning doesn't start out with sunshine it was because of something you did wrong.'

'It is up to me to see to our meals.'

'Then you will just come up with something else like you always do. There's mint growing in some of the lower places and we could make tea with it.'

'You know the men are for coffee or nothing.'

'Then I expect they'll have nothing and be as grumpy as bears. But that isn't your fault and it's not mine either. I think we take right good care of them.'

'I feel bad denying the men, they are working so hard.'

'If Emily Walker was still with us, she would have said the men don't feel sorry for us working like squaws.'

'Women's days might have been the longest back when Emily was with us, but now the men have more than made up for it hauling the wagons. Perhaps it was the Lord's plan to rest them earlier to give them the energy for the mountains.'

'You are something, Rebecca, always trying to turn the bad things around to make them good – except when you're being hard on yourself.'

'Well, I don't know any other way to face the day, Sarah.' Rain started to fall, the first in a long time. Groundboards and water-proofing were stored in the very bottom of the Springers' wagon and everything had to be pulled out to get to them. The tents had grown so brittle, they leaked prodigiously, so everyone crowded into the wagon to sleep.

John pulled himself in as small as he could, which wasn't easy for a big man. There was just enough room for everyone to fit snugly if Sarah slung an arm around Laurie.

The Journal of Rebecca Springer

September 21, 1846

The rain continues and we make what progress we can, getting soaked in the process. The wagon smells of wet clothes and there is no space to dry them.

Even with the warmth of our bodies, the canvas doesn't keep out the draft. The half of my body not pressed into John's side at night feels the cold and I am hesitant to turn over and disturb him. I am not warm-blooded the way he and Sarah are. I wear a shawl all day, but by mid-morning she has thrown hers off and usually forgets it on the top or the bottom of one of these infernal rises.

I can't scold her. She has changed in other ways – more than is good for her. Elizabeth and Margaret were settled women, resigned to the duties of motherhood and hearth. But Sarah has has to take on such heavy responsibility so young I fear she will soon be aged beyond her years.

Lord, I know You sometimes give us what we wish for just to teach us a lesson. I had wanted to tame Sarah, but not to break her spirit. I hope to make things up to her once we get to the Willamette Valley. I hope You will be thinking the same.

The rain turned to snow. What trail there had been was now mostly washed away. In some places it looked as if half the mountainside had been undermined and fallen. There was little choice: the men had to chop their way through the Blue Mountains. Their clothes were soon plastered to their bodies with sweat and melting snow, and any exposed patch of skin was raked by the pine branches they cleared.

Now Sarah ferried Laurie up and down the hills on her back, as Tom was fully occupied. John took the time to help Rebecca pick her way. While the Springer wagon waited its turn for a team to haul it uphill, Sarah, Laurie and Rebecca tumbled inside and huddled together, wrapped in blankets like Indians, trying to fight the growing chill.

Laurie amused himself by identifying the alphabet in what was left of the guidebooks. He was delighted to find he could sound out whole words here and there, if they were simple such as 'dog' and 'ox'.

Sarah and Rebecca took turns reading *Romeo and Juliet*.

It was growing harder to get the oxen to cooperate, as they slipped in mire and dung with each step. Two collapsed and died in their traces. They were cut out and roughly butchered; the men needed all the energy they could get. With the cold, there was no concern for spoilage. Then the carcasses were pushed out of the way down the mountain-side to make a feast for scavenging animals.

The company was stopped dead by a cataract pouring down the side of the mountain with a roar. It took a full day to turn around to try a different tack. The oxen had to be unhitched and led around the wagons and then the men had to turn the wagons by hand. They would head lower and cut a new trail in the morning.

The Journal of Rebecca Springer

September 24, 1846

Some time during the day, Ivy Bingham left her wagon. The Reverend retraced our way, but if she was hiding among the trees, she didn't want to answer his call. I imagine she was trying to get herself back to Nellie's grave.

It seems the closer we get to Paradise, the more unobtainable it is becoming. Help us overcome these obstacles, Dear Lord, and watch over Ivy Bingham's soul, as she can't last long wandering around these mountains.

Sarah

Even though we wore waterproofs, my skirts grew so wet, they hung like lead weights. We got a small fire going for soup and I hoped to dry out my socks, but the soup scarcely got warm before the snow doused the fire. There didn't seem nothing for it except to try to get some sleep while Papa and the other men kept on cutting the way.

Rebecca put Laurie next to her and covered him up with blankets and even an old smelly buffalo skin. They soon fell asleep, but I was restless and started rummaging about in the clothing trunk to see what I might find that wasn't either ripped to tatters or damp and smelling of rot.

There were trousers and shirts that had been intended for Joe and Willie; the sight made me sad, but I had to think practical: I put on a pair of Willie's woollen britches, and followed that with two of Joe's shirts and Willie's jacket on top. I found a felt hat at the bottom of the trunk and I jammed it down over my ears.

By then, I was starting to warm up, so I made myself a place next to Laurie and Rebecca and lay down for a nap. I woke up to see Rebecca giving me a sharp look.

'Well, I guess you have gone about as far as you can go, Sarah Springer. At least you haven't chopped off your hair – but I don't want you getting any ideas.'

'Rebecca, it doesn't make sense to keep on wearing skirts. You know yourself they are weighting us down.'

'This makes it appear there is no difference between men and women. It will lower the moral tone of the company.'

'Don't you think we are about as low as we can get? You have always been the practical one, Rebecca, and you'd best do the same yourself, as you are down to wearing wet clothes and will catch yourself a chill like Miz Stokes has done. Besides, you are something more than clumsy with that belly. If you keep tending to your skirt instead of looking where you are going, you will twist your ankle good. Papa's got more than enough clothes to cover himself; you were generous sewing for him.'

I waved a pair of Papa's longjohns in front of her nose. 'There is so much mud out there, no one's going to notice we aren't men anyhow.'

'I am not about to make myself look so loose!'

'I think you are worried more about looking ridiculous.'

'I am not!'

Rebecca was never one to lie, so right away

she 'fessed, 'Well, that too... I can see the practicality. I am not a fool.'

'I know that, so put them on.' I gave her the longjohns, daring her to take me up.

'Well, I'll try them on – but just inside the wagon.'

Rebecca took off her skirt, then struggled into the longjohns, banging her head on the wagon stays in the process. When she finally succeeded in covering both her arms and her legs, I had to laugh at the sight of her: the longjohns were far too big except where they stretched over her belly so tight it looked like the buttons were ready to pop.

Laurie woke up and commenced to giggle as well. Rebecca larked about for his benefit, sticking out her big belly and wiggling her behind with the flap hanging half open. She was in such an agreeable mood, she let me dud her out in Papa's clothes the same way I was in my brothers'. Then the three of us went outside for a stroll and I was right that nobody paid us any mind, as the men were all occupied with their own business and anyways most everybody was starting to look the same, covered with black grime and dusted with white snowflakes.

Our high spirits got us through the next few hours of snow mixed with rain. After a while, it turned to steady snow and that made the way seem easier, because the mud froze and got covered with a layer of snow. But just when we figgered things was finally looking up, one of the Stokeses' wagons skidded over a frozen puddle and tipped over. Miz Stokes lost all her china, except for one saucer which landed on a feather pillow.

'I guess I will just keep it as a memento,' she said, not seeming to care that she had carried that fine china all the way across the country. Her cold was going from bad to worse and I had a suspicion she might have been turning to the whiskey bottle to treat it.

The men broke up what remained of the wagon and were able to get a good fire going with such nice dry wood. Another animal was lost in the accident, and it was turned into dinner for everyone, huge chunks spitted over the fire. No one had any desire for side dishes, so Rebecca and me and Miz Stokes had little to do but stand about with the men, smelling the sizzling fat and feeling our empty stomachs turn over.

For the first time in days, they all felt warm and well fed. The men had stripped off the hide to make leggings and wrappings for their feet. Some of them had already become frostbitten.

A small group desperate for coffee experimented with scrapings from the inner bark of a tree, which they roasted over the fire, then pulverized. Sarah dared to taste the concoction, but spit it out, declaring it was as bitter as pure vinegar.

'Good coffee is properly bitter,' one of the men claimed.

'None of you denied yourself a spoonful of sugar when we had it,' Sarah teased them, 'so you can't like it too bitter.'

The mood of the company remained cheerful, with the snow falling so gently, it seemed to disappear in the heat of the fire. It reminded Rebecca of earlier times and bonfires around a skating rink on a frozen pond – some of the happier moments in her short childhood – taking a turn hand in hand with friends in a line, then falling down in a heap with laughter.

How strange it was, like the celebration of the first snowfall back home in Indiana, instead of being on a narrow mountain ledge in the wilderness!

Although no one else seemed to pay any attention to Rebecca's attire, her husband noticed.

'Seeing as how you have taken possession of my clothes,' he said, 'I reckon you will be going after my shotgun next.'

'Only if you persist in teasing me.'

'There's no fun in teasing a woman who looks like a man.'

'Do you wish me to go back to wearing more womanly attire?'

'It seems the better thing to be wearing pants right now, but I hope you don't plan to make it permanent.'

'I would never do something so un-natural.'

'Anyhow, you don't look like a man with that big stomach sticking straight out, not to mention the way you are filling my old jacket.'

The following day began as the previous had ended, with good nature and high hopes to reach the summit. Snow was easier on the oxen than mud.

The Journal of Rebecca Springer

September 29, 1846

I don't mind the cold so much now that the sun is out, and walking is a lot easier since I have accepted trousers. But however fine trousers might be for our circumstances, they provide no modesty for private matters.

It didn't take us long to reach the summit today; in fact, it came as a surprise it had been so near our camp. The trees are so close and dense, there was no way of knowing until the work party clambered up a rise and suddenly could see all around with no other rise in the way. Some claimed they saw the Columbia River, though I doubt it.

Several men have fallen ill after days of wetness and cold. Harriet Stokes also is much afflicted. Sarah swears she is drinking, and I guess I can forgive her for it as it might help take away the chill; we have little other remedy for ague and no way to dry out.

Lord, shed Your warmth on us; it will suffice.

If it had been hard to reach the summit, it would be equally difficult to descend the far side. First, trees had to be cleared as the train was far from any trail that might have existed before the storm. And while the snow had eased their ascent, it would make the way down so slippery there would be the danger that a wagon might get out of hand.

Sarah found a rocky outcropping that had been dried by the sun, and she and Rebecca perched there with Laurie while the men prepared the way. The end now seemed in sight, with the sun shining so brightly it seemed it would melt the snow. Rebecca took the opportunity to tend to her darning, while Sarah scratched letters on to the rock with a sharp stone for Laurie to decipher.

The men stacked felled trees to retain the steeply sloping sides of the new trail. It wasn't safe to use the oxen on such treacherous ground; they had been unhitched, to be later carefully led downhill. The wagons would be lowered by ropes. Most of the men were positioned at the summit as rope handlers, but a few took stances further down, ready to throw log chocks under the wagon wheels when the men on the ropes needed a break.

Rope duty was strenuous, and only the most fit of the men were assigned to it. Even so, the crews could only work in short shifts, spelling each other every few minutes. Not everyone still had gloves to wear; some wrapped rags around their hands to keep the ropes from gouging out deep welts.

John was on the rope crew for the first wagon, and then was sent downhill for the easier job of placing chocks. He looked up and waved to his family on their sunny ledge. They vigorously returned his wave, Laurie quite as happily as if he was his own papa, Sarah thought.

Even with breaks and shifting of jobs, the men were tiring. When the fifth wagon was being let down – slowly and painfully, hand over hand on the ropes – one handler reached the limit of his endurance and collapsed into the snow. Without him pulling his equal share, the other men lost their pace and the ropes began to slip through their hands, first so slowly it seemed they could regain control, but then faster and faster until they burned their skin and it became impossible to retain a grip. A large pine, branches and all, was dragging behind the wagon as a brake, but the pitch was so steep, it accelerated down the hill in spite of it.

Squinting uphill in the sun, John could

spot trouble coming and tried to drag a tree across the trail to stop the wagon. It seemed the sensible thing to do, but the wagon had gained such momentum, it wasn't but seconds before it was almost on top of him. He tried to jump down the sideslope, but his jacket caught on a branch of the tree he'd been hauling.

He tugged at it, and was frantically trying to unbutton it when the wagon pitched sideways over the tree and hit him broadside. It threw him off the trail into a snowbank, which collapsed under him, turning into a miniature avalanche that swept him further down the slope.

It all happened in a flash – and John's family had witnessed it all. They stood frozen for that awful instant, then Sarah began to scramble down the slope, tumbling in the snow, then dragging herself up and slipping and scrabbling her way down further, scraping herself on the pine branches and the ice.

Rebecca numbly watched Sarah for a few moments, then felt she must do something herself. It was difficult to find the words to caution Laurie to remain where he was; harder still to move her legs and try to find her own way down through the snow.

She could barely move and threw off her coat to have more freedom, trying to see some sign of John far below. She fell and rolled to her side, wrapping her arms around her stomach to protect the baby.

When she managed to get to her knees and wipe the snow from her face, she was finally able to locate her husband: the snow hadn't completely buried him, but he was so far away, he was just a dark dot, not seeming to move.

Someone came up behind her and pulled her to her feet. Some other dots that were moving toward John called out, 'He's alive!'

Rebecca murmured her thanks to the Lord and found new energy to push forward until she reached a bend where she could clearly see John – and Sarah plowing through the snow toward him. He looked so still, and was so far away! She knew she would never be able to get down to him without injury to both herself and the baby. She could only stand at the edge of the cliff helplessly, without even enough breath left in her to try to call down some encouragement.

Sarah

When the men hollered out that Papa was still alive, that made me go faster. Now I could see Papa's face between the men round him, and he didn't look good at all.

The men stepped away and I laid down in

the snow next to Papa, pressing myself close to help keep him warm. 'Oh, Papa ... oh, Papa...' was all I could manage to say.

Papa was scarce moving, but he put one arm around me. 'Hush up, Sarah, I am all right.'

I knew he wasn't, with his body so twisted and his face so pale. I had heard him groaning when I came near, but now he was biting back the pain for my sake, so I tried to hold back my tears for his. I could feel his chest rising against me and the sound of it was bad, rattling, and his breath breaking.

One of the men brought a thick blanket and others started to chop down saplings to make a stretcher. But when they tried to move Papa, it caused him such pain he gave a moan, which scared me as I had never heard such a sound coming from him.

'I think it would be best to just leave me here,' he said. 'I am not going to make it.'

I didn't want to hear that. 'You're wrong, Papa!'

Papa was so brave, he even managed a smile. 'You always were a stubborn mule, Sarah, but this time I know better than you.'

I just shook my head and held on to him tighter, but that brought him more pain, so I loosened my grip even though I wanted to cling to him for ever. He put his fingers in my hair like he always did when I needed comforting.

'You are going to have to help Rebecca with the baby, Sarah. I know that is a lot to put on you...'

'We'll be joining up with Joe, Papa, and then we'll send word to Daniel and Matthew and everything's going to be all right! But you just got to stay with us!'

'I am sure that if anybody could get this family back together, it will be you, Sarah. I wish I could see the sight...'

He had to stop and close his eyes with the pain, trying not to moan again, as he knew how it had frightened me. It was becoming harder for him to breathe, and each breath came with another rattle.

'Tell Rebecca that I love her and our baby, and that I apologize to her for not telling her so more often. You know I love you as well, Sarah. There is enough room in my heart for all of you.'

'I know that, Papa.'

'You are a good girl, Sarah; as good as any son I've had.' Papa wanted to say more and I wanted to hear it, but he had run out of breath. I kept my head close to his chest, but the rising and falling was getting slower. When it finally stopped, Papa got cold so quick I started to shiver.

The men were waiting respectfully a few paces off, their hats in their hands, and I knew I shouldn't be keeping them standing in the cold. It was hard to take my arms from Papa and stand up, but I did it, numb with the cold and something more.

The men came forward now, splitting into two around me, then joining again around Papa. I looked up and could see a dark figure on the edge of the trail high above that I knew was Rebecca. That was where my duty was now, not with Papa, who didn't need me any more.

When the men brought him up on the stretcher, Rebecca knew from Sarah's face that John was dead. She tried to take a step toward them, but her knees gave way. Sarah grabbed her under the arms before she fell and the two of them stood locked together until the men put the stretcher down at their feet.

It was a great effort to break away from Sarah's comforting embrace, but Rebecca willed her knees to bend and her body to follow She kissed her husband's lips; they were icy cold and not his any longer. She pressed her face to his cheek and closed her eyes, imagining that the power of love and faith could make the cheek grow warm again.

'He wanted me to tell you he loved you,' Sarah told her. 'And the baby. That was the last thing he said.'

'I love you too,' she whispered, and prayed the Lord would let him hear.

John was a large man, and the men moved

slowly carrying him back to the wagon. They wanted to carry Rebecca as well, but she was determined to walk beside her husband for the last time, mechanically putting one foot in front of the other, not even able to cry.

The Journal of Rebecca Springer

September 30, 1846

I don't know how long ago it was that I closed the wagon flaps and was finally alone with my husband. I washed John's face and cleaned off his clothes as best I could. A pale pink foam was dried on his lips, but there were only a few scratches on his body. The flickering lantern has seemed to give life back to his form – it is impossible that it has departed. I still can't believe he will never speak to me again, or touch me. I have been sitting next to him, holding his hand, and trying to tell him my feelings in a way I regret I never managed in his life. I am setting those feelings down now so that our child will one day know of it, and know that he or she came on to this earth as a testament of devotion.

I told my husband that I didn't think it possible, but I had loved him more and more each day that we had lived together. I told him that love had not been anything I expected at the beginning, and that I was just grateful for his giving me a chance to live out the rest of my life as a married woman, but that all he had said and done had brought out the best in me, which was that I could love someone the way I loved him. I told him I would hold close the rest of my life that he had said he loved me before he went. I only regret I could not hear it with my own ears or tell him the same myself. I didn't think I would see this day for many years to come. I pictured us with our new baby in our new home and then maybe more babies to come. I didn't think it possible it would be otherwise.

You have had Your reasons for doing this, Lord, but I fail to see what they are.

Sarah

I never thought anything could happen to my papa. I always thought no matter what, he would be there. I should have known you couldn't depend on anything after Willie was taken. Rebecca had always said to try to turn the bad away and look for the good, and Papa was always the good for me and I could depend on him to see me through. Now I had only me to be depending on, and I was feeling all alone in the world.

After Rebecca laid out Papa and had her time with him, she kindly gave me my own time, even though I had been the one with him in the end and I felt real sorry she hadn't been able to get to him herself. I told her him and me had prayed together, though it wasn't the truth, but it was a thought that might bring her some comfort, and if Papa had been able to find the words at the end, maybe it would have been to call upon the Lord, so it wasn't really a bad lie.

It was the last I ever would see his face and I looked at him real hard so I would never forget him, though I doubt I ever can. It came to me that it was up to me to take my papa's place in the family now. So I wasn't really alone: I had to take care of Rebecca and the baby and Laurie too.

It was hard to dig a grave in the frozen ground, but John Springer had been a well-respected member of the train and the men who were fit took turns with the shovels, even though their hands were ripped to shreds and their backs ached so much they were bent over. I took it upon myself to organize the service, as Rebecca did not seem capable of thinking of any practical matters and allowed me the lead. Miz Stokes didn't try to boss things neither, as she had got so bad off with the shakes she couldn't even attend.

Papa had taken preaching with a grain of salt, but he had his favorite from Ecclesiastes, and I read it aloud:

'To every thing there is a season, and a time to
every purpose under the heaven:
A time to be born, and a time to die;
A time to plant, and a time to pluck up that
which is planted;
A time to kill, and a time to heal;
A time to break down, and a time to build up;
A time to weep, and a time to laugh;
A time to mourn, and a time to dance...'

I didn't get any comfort from the words, but honor had to be paid to my papa, though God has a lot to answer for in my mind.

Snow started to fall again during the burial; at least a foot within one hour. It was impossible to do any work, so the train remained split, with four wagons at the bottom of the hill and the rest still on the top, which meant camp was made on the summit, even though it was not well sheltered. A steady wind soon mounded drifts of snow high enough to cover the wagon wheels, and those men who hadn't taken sick from the cold made makeshift crews to clear paths between the wagons to maintain communication.

Whoever wasn't on duty just sat in the wagons, which were dark and thick with the smells of damp clothing and unwashed bodies. Nobody went out except to empty their slop buckets. They chewed on what was left of the oxen feast and waited for the storm to blow itself out – and hoped it wouldn't take long to do so.

The long hours confined inside the wagon without any possibility of activity were agony for Rebecca. Hard work helped dull the pain when she'd lost Elizabeth and Margaret, but what she was feeling now was a hundred times stronger. There was Harriet Stokes to tend to, which gave her some concern other than herself. Captain Stokes had moved out of their wagon to avoid catching his wife's contagion, which had steadily worsened. Several of the men were as bad off as Harriet, and a sick-wagon was set aside for them.

The only available relief was to drape a cloth over their heads so they might inhale the vapors from a pan of boiling water mixed with herbs. The heavy snowfall made it difficult to maintain a strong fire, but Sarah coaxed the coals high enough to boil several kettles. These she placed on both Harriet's and the sick-wagon's tailgates every few hours.

But heating water could only take up so much time. Mostly it was talk that helped to count off the hours. Rebecca could find little to say, and Tom was naturally quiet. Sarah tried to fill the silence with chatter, often engaging Laurie in conversation.

'What did you do when you were a little

girl?' he asked her. 'Did you have a dolly like the girls in Albany?'

'I didn't play with dolls.'

Laurie was unbelieving. 'Then what did you do?'

'I played with my brothers, Willie and Joe. Do you remember them?'

Laurie shook his head. A child's memory was so short! So Sarah told him at length and in detail about her brothers and all they did together. A few of her memories were also Rebecca's, shared with her husband. It sent daggers into Rebecca's heart to have those moments recaptured, but it was a sweet agony; each memory allowed her to see John again, if only in her mind.

'We used to pretend we were overlanders going to Oregon,' Sarah told Laurie. 'Can you imagine that? We dreamed about being on a wagon just like this one. We called them "prairie schooners", which didn't mean much to me until one time we saw a line of wagons on its way to Oregon, far off across the fields. We could only see the tops, the grain was so high, and they looked just like they were sails moving through a waving sea of wheat. See, a schooner is a kind of boat. My papa explained it to me.'

'I know that,' Laurie said indignantly. '*My* daddy told me, too! He had a book with pictures in it. He used to read to me. Every night. Mommy, too.'

'You are lucky, as I had nobody who read to me when I was little,' Sarah said.

'Were you an orphan like Tom?' Laurie asked. 'Mommy read to him 'cause he didn't have anybody neither.'

It was perpetually dark in the wagon, so Tom's reaction, sitting quietly in one corner, remained hidden.

'Oh, I had lots of folks around back then, but they weren't the reading type. Then your ma showed me all about reading and now I don't know what I ever did without it.'

'I can read,' Laurie said proudly.

'And you'll be reading even better, and writing long sentences, too. Me and Rebecca will see to that, only Rebecca is a lot better than me at it.'

Sarah hoped to draw Rebecca into the conversation.

'I mean that, Rebecca,' she said firmly, trying to hold her eye. 'Margaret wanted Laurie educated, and if it is left up to me, he will be a disgrace.'

There was no denying Sarah. 'Only in his grammar and spelling,' Rebecca said. 'Your hand has become right graceful.'

Sarah looked pleased. 'I am thinking of taking up Mr Shakespeare's *Taming of the Shrew*. It is one of the comedies, and I could use some cheering after everybody dying in *Romeo and Juliet*.'

'Yes, so could I,' Rebecca admitted.

'And Tom, too,' Sarah added, warming to her subject. 'He has his reasons to be low as well.'

Tom was part of their small family now. He had already become the only man in Laurie's life, and now he had tacitly assumed Sarah and Rebecca as his responsibilities as well. Ironically, his family had grown as theirs had vanished.

The Journal of Rebecca Springer

October 3, 1846

When Sarah took hot water to Harriet Stokes this morning, there was no answer to her call.

She climbed inside the wagon and found Harriet already rigid. Captain Stokes and his remaining sons accepted the news as well as could be expected. Two of the sick men also died overnight.

As there is now over three feet of snow on top of the frozen ground, there was no consideration of digging graves. The dead were placed in a spare wagon until we can reach lower ground. This has made everyone in the company uneasy and I do not like to think of Harriet's body mixed with the men's, though I know this is foolish as the dead have no modesty. Captain Stokes tried to get Reverend Bingham to at least offer a few prayers for the departed to ease our minds.

'It is not just for my family,' Captain Stokes said, 'but for everyone; they need to feel there is still some order.'

'I apologize for not doing better by you,' Reverend Bingham told him, 'but God will no longer listen to me.'

As the bodies soon froze, there is no fear of putrefaction.

With Harriet gone, Sarah and I are the only women left in the company. I used to think I would be lonely without other women around me. But I don't miss having other women about as much as I miss having a husband.

Sleep is the only real release for me. In my dreams, I am still back home and John is still alive. I wonder if Sarah dreams of standing with Willie and John looking at the mighty Pacific Ocean?

Lord, grant me more sleep. I can no longer try to count my blessings. Why have You taken so much from me? I cannot fathom Your intent.

It stopped snowing and the men started to move the wagons again. They cleared a short way with their shovels, moved the wagons, then shovelled again. At least the heavy accumulation of snow made it easier to lower the rest of the wagons down the mountain, as it acted as a natural brake.

After the wagons and oxen had packed down the snow, it was not difficult to walk. It did Laurie good to be outside, as his damaged leg had stiffened from inactivity.

They didn't make a mile, but it felt like real accomplishment to reunite with the other four wagons, which were buried in the snow. Three were shovelled free, but the fourth was one of Captain Stokes' and it was broken up for kindling. Much of what it carried had been Harriet's household possessions, and these went into the fire as well. The other wood around was so wet, it was hard to keep a good fire going.

Captain Stokes' decision to volunteer to torch his valuable property to keep his company warm was a token of expiation. He was responsible for their predicament and knew he was losing the men's respect. Rebecca could sense the ebb of authority and wished John were there. She was never frightened when she knew she could call on him.

Sarah

We were growing short of food. One of the men killed a skunk and cooked it, but no one would share his meal.

'It's them goats we should be cooking,'

one of the Stokes sons declared. 'They are of no use except to fill out our ribs a little.'

I was mad as I could be over that. 'Laurie needs his milk! Rebecca too!'

'They waller in the snow and always have to be dug up.'

'It's me that's doing the digging, so it's no concern of anybody else.'

I waved Papa's shovel at him as proof, prepared to use it as a weapon if a finger was laid on those goats.

Charlie Stokes backed off. 'I was just supposing.'

'Well, suppose in another direction.'

In the end, an ox that was too feeble to go on much further was killed for food. He was our Lucky and his dying made me feel even more gloomy.

There was only Jack left from our teams now, but it was either Lucky or the goats the way the mood was going, and I figgered the goats were worth more.

It was impossible to keep the cold away. Although she had sworn to herself to keep it for Oregon, Rebecca unpacked her friendship quilt and tucked it around her knees. She stared at the patterns on the quilt, running her fingers over the stitches and remembering her lost friendships. She also wore John's coat for warmth – the same one he had died in. She smelled him in it still and tried not to let her sorrow choke her.

Sarah kept up her chatter. 'From the top of the mountain, it looked like it would be all downhill. Of course it isn't, but there are more downs than ups now.'

Rebecca had been doing her mending, but now she put it carefully aside. 'Well, ups or downs, there is not much we can do about it except keep going. Sarah, I think I have reached my time.'

Sarah stared at her, dumbstruck. 'I am trying to get you to where we're going in one piece to have that baby – you can't be having it right here and now!'

Rebecca nodded, concentrating on what she was experiencing, as she folded up the mending. She checked to see that a knot was well tied here and a basket squared there as she waited for the next spasm.

'What should we be doing?' Sarah asked nervously.

'I think I should just keep on as I am. I have been told first babies are liable to take a good long time and maybe this is just a false alarm. I probably shouldn't have said anything about it, except that it took me by surprise.'

'What took you by surprise? What are you feeling right now? Is it still happening?'

'That's too many questions,' Rebecca said, with a faint smile that would have reassured Sarah if she hadn't been so agitated. 'Maybe

371

it would be good to just walk along the wagons for a while and see what happens.'

The wagons had packed the snow, and it wasn't difficult to walk alongside them, even though they were still gradually descending. Sarah was nervous, keeping an eye out as they walked. She wanted to be ready to jump in and snatch up the baby if it suddenly dropped out. She knew better from her conversations with Margaret, but couldn't help the thought, she was so worried. Rebecca was in a detached state, not seeming anxious, but frowning as if she were straining to catch something hard to hear.

They walked some way, slowly enough for Laurie, who poked at snowdrifts with a stick. When a rabbit darted out, all three hollered, but it disappeared before anyone could shoot it for supper.

The train stopped well before the sun set; the temperature had dropped considerably and the men were fatigued. Rebecca carefully climbed back into the wagon while Sarah saw about dinner; now that the snow had stopped, she was able to prepare something hot. Laurie stood by the fire to get warm, but he knew not to get too close. While the rice cooked, Sarah warmed up Rebecca's flatiron, then wrapped it in a blanket and took it into the wagon.

'Put this on your feet. How are you coming along?'

'I guess I should be happy these pains are coming on regular as clockwork, because that is how they should be.'

Sarah looked alarmed, and Rebecca tried to make her feel easier. 'They are still far apart. All we can do is sit and wonder what is going to happen next since both of us are new at this.'

'Well, you don't seem too scared about it.'

'There's no use fretting, Sarah, as there's nothing to be done but endure it. As long as there is another woman with me, I know I can bear it.'

'You can count on me, Rebecca – I had good learning from Margaret on the subject just in case it came down to me.'

'I reckon it has, Sarah, and I appreciate you have had the foresight, as I have not had much myself.'

'I will see you through. What can I do?'

'Just talking helps.'

'Well, then, we will talk once I fetch our supper.'

After the rice, mixed with jerky, had been eaten, Laurie settled down by Sarah, snuggling up like a kitten and nodding off immediately.

Sarah thought hard of a subject of interest and decided on one of Rebecca's favorites, which was the need for cleanliness. 'I'm going to have to see to Laurie's hair – it's all sticky and full of woodsmoke.'

'I would love to wash my hair,' Rebecca mused, running her fingers across the top of her head. Her hair was so matted, she couldn't separate the locks.

'You have been fussing over your hair ever since I met you.'

'It is my best feature ... or it used to be.'

'I wouldn't say that.'

Rebecca shifted uncomfortably and gritted her teeth. She closed her eyes and tried to concentrate on something other than the pain she was feeling. 'Rainwater ... that's best for washing ... maybe a little borax when the water is hard or some lavender scent ... and giving it a treatment now and then with castor oil mixed with whiskey. I don't know why I am acting the expert, as that is the sum total of my beauty receipts.'

'Well, I would say it has been quite enough. You are a fine-looking woman, Rebecca.'

'And you are a liar. You never used to be one before, except when it served your own purposes.'

'Well, maybe that is true, but this time I do mean it.' She saw Rebecca wince and tried to keep on with the topic. 'And I am sure that is not all you know. Tell me more, as I might want to be taking better care of myself once we settle down.'

'Well, when I was washing regularly, I always put a few drops of spirits of ammonia in my washing-up water to prevent odor.'

'Sure wish we could be doing that now.'

'Some women use sour milk as a skin bleach at night, and there are store-bought salves made up of white wax and sweet oil,' Rebecca continued, frowning with another spasm. 'Honey's good for the hands – and for softening up the teats of a milk cow, too ... or putting into soap.'

'I guess it all comes down to soap.'

Rebecca screwed up her face. 'It is hard for me to go on talking nonsense. Maybe you should see if Tom can take Laurie for a spell. I don't think I can go on much longer without agitating him.'

Sarah ran out to rouse Tom. The men were so exhausted, they had long since been sleeping, several sharing a wagon so their combined body heat could sustain them through the night.

Laurie scarcely stirred when Tom carried him over to his wagon, though he whimpered when the cold hit his face in transit. 'This child is moving in with us for the time being,' Tom told his bunkmates, 'so you better watch your language, and that goes for talking in your sleep.'

As soon as they had left, Rebecca gave in to the pain, panting in animal-like fashion. It frightened Sarah when she saw a wet patch growing on Rebecca's pant legs, but then she remembered it must be her waters breaking and helped her remove her britches and roll off the wet blanket. She laid down a dry one, and tried to put another over Rebecca's naked legs.

Rebecca shook it off. 'Take a look and tell me if my baby is being born. It sure feels like it!'

Sarah felt awkward and couldn't figure out what she was looking for at first, but then it dawned on her that the baby's head was pulsing between Rebecca's blood-streaked legs.

'I see it! I see it!' she yelled excitedly.

'See what?' Rebecca panted. 'And you don't need to yell.'

'The baby!' Sarah yelled. 'And it's got black hair!'

Rebecca didn't reply; she was too busy working, trying to push the baby out.

Once the head emerged, the rest of the baby slipped out easily. It didn't look alive, but Sarah remembered what Margaret had told her and stuck a finger in its mouth to clear it, blew on its face, then gave it a smack on the back. It started to cry, and Sarah cried with it in relief, but she still had to cut the cord and tie it off.

Rebecca always kept the medicine chest handy, but Sarah felt so shaky, the job seemed to take for ever. It wasn't until she laid the baby on Rebecca's chest that she saw it was a girl. And it wasn't until then that she started breathing halfway normally herself.

The Journal of Rebecca Springer

October 10, 1846

Johanna Elizabeth Springer was born today. She has surprised me by more than a month but Sarah says she is just like herself – impatient to get going. It is right for her to be named for her father, because her name will keep him alive in her mind each time she is called. It is a good name too, from the Bible. Her second name will always remind us both of my dear Lizzie, whom I pray she will be able to meet one day.

I have examined all parts of Johanna and she is perfect in every way. She has her father's coloring and hair, which is to be expected as it runs so strongly in the family, but I think her nose is more like my side. Sarah swears she and Johanna have the same eyes and I agree with her as it pleases her so much.

Sarah fetched me the new Bible from the trunk. I didn't think we would be bringing it out again so soon after entering John's death, and I am happy to note an arrival instead of a passing. My tears have finally come back to me, but they are of joy.

Lord, I suspect You have sent Johanna a bit early to bring me comfort. Thank You.

Sarah

It wasn't but an hour or so after Johanna's birthing that Tom gave a low whistle from outside.

'I know it is still the middle of the night,' he said when I poked my head out, 'but I ain't grabbed but a few winks for worrying.'

'We have ourselves a fine baby girl. Her name's Johanna and she and Rebecca's both sleeping.'

'Laurie is dead to the world, too. Our wagon stinks, but it's right warm. You be needing anything?'

'You will be sorry you asked, Tom.'

Tom fetched hot water so I could do a more thorough cleaning, and warmed up the flatiron and a skillet as well, so I could make certain Johanna didn't catch a chill, even though the wagon was close.

In the morning, I cleared the snow from around the goats to do a milking, then started breakfast. Rebecca was able to wake up to the smell of hot gruel made of cornmeal and goat's milk.

'I am quite ready to get up and help,' she said. 'I am not sick.'

'You still have a heavy flow and it isn't good

for your milk to be trying to rush about.'

'Sarah Springer, you are sounding quite like an experienced midwife.'

'And I figure that is what I am now. Eat your breakfast. It is your job to become an experienced mother.'

'I reckon mothering is something that just comes natural.'

Before we commenced to get going again, Captain Stokes and the other men came to offer their congratulations. They all acted like they were right pleased, but I knew they were thinking Johanna didn't have much of a chance out in the wilderness. I didn't allow anyone too close for fear of contagion.

When we got underway, I took Laurie to walk by the wagons so Rebecca and Johanna could rest. I was glad for once we were barely moving and that soft snow took out whatever bumps there might have been. Me and Laurie were able to go to the lead wagon and back before the train gained twenty feet.

The trees that were cleared got piled up and set on fire. The green wood sent up clouds of greasy smoke, but it was right warm.

The men claimed they didn't mind drinking plain hot water when they took a break, but I added what was left of the bones and gristle from poor Lucky's carcass to give a bit of flavor. Everyone else put what they could find into the common pot and the men on break cared for those who were still working. There was no consideration of what might be called women's work and what was men's, as I was the only able woman left and they knew I had to be taking care of Rebecca and Johanna, not to mention Laurie.

Rebecca wasn't sure if her milk had come in strongly enough, but she imagined that all babies cried. She didn't know if it was normal to feel so weak or still have such a flow. Her own mother had never taken but one day in bed until her last child, but that was the one that had ruined her good health. She had questions that Sarah could not answer, and there was no other woman to consult.

It felt stifling in the wagon; she could scarcely breathe. It couldn't be healthy for Johanna. If only she could go outside! The cold might slow her flow – she was going through so many rags Sarah could scarcely keep up with a fresh supply.

Sarah scoured the medicine chest for something to help. But there had been so much illness in the train, most of the contents had been used.

'What about a nip of whiskey?' she suggested.

'You know that cure is worse than sickness to me.'

'It's downright warming – and I was thinking for the purpose of celebrating as well. If

Papa was here, he'd consider you bringing Johanna into the world a right special occasion.'

Just the mention of John's name made Rebecca cry. Her tears had returned, and now she didn't seem able to stop them. She dabbed at her eyes with her shawl. 'I am sorry, Sarah; I seem to have lost control over both my body and my emotions.'

'That is just natural for a woman in your state,' Sarah said, looking wise. 'We should be marking Johanna's birth day, Rebecca, and if you're not up to it, I will do it myself.'

Sarah made a show of toasting Johanna. It was her first taste of whiskey and it made her gasp.

'It *is* right warming!' she said, trying to cover up her choking and offering Rebecca the bottle.

'Tea would be better,' Rebecca said. 'I will add some of the plants we collected with the squaws.'

Sarah made a brew of the leaves and stems Rebecca selected. Rebecca swore that it gave her relief. Sarah didn't tell her, but she had slipped a drop of whiskey into her tea.

She took the bottle outside and passed it around to the men, all of whom took a nip in honor of Johanna. Some were eager to take more than just a nip, but Sarah made sure at least an inch was left in the bottom for future medicinal use.

Rebecca slept heavily. Sarah replaced her bloody rags, rinsing them out in a bucket of melted snow, then used a separate bucket to soak Johanna's napkins. She wrung everything out as dry as she could and strung a washline inside the wagon, then sorted through the bedlinen, ripping up the most worn to make more rags and napkins.

She went outside again to retrieve Laurie from Tom's care; as good as Tom was, he had his own work and Laurie was her responsibility.

Wolves were howling somewhere. 'I am worried about the goats,' she told Tom. 'They will either get eaten or buried alive in the snow if I leave them outside. I better bring them into the wagon.'

'I should put them in my wagon. It can't smell any worse.'

'I need them close at hand for Rebecca and Laurie. It will be a convenience.'

'Most folks wouldn't look on sharing a bed with two goats as a convenience!'

Sarah was glad to see he had some humor in him. He was always so serious, and had become even more so since Margaret's death.

It wasn't easy getting the goats into the wagon, even with Tom helping. Sarah tied them close to the box and Tom brought in some young pine boughs for bedding and to soak up their piss.

Laurie thought it a treat to have his pets so

close at hand, but their bleating disturbed Johanna, who began to cry. Sarah had to help Rebecca sit up to nurse her, and she worried she had put too much whiskey in the tea.

The bedding beneath Rebecca was soaked with blood and she was shivering, even though her forehead burned with fever. She couldn't bring much comfort to Johanna, who turned her head away from the nipple and continued to mew.

Sarah crawled over to the goats and did a quick milking. After a few fits and starts, Joanna understood to suck the milk off the end of a rag and went back to sleep after she was changed.

Sarah took the axe and filled a water bucket with chips of ice, which she wrapped in towels. She placed one across Rebecca's forehead and packed the others around her stomach. But the ice did nothing to slow down Rebecca's bleeding, only making her shiver more.

'Lay down next to her,' Sarah instructed Laurie, as she removed the ice packs. 'It will help both of you keep warm. Rebecca is just feeling a little sick. She will be fine by and by. I have to go out again for a spell, so don't move an inch, even if Johanna bawls her head out.'

She didn't trust leaving Johanna in the basket with the goats around, so strapped her into a sling lined with rabbit fur and hung it high on the wagon frame, out of harm's way.

Another snowstorm had blown up and Sarah had to force her way to Captain Stokes' wagon. She could scarcely recognize him among the men packed closely together in the narrow confine. His ragged beard dripped ice and his eyes were red. Black streaks ran down his cheeks from the charcoal he'd rubbed under his sockets to help cut the snow glare. His feet were so swollen with the chill, he couldn't get his boots on and had wrapped them with rags. The other men were in much the same condition and the stench coming off them was made worse by the shaved bark tobacco they were smoking. But at least their bodies put a warmth in the wagon that took the edge off Sarah's own chill.

'Rebecca's in a bad way,' she said. 'She's been bleeding ever since the baby came.'

'You tried something cold?' Captain Stokes said. 'That did the trick for my wife, rest her soul.'

'Ain't nothing that ain't cold around here,' a man said. Sarah couldn't recognize him, everyone's appearance had changed so much.

'A knife edge's good for staunching a cut,' a second man suggested.

'Ain't that kind of cut,' a third man told him.

It was only Tom who offered help in the end, and there wasn't much he could do but muck out after the goats and help move Rebecca on to fresh bedding.

'I will take Laurie for a spell over to my wagon again – we ain't going nowhere in this snow and I been promising to whittle him a hobby horse.'

'That would be a blessing, Tom. I can't take the time to coddle him.'

After bundling Laurie off, Sarah took Johanna down from her high nest and tied her to her chest with the rabbit fur. She could feel her tiny heart beating next to hers. There was still some warmth in a jug of broth she'd kept wrapped in a blanket, and even though Rebecca spluttered and choked, she swallowed at least some of it.

'Johanna...' she murmured. Sarah no longer hoped whiskey was the cause of her stupor.

'I've her strapped to me to keep her warm.'

She untied the bundle and laid the baby on Rebecca's chest. Rebecca tried to stroke Johanna's fine hair, but the effort was too much, so she just cupped her hand around her skull.

'Sarah ... I have made so much work for you...'

'I am only making up for the grief I have caused you along the way.'

'Johanna will be safe with you.'

'I will keep her safe and warm until you are better. She seems to be taking to goat milk, so she is already better than me.'

'Make a home for John in Oregon ... it means so much to him...'

Sarah was taken aback: did she think her papa was still with them? Maybe she just meant to make that home in his memory so he could look down from Heaven and feel a part of it. Sarah was planning to tell Rebecca as much when she said, 'I am letting you both down... I am sorry...'

The Journal of Rebecca Springer

October 13, 1846

These words are being writ by Sarah Springer. Rebecca Springer is with us no more. She passed away today, somewhere in the Blue Mountains. She has reached Oregon, even if she has not made it all the way.

I don't think she would mind if I used her pages to tell the end of her own story.

She was a good woman, always trying to do her best by everyone without thinking of herself, and always harder on herself than anybody else. She went out of this life thinking she hadn't done what she could, but that is not true. She did the best under the conditions.

I hope my lack of knowledge didn't have anything to do with it.

Sarah

Rebecca's dying happened so sudden I couldn't take it in. I had been so busy I didn't see how badly she was slipping, or maybe I just didn't want to see. One minute she was talking to me in a way that didn't make much sense, and then the next she was gone and what she had been saying suddenly made sense. I went on sitting there for a spell, leaving Johanna lying on her chest as she needed to say her goodbye to her mama too. Then I let her suck on some more goat milk and I took care of her duty and put her back to bed hanging up on the wagon frame.

It had always been up to the women to do the laying out when somebody died in the train, and now it was down to me, but I wouldn't have let anybody else touch Rebecca anyways. I wrapped her in the friendship quilt her friends had made for her before we left Indiana. It was all she had left of that home she had never wanted to leave and only fitting she should keep one part of it with her for ever.

Now that I finally have ears to listen and

eyes to see, I know Rebecca must have been hurting inside all those months on the trail. I was so excited about what lay ahead, I never gave it a thought some others might not share my own convictions. I have regrets over all that time I wasted not doing right by her, and it is no excuse to say I didn't know our time together would be so short.

It is sad to think Rebecca will remain in the mountains all alone and far from those she loved. She loved my papa, though, and he is resting in the same mountains, so at least they are together.

I would not let Rebecca get put with the other dead folks, all piled together in a wagon. The men had kept fires going along the trail they were cutting, and Tom helped me clear away the charred logs from one. The ground underneath had thawed enough for him to break it up with a pickaxe, but it was still hard going. I helped by prying up the rocks with a bar. As tuckered out as the men were, it still shamed them to see a woman doing such hard work and a few pitched in. They all had respect for Rebecca as she never treated anyone badly, and if they were short on their rations or ruined their own dinner, she had always invited them to our table.

I read from Rebecca's Bible – I had already writ in her dates under my papa's in my best hand. She always had God on her mind and it wouldn't have done to put her to earth without Him, though I wasn't of a mind to pray, and of course Reverend Bingham was of no use.

This is what I read from the Book of Proverbs:

'Who can find a virtuous woman? for her price is far above rubies.

The heart of her husband doth safely trust in her, so that he shall have no need of spoil.

She will do him good and not evil all the days of her life.

She seeketh wool, and flax, and worketh willingly with her hands.

She riseth also while it is yet night, and giveth meat to her household, and a portion to her maidens.

She layeth her hands to the spindle, and her hands hold the distaff.

She stretcheth out her hand to the poor; yea, she reacheth forth her hands to the needy.

Strength and honour are her clothing; and she shall rejoice in time to come.

She openeth her mouth with wisdom; and in her tongue is the law of kindness.

She looketh well to the ways of her household, and eateth not the bread of idleness.

Her children arise up, and call her blessed; her husband also, and he praiseth her;

Many daughters have done virtuously, but thou excellest them all.

Favor is deceitful, and beauty is vain; but a

woman that feareth the Lord, she shall be praised.
Give her of the fruit of her hands; and let her own works praise her in the gates.'

This has been the Devil to copy out from the Bible, but if it doesn't sum up Rebecca, I don't know what does.

The men were hot to take advantage of a lull in the storm, so went back to felling trees and moving the wagons forward after Rebecca's burial. But only a few yards were gained before the snow began to fall in thick sheets.

'You want to come into our wagon for a spell?' Sarah asked Tom. 'I don't feel like being on my own just now.'

They sat side by side for warmth, Tom whittling for Laurie and Sarah holding a rag for Johanna to suck.

'It is strange to think Johanna is my sister,' Sarah said. 'I keep thinking of her as my baby.'

'I guess we are all orphans now,' Tom said.

'At least I have Johanna. But you have no blood relation, Tom.'

'Blood ain't everything.'

'I suppose not. I reckon Laurie is bound to you as much as Johanna is to me, so he's really your family.'

She could tell that had hit home with Tom, as he pushed one of the goats away from where it was trying to nibble the ragged sole of his boot.

'You know we are all in the same fix when it comes to food,' he said, trying to change the subject. 'We'll kill another ox if we have to, but we're depending on them to get us out of here. I don't know how long you're gonna be able to keep these goats.'

'Johanna can't stomach any other kind of food. As long as they keep producing, they're staying.'

'Well, I will go along with you in standing up for Johanna. I just wanted you to know how hard things are getting.'

'You think I've been so busy with my own affairs I didn't see the men smoking wood-mice out of logs and roasting them?'

'They say they are better than skunk.'

'I bet no one of us would pass up a skunk now.'

The company boiled deer and buffalo hides for soup, along with what scrapings of vegetables and grain were still in the sacks, and then the sacks were boiled up separately and fed to the oxen, who needed nourishment as much as the humans. But only the goats did well on this type of diet; the oxen needed grass or grain and they were barely alive.

After a week of almost continuous snow-storms, they had progressed such a short distance, Sarah could've still paid Rebecca's grave a visit if the drifts weren't so deep.

As Tom had predicted, Captain Stokes came after the goats, and Sarah stood firm.

'An ox would stretch a lot farther than these goats, and I don't see as how it matters anyway. We are never going to get these wagons down the mountains.'

He gave her a sharp look, but she didn't break her lock on his eyes. Then he turned around and walked away. A few minutes later, she heard the bellow of an ox as an axe struck deep into its throat.

While sometimes the snow intensified into a whirling white torrent, other times it stopped altogether – but, as a mean trick, only at night when they couldn't see far enough ahead to use the opportunity to make some headway.

Another ox was killed, which meant another wagon was broken up for firewood as there wasn't a team left to pull it. They weren't starving yet, but it looked like winter had settled in for a good long spell.

Tom was almost always with Sarah, taking over when he saw she was close to her limit trying to keep Johanna and Laurie clean and fed and warm. Laurie's spirits had sunk and he now cried almost as much as Johanna. Sarah worried the goats' milk was not suiting her.

'I don't know why you don't just bunk with us,' she finally told Tom. 'It would be a damn sight easier.'

Tom looked flustered by her suggestion, so to save him embarrassment she added, 'I forgot your feelings about goats.' After all they had been through together, he was still just about the shyest person she had ever met. 'At least let me do something for you for a change,' she urged.

'I don't have nothing needs doing.'

'I could give you a shave – Rebecca used to do it for Papa when all the mirrors got broke.'

Tom looked as wild as any mountain man now.

'I thank you, Sarah, but this beard of mine, as sorry as it is, is keeping my cheeks and chin from freezing off.'

'If that's the case, I guess I will not mind you going on looking like a muskrat, but it's a shame I can't do the same, as my whole face is froze up.'

They had a laugh over the thought of her with a beard, then just sat a while more without talking.

'What are you thinking?' Sarah finally asked, as talking was about the only activity they could do.

'Remembering how things was back when everyone was still with us.'

She knew he was thinking of Margaret. 'I liked when we all used to pass Margaret's Shakespeare around and read,' she recalled. 'My eyes are too far gone from the snow glare to be reading much now, but maybe I could teach you to play chess, Tom – remember when she learned me?'

'Yep, but I am too dumb to learn it.'

'I am far more ignorant than you, and I caught on. There is little else to do and that is a fine set you carved.'

Sarah

Playing chess helped pass the endless hours. Even when the snow fell so thick it was almost like midnight in the wagon, we could feel the pieces. I kept saying to myself that if we hung on just one more day, the sun would break out and things would get better, but it didn't and they didn't.

Captain Stokes finally stirred himself enough to call the men together. That meant everybody in the company except me, which didn't make any sense, so I was invited along as well.

'If we continue to sit here doing nothing we will be lost for sure,' he said. 'We need volunteers to try to walk down the mountain to find some help. I would go myself, but I am too old to make it.'

'There ain't much chance anyone can make it,' one man said.

'And there's no chance unless we try,' another said.

Tom was one of the fitter men, and I could tell that he was torn in his feelings.

'Tom, I know you want to go,' I told him.

'I got to take care of you and the children.'

'The best way to do that is by finding a way to get us out of here. If anyone can do it, you are the one.'

That fixed it for him, and he and three other of the huskier men made up the rescue party. They were given the best cuts of the latest ox that had been slaughtered, along with a shotgun, blankets, shovels and a pickaxe.

They lashed the gear to a sled made from a half-barrel and wrapt their feet in more blankets, then slowly made their way down through the woods, taking turns at the lead to break the snow, with the last man cutting blazes in the trees to mark a way back.

The rest of us shaded our eyes against the glare, no matter how much it stung, trying to keep track of them, but even as slow as they were going, the thick piney woods and the whirling snow soon swallowed them up, even muffling the sound of their axes.

The loneliness practically swallowed me after Tom left. It was just more sitting and waiting and no Tom to talk to. I missed having him there to share some small secrets or minor complaints (it didn't do no one any good to really bellyache) – even sometimes a joke. Tom and me had got into almost the same habits as me and Rebecca, and without continuing on with such habits, I felt her loss even more keenly. Lord, but I was lonely.

Laurie had got lice from spending time in the men's wagon, and I was able to occupy myself a bit combing the nits out of his hair, which was so tangled he bawled and hollered, but I cut out the worst snarls, and once the rest hung straight, he started to get some comfort from my brushing. And it gave me solace that I was keeping him and Johanna as fit as possible under the circumstances.

But I couldn't stop thinking of Rebecca and how I could have done better by her and then maybe she wouldn't have died. I began to dwell on how very little I knew and my general ignorance, and that was a dangerous thing to do as it put me down mighty low.

It was hard just holding on to my senses with the children crying almost constant, so I found myself sleeping when Johanna did, which was a great deal of the time. I lost track of how many days the men had gone walking off, but I had reached bottom and it didn't seem to matter. I couldn't hardly move now except to take care of natural functions and clean up after the others. My only thought was to keep the children alive, and to do that trick I had to go on living myself.

Some of the men that were still in decent health got in the habit of going down the mountainside as far as they could without losing their way. It gave them something to do more than just waiting. They'd tie bits of colored cloth to the trees or cut more slashes on the bark to show the way back to the wagons. With the snow almost continuous, there wasn't a trace left of the trail made by Tom and the others. When the wind wasn't howling, they hollered out, asking if anyone was out there.

And finally one day, someone hollered back.

When they heard a commotion outside, the remainder of the train emerged from their snow-covered wagons, resembling a strange tribe of half-human snow creatures. They were all so weak and light headed, it took a time for them to realize the men hadn't come back up the hill by themselves. Then everyone began to shout and laugh and cry all at the same time. Like the rest of the company, Sarah was suffering from snow blindness and had to squint hard to make out the shape of someone on a horse coming toward her. When it grew closer, she could make out a man wrapped in an ice-covered blanket. There were a couple of other men on horses behind him and a string of mules following them.

It wasn't until he stopped in front of her and climbed down from the horse – in fact he had to rub the icicles from his beard first – that she recognized Ben Cooper!

'Are you an angel come from Heaven to take us?' she stammered.

'Sarah, don't you know I am headed for the hotter place?'

'It is you! It is really you!'

She grabbed him in a bear hug, but was too weak to do any damage. 'How did you find us?'

'It was us that got found by the party you sent down.'

'Where is Tom? Did he make it all right?'

Ben nodded. 'He and the others got themselves almost all the way down the mountain before they bumped into us, and it was a good thing they did, as they was frost-bit and close to starvation. We sent 'em on so they could get doctored up.'

A celebration broke out to rival the Fourth of July, everyone feasting on biscuits, cheese, and smoked fish. The rescue party warned they'd get sick if they ate too much at one sitting, but they ignored the warning; no one cared if they got sick if it was from something that tasted so good.

Sarah took Ben into the wagon to show him Johanna.

'I want to hear all your adventures, Ben.'

'What has happened to you, Sarah, has put my troubles to shame. I am so glad to see you again, I have half a mind to give you a good hug myself.'

'Well, that would be fine by me.'

'It was the food and water you brung me kept me going.'

Sarah still felt ashamed. 'Half of it was from Nellie Bingham. It has been on my conscience a long time that I kept that fact from you.'

'Tom told me about Nellie dying, and I heard more of your troubles when I was finally able to get myself to The Dalles.'

'You got all the way to the Columbia River on your own?'

Ben nodded. 'I was looking to raft down to Oregon City, but the injuns charged so much I had to find some work to save up the fee. Folks'd come in now and then saying they had seen you, but then I stopped getting news. When you was so long overdue, this party got made up to go looking for you.'

'Folks knew about us? I figgered we had just plumb disappeared!'

'I reckon there ain't nobody don't have someone worrying for them somewheres.'

'I am glad it was you doing the worrying, Ben, or otherwise we might never have got ourselves rescued.'

'It was these other folks was the ones knew where to look.'

'But you came with them and that's what counts. You don't know what it feels like to see someone you ... you thought was dead.'

'Well, I am glad to have brung you that pleasure, Sarah. And I am sure you will find the others in your family that's been lost to you. I'm damned sorry about the ones you can't.'

'You hear any word about Joe?'

'No, but that don't mean nothing.'

Sarah was fast regaining her spirit. 'If you could find us, Ben, I will find him – and Daniel and Elizabeth too. This mountain got me down, but I am sure not staying there!'

The rescue party was anxious to head back down off the mountain before they became completely snowed in. The company was allowed to take what they could manage to load on the back of a mule, three people to an animal. Sarah didn't have much beyond the clothes on her back except for Rebecca's journals and Bible and Margaret's books. It made for a heavy bundle, but the mules were sturdy. She argued that with two children she merited one whole mule, no matter how tiny they might be. Being the only woman, she was given her way.

She carried Johanna in her sling. Ben strapped Laurie behind her, and the goats trailed behind on tethers. Some of the weaker men were also strapped on to mules, but the rest walked. The wagons were left behind and the oxen shot out of mercy.

'We got some two hundred miles to go before we hit The Dalles,' Hiram Oakes, the leader of the rescue party, told Captain Stokes. 'It's no trip for small children.'

Sarah didn't make any bones about overhearing. 'This child has made it thus far and the baby isn't going to be walking.'

'The Whitman mission isn't far from the foot of the mountains,' Oakes explained. 'That will be the best place for you and the children.'

'Those missionaries will want to take the children away from me.'

'Narcissa Whitman has taken in many orphans,' Mr Oakes resassured her. 'They'll be in good hands.'

'Johanna's my sister,' Sarah replied, 'and Laurie isn't an orphan because his mother left him to me, which should mean something. He has got Tom Miller who is like his father and it would just kill them both to lose each other. Tom and me are just as good as that Narcissa Whitman, even if we don't spend all our time in praying but in doing things.'

Ben put a hand on her shoulder. 'Whatever you decide to do, I will stand behind you, Sarah.'

She stopped to think a minute. It wouldn't do to let her hot head run away with her as she would have to be making sensible decisions for all of them to survive. 'Where will you be heading?' she asked Ben.

'I've settled for now at The Dalles. You can't get much farther until the spring.'

'Is that where Tom and them got took?'

'It is.'

'Well, I owe Tom much, so I reckon I'd best be heading there myself to see how he's getting on. Then I want to get to Oregon City so's I can see if Joe is waiting there for me.'

She hoped Ben could be talked into going on to Oregon City himself.

Captain Stokes stroked his beard. 'Well, I am also wanting to go to The Dalles. When they can get through from Oregon City, that's the first place the rest of my family will be looking for me. I guess I am still responsible for Sarah's welfare, even if I have let her down badly.'

'You haven't been half bad, Captain,' Sarah reassured him. 'And you've had to bear your losses along with the rest of us.'

Oakes shrugged. 'Well, I guess that clinches it, but you are too young to be taking on such a responsibility.'

'I'm not as young as I look.'

He turned on his heel, having no use for argument with crotchety females of any age. 'We better get moving!'

As they slowly descended the mountain, the snow turned into rain, which grew warmer as it diminished to a drizzle, melting the snowdrifts. Gradually, the snow was left behind and it was a wonder that there was still green grass in the world and streams that weren't frozen. They could open their eyes again without being blinded by snow glare, and drink in the beauty of the Walla Walla Valley.

An Umatilla Indian village lay at the foot of the mountains. They were farmers and had fresh food on offer, as well as a wagon in which Sarah and the children could ride. The rescue party split in two, half going with Hiram Oakes to the Whitman mission. Reverend Bingham chose to accompany them.

It started to softly rain again, but at midday on the plain, it wasn't particularly cold. Sarah had no soap left for a wash, but she raised her head and felt the grime and grease and soot run down off her face and clothes. She stripped off her heavy jacket, but the men paid no attention to the way her shirt was plastered to her body; no one was possessed of modesty any longer. Some of the men stripped naked for the first time in months to let the rain clean away their dirt if not their nightmares.

Sarah caught enough rainwater in a feed-bag to give Johanna a bath after she warmed it by the fire. Laurie also received a scrubbing from Ben; he was too old to be washed by a woman, he insisted.

Well provisioned by the Indians, they

regarded the remainder of the journey as no more than a stroll. The wagon was well sprung, and after the one rain, the weather held, even though the temperature dropped. They came into The Dalles in late December – Sarah had long lost track of the date, but it seemed as if it were Christmas with the entire population giving them a welcome and offering all sorts of things to make up for what they had lost.

A young woman ran up and threw her arms around Ben. Sarah tried to smile and express her congratulations convincingly when he introduced her as his wife. Her name was Fleur, and she was the daughter of a French trapper and an Indian Squaw.

Sarah chided herself; she was still much a fool, pinning her hopes on Ben. She would have to have another think coming about getting him to go to Oregon City! She told herself she should just be glad he had come out all right and settled, and the fact that he had wanted to see that she came out alive as well meant something. With Fleur, Ben had gotten just about as close as he could to being an Indian himself, which was what he had always wanted.

Fleur invited Sarah and the children to stay with her and Ben in their small cabin. When Sarah tried to protest there was no room, she explained that as one of eleven children, their addition would be no imposition – as long as Sarah did not mind the cramped quarters.

In spite of herself, Sarah couldn't help but warm to Fleur. 'Thank you, then, for your offer; I'm sure the surroundings will be downright roomy after seven months in a wagon.'

Sarah

Tom had to have three of his fingers cut off, but only one toe. But he fared better than some of the other men that went with him trying to get us rescued, one of whom had to have a whole foot cut off from the frostbite. Tom said he was not of much use now, but I told him he was of enough use to drive us all to Oregon City once we could get through, as I would have my hands full with the children.

There are two ways to get to Oregon City. The first is by way of an evil branch of the Columbia River, with steep cliff walls and swirling water. You have to pay an injun to ferry a canoe through the rapids, and it is a rugged trip likely to give anyone who attempts it a good dousing and not recommended until late summer when the water is low.

The second way only opened up last year,

cut through the Cascade Mountains by a man named Barlow, who charges a toll for his trouble. Soon after we arrived, deep winter set in and shut down the road. Since I had no intention of taking the children on a raft, I had to wait for the spring thaw.

When the weather lifted for a spell, I visited with Tom, who was sharing lodgings with some of the other men from the train. It took him a while to get steady on his feet and he used a stick for balance. Laurie reminded him how he had used a stick himself but now he could walk almost perfect. To his mind, Tom was his papa.

Somehow, it made me feel lonelier when I saw the looks Fleur and Ben passed and the way their bodies brushed when they went by each other. And I could hear them at night from the annex I shared with the children. I escaped into sleep as much as I could. It was a long winter.

Eventually the ice on the river began to break up, sometimes whole shelves crashing into the water, and spring rains started to melt the snow, revealing brown patches of grass and creating a thousand rivulets which found their way to the river.

Before anyone on the eastern side of the Barlow Trail from the Willamette Valley knew it was finally passable, the first man came through. He was Robert Stokes,

Captain Stokes' oldest son.

It didn't take him long to locate his father, as Captain Stokes and what remained of his train were so much in the habit of being together, they met each day to take their meals in a tent that gave such services to those without a hearth of their own. It wasn't free, but they had been given credit until they got themselves on their feet again. The people of The Dalles had known their own hardships.

Robert Stokes stood in the tent opening, looking around in the dim light for a familiar face. It took him some minutes before he recognized a thin, gray-haired man sitting at the far table as his father.

'Pa! I have found you!'

His son was hugging him before the Captain could get up.

'We have been worried to death all winter, wondering what had become of you.'

'We have lost your ma, Bob. Grammy too.'

'I knew of Grammy and I'm right sorry about Ma.'

'How did you know? We have been cut off all winter.'

'There was a family in your party got separated from you quite a ways back and they come into Oregon City in October looking for you.'

Tom sat with the others at the table, listening more than eating. It was not his conversation, but he had a stake in it.

407

'Was their name Hansen?' he asked.

Robert didn't seem to consider him rude. 'That it was. And is. They are still waiting there in Oregon City.'

He looked around.

'Are any of you named Springer? A boy of that name is with them.'

Tom didn't stay to hear any more. He bolted from the table, not even remembering to take his cane.

The Journal of Sarah Springer

March 30 1847

I have brought this long tale of my short life right up to today, so I am starting fresh with my own journal, since we leave for Oregon City tomorrow and from now on all that I write will be about the future, instead of the past.

They say that the West is no place for a woman. Men might do what's called the heavy work, but hauling water and firewood and bending and stooping from before the crack of dawn until well after dark cooking and washing and cleaning and mending and minding the sick is hard work, too. I am not complaining, and I will be doing more of the same. I am just stating the facts.

I am about as tough now as any man and

can make a go of things in Oregon the same way. Joe will be getting his acres even if they don't allow women none, and Tom didn't say no to coming with us. He is just as much a part of this family as Laurie and Johanna, and he can get his own land, too, but he will still be needing cooking and laundry, so I hope he will stick with us.

I don't know what state of civilization they got over in Oregon City, but I reckon I have learned enough from Margaret to pass myself off as a teacher, if one is wanted. If not, well, I will find some way to earn my own living, which I think is necessary for both man and woman in the West. I have come through far worse.

Once Daniel and Elizabeth in California hear what has happened, I bet I will be able to get them back with the family again. And we got so delayed up in the mountains, folks got to Oregon City who left after us. One such was kind enough to send word he had met Letty and Matthew back in Independence well on their way home. I know I could talk some sense into Letty if I had the chance, as I have gained some sense myself. So, I've still got plenty of family, even if we aren't all blood kin.

Rebecca wasn't my blood, but we went through the fire together, as they say. I have taken the liberty of reading her journal. I debated the seemliness of it, but she said she had planned to pass down the tale of our journey to her grandchildren, so that is my responsibility now to see that Johanna knows all about her mama. Rebecca's writings made me live again each day she noted, though often I lived them contrary to her. It is a waste of time to linger in regretting my behavior; nothing can be done about it now. And Rebecca and me wound up closer than any two women can be, I reckon. And that is what counts.

I am thinking of Rebecca's quilt. The ladies who gifted it felt that part of themselves would live on in each patch they sewed. Well, Rebecca will live on in Johanna and Johanna's children, and as long as I live, I will see that she lives along in mine as well.

Rebecca always ended her days with a prayer and I will copy her habit as my faith has been restored. That Ben came through alive was Your miracle, Lord, and it was Tom who was able to bring him to rescue us all at our darkest hour. And now Joe is good as back again, so I have much to be thankful to You for. There is a new life waiting for us all in Oregon and I hope You will allow Papa in Heaven to know his children will thrive there. And I am sure that in Your wisdom you have seen that Rebecca has joined him and that she knows that I could not have come as far as I have without her.

Amen.

Author's Note

Several years ago, I was given a wonderfully thought-provoking book, *Women's Diaries of the Westward Journey,* by Lillian Schlissel, which pointed out how different women's experiences on the Oregon Trail had been compared to men's. I have taken the liberty of putting her premise that the two sexes took a 'parallel journey' into one of my character's mouths, and these words have driven my writing.

As things so serendipitously seem to happen sometimes, it was not long after discovering Dr Schlissel's book that I became an avid cross-country skier in the West, my trails often crossing those of the Oregon pioneers. At a small bookstore in Bend, Oregon (alas, no longer in existence), I discovered reprints of Oregon Trail diaries compiled by Bert Webber. These often mundane, day-to-day accounts of life on the trail were, in their way, as illuminating as Lillian Schlissel's insights.

One day when I was skiing on the Emigrant Trail at Donner Pass in California, I paused to contemplate the snowcapped peaks rising so high above me and was filled with admiration and awe for the pioneer women who had been here before me under far different circumstances. This novel is my tribute to them.

Although the characters are fictitious, many incidents in my book are based on fact. Ben's joke about selling Nellie Bingham to the Indians actually happened, but after being banished, the real prankster wound up in the California gold-fields rather than in Oregon.

Marcus and Narcissa Whitman and eleven others at their mission were killed by Cayuse Indians in November 1847. The Indians also kidnapped several of the orphaned children the Whitmans had been caring for. Emily Walker, Sarah and the children all made the right decision not to join the Whitmans.

However, Daniel Springer's decision to join the train led by George Donner was most unwise, as the Donner Party, who had left Illinois in April of 1846, tried a cutoff around the south side of the Great Salt Lake which resulted in their being stranded at Truckee (Donner) Lake in the Eastern Sierras by the end of October. Forty of the eighty-seven emigrants survived, including some of the women and children. Daniel and Elizabeth's inclusion in the party is entirely fictitious, but though Daniel was stubborn, he was strong, experienced and brave. He could well have kept his family alive, including a new baby. Stories of cannibalism aside, it is said that the women of the party survived the ordeal better than the men.

As Dr Schlissel has indicated, much in the pioneer women's diaries was written between the lines. I hope I have been able to fill in some of the gaps in presenting my own version of how the perseverance of a few women helped to win the West.

The publishers hope that this book has given you enjoyable reading. Large Print Books are especially designed to be as easy to see and hold as possible. If you wish a complete list of our books please ask at your local library or write directly to:

Magna Large Print Books
Magna House, Long Preston,
Skipton, North Yorkshire.
BD23 4ND

This Large Print Book, for people
who cannot read normal print,
is published under the auspices of

THE ULVERSCROFT FOUNDATION